As always, his memorie prodded places inside him that he habitually left undisturbed, and he was troubled and unaccountably annoyed at the innocent pedlar.

Elden, who used to be Lina's husband until she got fed up with him and joined another camp to the east in Chrj, moved to stand behind the handsome pedlar and looked him up and down like he was a piece of meat he had a mind to purchase, leering in a suggestive manner. Liall found this distasteful and he gave Elden a scowl until the man retreated.

"Well, red-coat, and what does a pedlar have for the Wolf?" Liall asked, giving the pedlar a warm look that was rewarded with a frown of suspicion and dislike.

"It's been a lean year, Atya," the pedlar began, dropping into the customary speech of a born haggler. Despite the frown, the lad addressed him respectfully enough and gave him his proper chieftain's title. His voice was low and pleasant to the ear.

More than pleasant, Liall admitted privately, to look at as well as to hear. He studied the pedlar's face and decided the Hilurin was exceptionally attractive, despite the smallness.

"So I hear, but luckily we have had good trade this week," Liall said. "My krait is fed and warmed by city garments, and my needs are not what they were a month ago. Otherwise, you would not get through for less than everything you carry and what is on your back besides."

"And then I'd freeze in the snow," the pedlar said resentfully. "A real wolf wouldn't be that cruel. He'd kill me quickly and be done with it."

Scarlet and the White Wolf Book One: The Pedlar and the Bandit King
TOP SHELF
An imprint of Torquere Press Publishers
PO Box 2545
Round Rock, TX 78680
Copyright © 2006 by Kirby Crow
Cover illustration by Analise Dubner
Published with permission
ISBN: 978-1-60370-488-5, 1-60370-488-4

www.torquerepress.com

First Torquere Press Printing: September 2008
Printed in the USA

**If you enjoyed The Pedlar and the Bandit King,
you might enjoy these Torquere Press titles:**

Scarlet and the White Wolf Book 2: Mariner's Luck by
Kirby Crow

Scarlet and the White Wolf Book 3: Land of Night by
Kirby Crow

Windbrothers by Sean Michael

The Pedlar and the Bandit King

Scarlet and the White Wolf Book One:
The Pedlar and the Bandit King
by Kirby Crow

romance for the rest of us
www.torquerepress.com

for J.

The Pedlar and the Bandit King

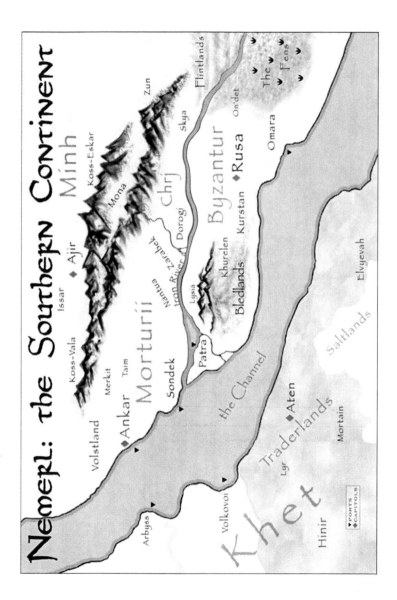

Nemerl: the Southern Continent

The Pedlar and the Bandit King

Scarlet and the White Wolf

Book One:

The Pedlar and the Bandit King

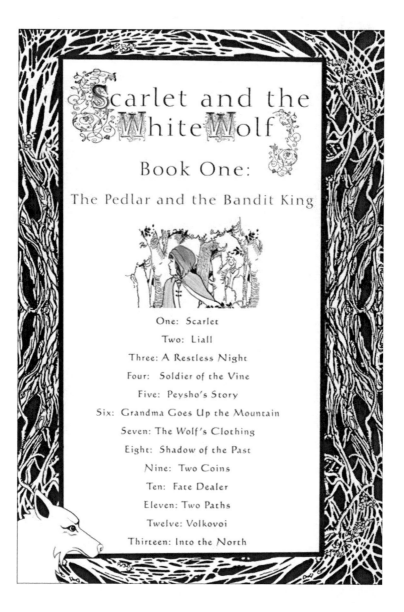

The Pedlar and the Bandit King

1.

Scarlet

Autumn, the Month of Ashes.

The serpent banner of Om-Ret fluttered over the great *souk* of Ankar, crowning the jumbled din of camels, horses, men, slaves, tinkers, dogs, whores, hawkers, cutpurses, soldiers, and merchants with a constant flapping sound like the wings of gulls. Scarlet, son of Scaja, swiped at the gritty red dust on his face and surveyed the colorful row of furled ribbons the tradeswoman laid out for him.

"For your wife, little Byzan?" she asked him coyly, her golden eyes glittering above the hem of her embroidered veil. Here, far north of Byzantur, all Morturii men and women who were not soldiers or whores hid their faces behind layers of filmy gauze or bright-colored cotton or jeweled silk. Scarlet was not Morturii and hid nothing.

"Sister," he answered shortly, and pointed to the red ribbons. "The blue and green, too, and a yard of the white silk and a yard of the green," he added, mentally wincing at the price. The woman bowed as he paid her with half of a silver *sellivar*. He collected his package and left, threading his way through the crowded, stinking alleys of the marketplace. Avid seagulls, fresh from feeding on entrails thrown from the many fishing vessels crowding the glittering bay, swooped low over the crowds. One black-winged gull darted past him, wings slashing, and stole a fragment of flesh from a meat-sellers stall.

"Greedy!" the man cried, shaking his fist after the departing bird.

Scarlet came to the Street of Doves and Flowers and pursed his mouth in distaste, for he disliked having to take this route. He navigated his way past a noisy *ghilan*, a two-story dwelling whose function was made known by the series of carved frescoes that depicted a young, shapely woman being chased through a lush forest by an armored Morturii soldier. The soldier pursued her through various stages of undress, with the last panel culminating in the soldier mounting her thighs amid a flowering field.

Next on the street was a *bhoros* house, constructed almost identically to the white-walled ghilan, with fine bronze screens at all the windows and the doorways tiled in blue. The main difference were the frescoes, and in the last marble panel before the street opened up into the wide main avenue of the souk, a laughing young man lay sprawled on his back in the grass with a lean soldier kneeling over him, both of them very bare.

Scarlet came upon a kneeling Fate with eyes like two raisins pinned on a shrunken apple; all he could see of her behind her veil. The crone extended her wizened hand to him.

"Read your fate, red-coat?"

He shook his head and went on, intent on making his way back to Masdren's stall. Morturii, the land of metal and magic, abounded in soothsayers, seers, fate dealers, and crones. They were almost as prevalent as the blacksmiths, armorers, and master weapon-smiths, and in some parts, the land was under a permanent pall of black smoke from the smithies.

A pair of long-knives hanging in a corner smithy caught Scarlet's eye, and he stopped to admire them with frank longing. Like all Morturii weapons, the knives had smooth hafts made of spun wire and the blades themselves were black as jet. Inscribed on the blades were many curling designs of leaves, trees, human faces in torment, and stretched, eviscerated animal bodies, all swirling together in finely-etched silver lines to form a depiction of Deva's creation of the world. The weapons were ugly and terribly beautiful at the same time, and Scarlet lingered to stare as the foot-traffic flowed around him.

The burly Morturii smith stirred from his forge and pointed. "Ye want try 'em out?" he asked in poor Bizye.

After a long moment, Scarlet shook his head. He did, but he could never afford the smith's price.

"He'll take them," said a familiar voice.

Scarlet turned and frowned at Masdren. "I will not," he said in Falx, the local language. His accent was flawless. "Sit down, blacksmith. I don't have that much silver."

"But I do." Masdren nodded at the smith. Masdren was a black-haired Byzan as well, one of perhaps a hundred in all of Ankar, and much older than Scarlet. "Wrap them up. Never mind the sheaths; I've got better in my shop."

Scarlet opened his mouth to protest and Masdren put a restraining hand on his arm. "How many summers have you worked for me in the souk, lad? Four at last count? And your dad is still one of my best friends. Take the knives. I know you know how to use them, and I want Scaja to see his son again."

"But I don't want—"

"Do as you're told, boy."

Though he knew Masdren was right, Scarlet felt his tenuous hold on his volatile temper slipping. The roads in Morturii were safe enough, but he was headed home for Byzantur on foot. Many a young man or woman who traveled a Byzantur road alone often wound up as chained work-slaves for sale in Minh. More infrequently –depending on their beauty– they woke up from a drugged stupor as painted and perfumed bhoros boys or ghilan girls, sold into whoredom by any of a dozen slave brokers who eked a steady living from the southern roads.

Rannon, the lean and soft-spoken *karwaneer* who had led Scarlet's first caravan, had taught him the art of knives. Although Scarlet was no warrior, he could run swift as a deer and possessed an almost uncanny sense of direction. A foot-traveling pedlar's life is best paced slow and steady, but sometimes the only hope he had was to run like Deva's imps were after him. He was marked for luck: born with only four fingers on his left hand, a sign of Deva's favor. Running had saved his life more than once.

The smith was holding the cloth-wrapped pair of knives out to Scarlet and Masdren was reaching for his pouch to pay. He watched as Masdren counted out forty sellivar, almost half a year's pay for a pedlar, and he found himself ducking his head sullenly to thank him. He would have preferred to buy his own weapons, but Masdren was his elder, so he bit his lip and thought of how disgraced Scaja would be if he lost his temper in public again. His black moods and immodest speech had caused his father enough embarrassment over the years. The fact that Masdren was one of Scaja's oldest friends helped to restrain him, but he sometimes resented this man's ability to make him feel like an unruly boy in need of a good dressing-down.

The aged leathersmith waved Scarlet's thanks away. "None of that. Come on, I'll walk you to the walls." He was a big man compared to most Hilurin, black-haired and very pale-skinned like all those who belong to the First People, and with large, ink-dark eyes, shiny as obsidian.

They stopped at Masdren's shop and the leathersmith sent one of his many boisterous children for Scarlet's walking stick and a pair of tool-worked leather sheaths, black to match the knives. They were indeed far better than the ones at the blacksmith's stall. Masdren was a master.

"These are too fine," Scarlet said as a last protest, and Masdren smiled ruefully and pushed them into his hands. Masdren shooed his children back to their work and took Scarlet's arm to steer him to the gates as if he were five years old himself.

They were challenged briefly at the city's high, stone walls, but it was perfunctory. The bored, leather-armored bravos scratched and swatted at flies as they let the pair of foreigners through the gaping iron teeth of the massive gate into the flat, brown lands surrounding the port city. To the east was the wide Channel, its white-capped blue waters sparkling in the sun. A thin breeze of cooling air carried the taste of salt.

Masdren made him a final gift of a pair of storm-gray leather gloves, custom-fitted to accommodate his left hand with its missing fifth finger. Again, Scarlet's thanks were deflected gently. "What will you do when you get home?" Masdren asked.

Scarlet sighed and shot Masdren a tired, affectionate look. "You know I won't stay there for long."

"When did you ever? No, I'm only asking because I want you to think about working for me permanent next year, not just the summer."

He hesitated, surprised by the proposal. "You want me to move to Ankar, make it my home?"

Masdren's mood suddenly changed. He fidgeted. "It would be best," he said, averting his eyes. "I didn't want to worry you, but the news from Byzantur is bad: more Hilurin families killed, farms razed to the ground, cattle stolen, wells poisoned. There's been talk of public burnings, too, and worse." Masdren looked at him with large eyes. "Much worse. If you can, convince Scaja to bring your mother and sister out before it's too late."

Scarlet shook his head. "Scaja will never leave Lysia. I know he won't." Scaja was a stubborn man and Scarlet's second mother, Linhona, had already lost one family to Minh raiders. She had lived in an eastern settlement of Byzantur above the marshy lands known as the Fens, far closer to Minh than Lysia was. She would not want to leave her beloved adopted home, no matter how great the danger.

"He has to," Masdren said urgently. "Oh Deva, does he *want* to die? Do you? For the god's sake, leave Byzantur while you can. You'll never be able to hide what you are with that face, nor will Annaya or Scaja or Linhona. You're all Hilurin to the bone and they'll kill you for it."

Scarlet was alarmed, but some part of him still refused to believe that his own countrymen had turned so completely against them. Surely something would happen, someone in power would intervene, and the fighting would stop soon? "The Flower Prince..." he began.

"The *yeva bilan* can't stop what's happening," Masdren finished. "He's offered to step down."

Scarlet was dismayed. The Hilurin were a dying race outnumbered fifty to one by the Aralyrin in Byzantur, yet the only men of any power in the governing palace at Rusa were pure Hilurin, a thing that had garnered enormous resentment among the Aralyrin population. There had been a failed military coup last year, brought on by dissension in the army ranks, and it was then that talk began of electing a non-Hilurin for *yeva bilan* next term.

"The Flower Prince has been Hilurin for the past two thousand years," Scarlet said, shaken. It was a requirement, for the sacred legends taught that if the deified prince was not pure-blooded First People, he would not have the ancient Gift and Deva would not speak to him. Few remembered this except the priests of Deva and the Hilurin themselves. "What'll happen to us when they find out that the goddess only answers the Hilurin?"

Masdren only stared at him sadly, and did not reply. Scarlet found himself mumbling a promise to send word of his decision and to see Masdren next spring, at the very least.

The elder left him in the busy thoroughfare outside the walls, and Scarlet stood there for a little while after. The long road home would take him nearly ten days on foot, and he was not sure he was ready to begin. Passersby saw little to remark on: a slight Byzan youth of about seventeen with the beardless, flower-pale face of a Hilurin, black hair, and black eyes. If they were asked later to describe him, they would have remembered that he wore the long crimson coat of a pedlar with its characteristic broad hood, and that his face was very fair to look on, his features both delicate and masculine with a subtlety of secrets about the eyes. As Hilurin are a very handsome race and beauty is not uncommon among them, looks alone could not distinguish him, but the crimson coat would.

To see a Hilurin at all outside of Byzantur is a rarity, for they are, on the whole, a secretive, withdrawn folk, and a bold traveling pedlar with a Hilurin face would most certainly be noticed.

Scarlet frowned and sourly eyed the crowded southern path that would take him eventually to the Common Road and home. The winding road looped over the rocky hills as far as he could see, vanishing at last over a black knoll that hid the rising smoke from the city of Sondek. There were a few battered wagons outlined on the horizon, reminding him that there would be Kasiri bands thick as flies on the road. There would also be slavers, Bledlanders, bandits, and just plain rogues bent on whatever ill deeds kept their bellies fed and their hands to mischief. It would be a long and tiring trek.

The sound of his father's voice, brittle with disapproval, echoed in his mind: *This is no life for a proper Hilurin.*

"It's my life and I'll do as I please with it," he muttered resentfully, feeling once again like a scolded child. "No one pens me in." So saying, he gripped his walking stick firmly, adjusted his leather satchel higher on his shoulder, and started off.

Not being a true warrior, Scarlet had no defense against slavers, other than to be swift and on his guard. The trick with Kasiri is not to be too much of a temptation. A pedlar's long red coat is known everywhere, and it is a lure to some. For the most part, the nomadic Kasiri tribes roam the southern roads between Lysia and Rusa, and are shunned by all and welcome nowhere. They are petty thieves and cheap charlatans, dirty and underhanded and sly, and there is not a town or city in the whole continent where they are not despised. Yet, even jackals have their good qualities and no one had ever heard of a Kasiri gypsy taking slaves, though they would take anything else not nailed down.

To Scarlet's mild surprise, it was not a Kasiri who menaced him eight days later on the lonely riverside road outside of Sondek, but a grizzled Bled. The fierce, bearded warrior eyed Scarlet as he walked by on the rocky path, and Scarlet's hand tightened on his leather pack and he fretted at the thought of the good pouch of silver coins hidden in his belt.

The Bledlander's excellent knives and the ragged scars covering his bare chest recommended him as a skilled fighter, and Scarlet got a good look at both before giving the man a cursory nod and hurrying past. The spot between his shoulder blades tingled as he left the Bledlander behind, but he resisted the urge to look back.

The Bled were like dogs: show them an ounce of fear and they'd be all over you.

For Scarlet, who was a skilled woodsman and had no fear of beasts, bad weather, or hunger, survival depended mostly on his wits and his ability to outrun those predators who went on two legs instead of four. The Bled might give him some trouble in that quarter.

He glanced over his shoulder at the Bled as he continued to walk at a brisk pace, his legs moving tirelessly beneath him. There had been trouble between the lawless Bledlands and Byzantur all season, and it was a lean year; the roads filled with hungry men. He took no chances and looked back a minute or so later, only to see the warrior had vanished. His heart gave a little jolt, and a quick glance to the stand of spare cedars to the west showed him a glimpse of tall shadow slinking behind a tree. It was all the warning he needed.

He took off like a rabbit and left the skulking Bledlander in the dust, silently thanking Deva for her gifts. If she had taken the littlest finger of his left hand before he was born, she had made up for it by giving him two good legs. He did not mind never having the finger, honestly, though it did make his left hand too slender for any normal glove to fit, since the long bone that ran from the wrist to the knuckle was gone, too.

With the Bledlander far behind him, Scarlet slowed to a trot until he neared the turnoff to the Patra Ferry. He halted in the middle of the road, his hands on his hips, and caught his breath while he thought. The air had cooled, hinting of the mild winter season that was almost upon them. He fished a furled apple from his pack and bit into it with strong white teeth as he pondered his options. Walking all the way home presented problems: he was tiring from his run and would be less able to run again if more trouble presented itself. If he took a ship down the river all the way to Tradepoint, he would shorten his journey and avoid any further trouble on the road, but he was equally likely to run into slavers or bandit boats on the water.

Scarlet ate a little more of the apple, his clear brow furrowing as he chewed. This job was getting almost *too* dangerous, though once he would have insisted otherwise. His love for the pedlar's life was as strong as ever, but even he had to admit that he had been extremely lucky thus far. Numerous hazards had brushed past him, death and rape among them, but he had always managed to escape. He recalled Masdren's offer and toyed with the idea of settling in Ankar or Sondek, or perhaps even far south in Rusa, the colorful capital of Byzantur, where there were Hilurin who actually lived in walled cities instead of rustic, undefended villages.

Finishing the apple, Scarlet looked around at the dry, yellow country surrounding the road. He chose a likely spot: a little mound of earth out of the shade of a stand of wind-blasted oaks, and dug a shallow hole to drop the apple core into. That done, he glanced quickly around him to make certain no eyes would witness, scraped a little dirt over the gnawed core, and laid his palm over the earth. Warmth crawled up Scarlet's wrist as he closed his dark eyes and chanted the short verse, and then he was up and walking down the road to the ferry, dusting off his hands.

Behind him, a thin, fragile, tendril of green curled out of the mound and tested the air.

The boat was a skiff, the waters choppy, and the captain was roaring drunk. Not the best way to navigate the Iron

River from Patra to Lysia, but it had to do. The deck heaved under Scarlet like a wild Bledlands' mare, the captain stank like a distillery, and he was vastly relieved to finally see the lowland dock of Skeld's Ferry with the usual loiterers hanging around. He waved at a figure seated on shore just as the skiff's bow slammed into the dock and landed him on his rump.

One of the old men smoking his pipe in the sun grinned and raised a hand to him as he was getting to his feet. "High time you returned, Scarlet-lad."

He squinted to make out his features and waved. It was Old Kev, the village Watch and Teff Ferryman's uncle, who knew his father's father when he was a boy and never let him forget it. Lysia was a small village and everybody knew him and knew he was too restless to stay long in one place. Yet, his feet always seemed to find their way back.

"What do you hear, Kev?" he asked, stretching stiff muscles and trying to rub the soreness out of his backside. Teff and his son Keril were seated beside Kev in wide broomstick chairs, each with a smoldering pipe in their hands.

Kev gave Scarlet a dour look and dragged a puff from his pipe. "News is what happens somewhere else," he drawled, disapproval coloring his tone. Kev had made no secret of his dislike of Scarlet since he had turned fourteen, and wondered loudly and often in Scarlet's presence how in Deva's name any proper Hilurin man could choose a wandering life over home and hearth. Though he was invariably civil to Scarlet for his father's sake, Scarlet was painfully aware that Kev himself represented every reason he had left Lysia in the first place.

"Nothing much changes here," Kev went on.

"Steady as the Nerit," he agreed, nodding his head to the south, where the shadow of Nerit Mountain sketched a black and white hump across the sky behind Kev.

"True, true," Kev nodded lazily, smoke flowing from his mouth. "But as it happens, there *is* something new these days."

He pretended disinterest. "Oh?"

"There's a snot-nosed Kasiri king. *Liall,* he calls himself. A Northman, I gather. Some even say he's from frozen Norl Udur itself, and he's squatting on the mountain athwart Whetstone Pass. He was here a day or three ago, the Wolf himself: tall as a frost giant, hair like snow and pale blue eyes like a cat. Never seen the like. If you're going to sell your wares in Khurelen or the Bledlands, you'll have to pay his toll."

Scarlet smirked, unconvinced that a Kasiri could be from Norl Udur. Kasiri were generally from Chrj, the vast, arid desert east of the Iron River. Saying one was from Norl Udur was like saying he was from the moon. Still, he was glad of the chance to take Kev down a peg for once.

"You call that news? Since when is a gypsy rare, even one as strange as that? There's a thousand other Kasiri on the roads between here and Morturii."

"*This* Kasiri has got a well-armed krait at his back, and they've held the Snakepath to Khurelen for three months."

Scarlet blinked. Kasiri chieftains, or *atya*, generally did not allow their people to make camp in one place for any amount of time. To do so was to invite disaster, for no civilized place tolerated Kasiri for long. A sly Kasiri atya had more sense and kept his krait on the move.

"Why hasn't the army garrison in Patra ridden out to remove him?"

Kev tilted his head to blow out a thick stream of fragrant smoke. "As it happens, the Wolf does his squatting too near the Bledlands side of the pass, and the Flower Prince

–bless his name– does not look to brew trouble with the proud Bled lords."

Once every thirty years or so, the priests of Deva chose a Hilurin youth who would be known as *yeva bilan*, the Flower Prince, until he reached middle age. He was destined to be the Consort of the goddess Deva, she who threw down the cruel Shining Ones and freed the Hilurin people. The Flower Prince would be a living embodiment of her love for as long as he ruled, and would be treated almost as a god himself. In good time, he would step down and a new prince would be chosen. After that, no one knew what happened to him.

The news about Kasiri holding the pass was irksome. Scarlet had planned to spend a few days in Lysia before he ascended the path to Nerit Mountain. From there, he would take the Snakepath down the other side to skirt the eastern borders of the Bledlands, passing many homes and farms on the way, where the folk living there would buy his wares. The other road, the dangerous and deserted Salt Road, went around the mountain and the Bledlands entirely and took six or seven days longer in good weather. That fact was not only trying, it was costly.

He scowled. "Wolf or no, I won't be penned up in my own land. Perhaps I'll just take a walk up to the pass and meet this Wolf."

Kev gave a sharp bark of laughter. "Now that would be unwise. Didn't your mum and dad ever tell you to not to talk to strangers?"

Scarlet hefted his wide leather satchel meaningfully, shaking it at Kev a little to remind the old man that his entire livelihood depended on talking to strangers. He bid Keril and Teff a grumpy farewell before heading toward the Owl's Road, which would take him straight into Lysia.

He passed Tradepoint an hour later, a large and efficient

supply outpost for river traffic and the army, but only Deni and his father were there, mending a fence to keep their goats from getting into the grain stock. He waved at Deni as he walked past and Zsu, Deni's younger sister, came out onto the porch. Her apron was dusted with flour and she was holding a wooden bowl.

"Hullo, Scarlet."

He waved at her, suddenly sorry that he had only brought back a present for his own sister. Zsu's black hair, always in a tangle from climbing trees or chasing goats, would have looked pretty with new ribbons. She had been Annaya's best friend since they were in diapers, and had now grown into a petite young lady with a pert nose and large, inquisitive eyes.

"Hello, pretty Zsu." He winked at her and she giggled and hid her smile behind her hand.

"There's dinner soon, if you're in a mind to stay," she offered, shy and eager at the same time. Annaya said Zsu wanted to marry him one day, but he put that down to a girl's foolishness and paid no attention to her.

"Ask me next time," he said cheerily. He waved again and kept walking. "Linhona will skin me alive if she doesn't get to feed me herself tonight."

Zsu waved at him from the porch. He looked back when he was further up the road and she was still there, a small figure in a long blue smudge of a dress, her face a pale oval turned in his direction. When Scarlet raised his hand to wave a last time, she turned and went quickly into the house.

Hilurin houses are multi-roomed domes covered with

white plaster inside and out and then overlaid with bright paints in many colors. Walking through a Hilurin village is like walking through a Sondek carnivale, some said. Their love for colors and for detailed, intricate bits of art is known everywhere, and their embroidery and rugs are famous for their delicate stitching, bright dyes, and the incredible detail crafted into each design. Nowhere else could one find such workmanship, and the Aralyrin majority of Byzantur had contempt for little Hilurin people who made no weapons and could not read or write and never journeyed far from their homes, yet who could coax such astonishing skill from their hands.

Lysia was a Hilurin village. As such, there was no street of doves and flowers in Lysia, a surprising omission for any settlement in the Southern Continent. Even Patra, a smallish city by Morturii standards, had several such districts where men and women went to relieve their lusts. Any township that did not have a street marked thus or that was not riddled with bhoros or ghilan houses was invariably a Hilurin village, filled with First People: Byzans who were proud of their pure heritage and their undiluted bloodlines that went back to Deva herself.

Nemerl was a licentious world where sex could be bought, bartered, traded or thieved from any street corner. Yet, the Hilurin believed they were descended from Deva and scrupulously kept her few and simple commandments: honor to self, chastity until marriage, fidelity to one mate, honesty in trade, charity to strangers, generosity to travelers, kindness to children, and respect for all beasts. Hilurin commoners managed to keep apart from the corruption of civilization by settling in remote villages with poor farming land that no one else would want. Hilurin nobles and primes -- those above the commoners and slaves but far short of nobility -- lived in Rusa and the greater cities of the south, where they wielded much power.

Lysia would never see much progress or commerce, but after the raucous flesh markets of Morturii, a quiet tradesman village was a relief for Scarlet to come home to. Even now, he could see the familiar outlines of his father's small, domed house on the lane. Linhona, lean and strong, was outside taking down the last of the wash in the late afternoon sun. It had taken him three hours to walk up the steep Owl's Road from Tradepoint. When she saw him, she took off her bright scarf and waved it with a shriek of joy, her gray-streaked black hair tumbling around her shoulders.

"Scarlet!" He could hear her all the way down the lane. "Scarlet's home!"

She turned and ran around the side of the house to get Scaja from his workshop, dragging him by the arm as he laughed and slapped sawdust from his hands.

Scarlet dropped his pack and stick in the lane to clasp Scaja's hands, and then bowed his neck to touch his forehead to his before hugging his father so hard that his bones creaked. Laughing, Scaja begged him to stop before he broke his spine.

Annaya shrieked, too, but it was over the costly ribbons and silk. Like him, Annaya had pale skin that stubbornly refused to darken in the sun, and her hair was so black it shone blue in the sunlight. Linhona took charge, gathering up her son's fallen gear and shooing her family inside. Scarlet lingered on the threshold, looking at the front yard and the sky. Winter was nearly upon them, but in late spring, Linhona's wild roses would again burst into disorganized, riotous bloom, filling the yard with vivid colors and evening scent. He missed them and had to settle for bloomless, pale-leafed honeysuckle winding its creepers around every section of the wooden fence, vying for space with hardy lavender and leathery-green ivy. The very last of the mums bloomed in a bed near the kitchen door, yellow as butter.

"Scarlet?" Linhona sang out.

"Coming," he called back. He took a last look at the yard. How long had he been away this time? Three months? It seemed like more.

Scarlet closed his eyes and breathed deep of the familiar smells of hearth and home, vowing silently that *this time* he would stay longer and come back sooner. He never kept his promise, but thinking about it brought comfort, of a kind.

"So," Scaja said as they sat down to dinner, "how did you fare this time out?"

It was as close as he ever got to asking him for an accounting. Scarlet believed he hated to ask him at all, but business is business, and he would have felt like a baby if Scaja had not.

"It was a good run. No trouble, or little enough," he replied. Linhona looked sharp at this, and before she could open her mouth, he told her the rest: "I ran into a Bledlander on the road south from Sondek. Thought he had a mind to rob me, but he mustn't have been that desperate."

Annaya was listening intently. "Did he have a long beard?" she asked excitedly. "And were there horse-tails hanging from his helmet?"

"Annaya!" Linhona scolded.

He chuckled. "He had a beard, but more than that I didn't see. I was too busy running away. I did manage to work for Masdren in the souk for four weeks this time. I would have stayed longer, but with winter coming on

I thought I should come back one more time before the snow falls." He planned to weather the short winter in Khurelen this year, where it was warmer and where the souk was almost as prosperous as Ankar, but he did not mention that just yet.

Annaya stumped off to get the dishes, disappointed that he had no more tales of bloodthirsty Bled.

"How is Masdren?" Linhona asked.

"His wife has run off with a scarf merchant."

Annaya hooted from the kitchen and Linhona shushed her. Scaja looked startled. It was not every day a Hilurin wife ran away. Family was greatly important to them.

"This proves what city-life does to family," Scaja harrumphed. "Do see you send Masdren my good wishes the next time you meet up with him. Did he pay you well?"

"Better than Mekit, and he doesn't stink up the stall with his drinking, either." At Scaja's gesture, he slid a grimed leather pouch over the table.

Scaja picked it up and hefted it, though he did not tug the laces apart and look inside. His eyebrows went up.

"It feels like a goodly weight," Scaja judged, voice tinged with admiration.

He ducked his head at the praise and helped Linhona settle the iron pot on the table. Scaja and Linhona and even Annaya contributed the work of their hands to his pedlar's wares. Scarlet took a percentage for himself and sold it at what profit he could, spent a little for the road, worked when there was work, and brought the rest home to Scaja to hold against the lean years that always came, sooner or late.

"In fact," Scaja said doubtfully, again hefting the pouch that contained eleven sellivar, "perhaps too goodly."

"Scaja—" he began. Scaja always was proud, but Scarlet knew his father needed the money. How not, with so many raiders and bandits and Kasiri about? People were becoming afraid to risk a costly wagon on the highways, and no broken wagons or carts meant nothing for Scaja to repair.

Scaja held up his hand. "Not over dinner. Wait until the *che*." The pouch vanished into his shirt as Linhona lifted the lid on the stew with a flourish.

The argument averted, Scarlet smiled at her and looked into the pot. Thick chunks of pale meat floated in a crimson soup, surrounded by spiky bits of fragrant black rice. Stewed chicken with *persa*, his favorite dish.

"Thank you," he said with a grateful sigh. "It couldn't have been easy to get spices this time of year."

"I had to trade a good apron and an iron ladle for it, but I got plenty in the bargain," she said briskly, wiping her hands on a towel. "Well, dig in! I'll bring the biscuits."

She vanished back into the kitchen and Scaja watched his son with fond eyes as he dipped out a portion that would have fed two, well-grown men. "Thin foraging on the road, I gather?"

He shrugged and dug his spoon in, ignoring the heat from the fiery seeds of the persa. He usually ate well on the road, if plainly, and still managed to look hungry enough that he was invariably offered a meal at whatever farm or steading he wound up at near suppertime. Rabbits were a staple, as were wild hens and quail, berries and furled apples, and fish and mollusks from the river.

"Thinner than last year," he answered around a mouthful. "There was less growing by the wayside than usual. Less game, too. There are so many travelers on foot this year. They eat it before I can get to it." He fanned the air in front of his face and stuck out his burning tongue to cool it off. "It's good!"

Linhona slid a pan of biscuits in front of him and he filched two with a big spoon of butter on the side.

"Thanks, Mum."

Oh, she liked to be called that, he could see. As was the custom, Scarlet had called his parents by their right names since he was eight years old. Linhona had seemed sad at the change and never corrected him when he lapsed, but not Scaja. Scaja was a proper Hilurin and chivvied his growing son at every turn to be equally proper and correct, yet when Scarlet's feet took another path, he had not objected. His father could have been angry at him for not learning to be a wainwright and not wishing to spend his life in Lysia, but all he had ever done was sigh now and then and talk in a roundabout way of what daughters of Lysia were marrying this year or next. Scarlet ate while Annaya fiddled with one of her ribbons and nattered at him with questions about the road. Scaja ate his supper and occasionally cast a twinkling eye at his wife.

Scarlet finally pushed his bowl away with a sigh. "No more!" he laughed when Linhona would have put dessert –a raisin and apple pudding sprinkled with walnuts– in front of him. "I'll eat it later. Annaya, love, go help our mother. I want to talk to Scaja for a bit."

She rolled her eyes as she got up and began to clear away the dishes, but winked at him as she brought the little ceramic pot of green che. Scaja filled a second pipe and handed it to Scarlet as he poured a cup.

Scarlet flicked a glance to the kitchen, making certain that Annaya was engrossed in conversation with Linhona before he spoke. "There was a new farm on the Iron Path when I went to Patra last time, near the abandoned mines," he said very lowly, leaning his head closer. "They were Hilurin folk from Nantua. When I came back, they were gone. Burned out."

Scaja's eyes went stony. He passed his hand above the surface of the table as if brushing sand away, a gesture of negation. "Say nothing to your mother or sister."

Scarlet nodded. Hilurin families were being hounded and murdered all over Byzantur. There was no sense in worrying them with report of yet another disappearance. He bit his lip. The family had had two small boys, playful as bears.

"I hear tell there's a felon charging a toll over Whetstone Pass," Scarlet remarked while tamping the herbs into the pipe bowl with his thumb.

Scaja's tone was resigned. "So they say. Polite enough, I suppose, for a robber chief."

"You've met him?"

"No, but I got an eye full of him in Jerivet's shop. He came in to buy an iron rim for a wagon wheel," Scaja nodded. "To carry away the goods they extort from the travelers, no doubt. A big fellow, biggest I've ever seen, and white-haired like an old man, but with a young face and body."

"Shansi says that they're all armed like Morturiis," Annaya chimed in from the kitchen as she carried bowls to be washed.

His eyebrows went up. "Shansi?"

"Cousin of Jerivet's from Nantua," Scaja muttered aside to him. "He's courting your sister. A good lad, apprentice to the blacksmith, who is his uncle as well."

Hilurin bloodlines were tangled as nests of yarn and that did not bother Scarlet. The news that Annaya was being courted did. He stared at his sister, but she had grown up during his months away. She cast a sloe-eyed look over her shoulder at him as she carried the iron pot back into the kitchen, her silky black hair falling to the pit of her back. Suddenly, Scarlet had to admit that she was no longer a grubby little girl with skinned knees.

"I will have to visit this Shansi," he said, still a little stunned.

"As is right and proper," Scaja said.

"But she's only—"

"The same age you were when you left with Rannon and his caravan," Scaja interrupted mildly, refusing to be drawn into an argument.

From the kitchen, Annaya hooted again. Scarlet scowled. I'll have to have a talk with this Shansi, he thought. Hilurin daughters were prized, and some things never changed, such as lustful apprentices.

Scarlet ignored Annaya. "Well, anyroad, I'm minded to see what kind of toll this gypsy king charges to pedlars."

"No, that you won't," Linhona said firmly, striding in from the kitchen. "Traveling the roads is one thing. Thumbing your nose at the Kasiri is another."

"Who said anything about thumbing my nose? I was just going to—"

"Go up and see. I heard. And the minute this Wolf gives you an answer you don't like, you'll wind up in a fight with him, like always. Avoid the mountain until he's quit of it."

Scarlet began to think he would never get a full sentence out in earshot of his parents. "And when will that be? From what I've heard, he's been there for months already. I can't spend the rest of my life traveling back and forth to Patra." She did not answer and he got up and went around the table to her. "Linhona, you worry too much."

"And I don't have reason?" She was alarmed and trying to hide it with anger, twisting the damp dishcloth in her hands. "All the scrapes you got into when you were little, the fights and the bloody noses and elders rapping on my door because you sassed them. Now you want to go tangling with Kasiri. Didn't Kasiri kill my family?"

"Those were Minh raiders," he reminded her gently.

"Raiders, Kasiri, all the same. Bandits and nomads." She waved his answer away impatiently. "Ai, but you won't listen. You're too reckless."

He was stung. "That's not true. I'm careful as I can be, what with who I have to trade with and where I have to go. We'd starve if I stayed home, and that's the truth."

"That's not why you became a pedlar."

"No," he agreed. "It wasn't. But it's the truth anyway. I had a choice before. I don't now. When was the last time a wagon came through Lysia, or a horse needing shoes or tack? There's barely any work here at all for Scaja, and for me, nothing."

She sagged a little, and then reached out and hugged him fiercely. "I can't lose another child, Scarlet. Promise me you'll be careful. You've just come home and here you are talking about leaving again."

He kissed her cheek, a little unsettled by her worry. "I won't go today or next week. I'll stay and help Scaja fix the roof and the fence before I wander off into more trouble."

She smiled and wiped her hands on her apron and shooed him away, and that was the end of it for a while. He sat down with Scaja, who had grown silent and sad, and finished his che.

It was his second night home. He had gone with Scaja to survey the broken fence earlier, as an excuse to stroll and smoke a pipe or two while they caught up with each other. In the late afternoon, when the brassy sun turned the last drying stalks of hay to golden spikes in the fields, Scaja insisted on visiting the family *templon* to give thanks for his son's safe return. Scarlet stood beside him while he addressed the little stone shrine that was chipped into the shape of a turreted castle no higher than his shoulder.

Inside were two paper gods, Deva and Her Consort, He who is never named, dressed in red and yellow paper gowns. It was Scaja's job to clothe the gods and care for their symbolic house, and also to make periodic offerings of incense and fragrant oils. As a chill wind blew from the Iron River, Scaja lit the sticks of incense, placed them carefully in the holders, and then bowed his head over his clasped hands, nudging Scarlet to do the same.

"On danaee Deva shani," Scaja intoned, and Scarlet followed lead.

The prayers were short and simple and he had learned them all while he was still toddling. He repeated the *cantos* after Scaja, made the customary low bow before respectfully backing several paces away (never present your back to a god), and after that they made for home. On the way, Scarlet mused in his head how strange it was that in Heaven a woman should rule, but on plain earth she always chose a man to see to her realm. There must be something to that.

Thinking about the Flower Prince reminded him that he still had not spoken to Scaja of Masdren's invitation. "Masdren has offered me a place in his shop," he said carefully, broaching the subject as delicately as he could.

Scaja was surprised. "And do you have a mind to apprentice with him?"

"I might," he hedged. "That depends."

Scaja stopped walking. They were on the muddy path bordering Imeno's field, and the rich, loamy earth under their boots was nearly black. "On what?"

"He wants you to leave Lysia. Linhona and Annaya too, of course. He says he'll find a place for us in Ankar."

Scaja was shaking his head before Scarlet got the last words out. Scarlet sighed and crossed his arms over his chest as he stood facing his father.

"Not Ankar," Scaja declared. "Never."

"Where then?" Scarlet demanded. He was beginning to understand Masdren's exasperation. "It's only a matter of time before the Aralyrin get around to burning us out, too. How much longer are we going to wait?"

"It's not all their doing," Scaja protested. "It's the Bled and the regular army that's—"

"That's full of Aralyrin soldiers!" Scarlet finished. "Wake up, Scaja. The Flower Prince isn't going to stop them. No one is." He watched the lines on Scaja's face rise up into ranks of worry before settling into their old, familiar pattern of stoicism. Hilurin denial, solid as rock. Scarlet knew he was defeated.

"It can't go on forever like this," Scaja said gruffly. "Mark my words, son: there will be an end to it."

Scaja would speak no more of leaving and forbade Scarlet to mention it to his mother or sister, and he had no choice but to swallow the angry words that arose and submit.

The hour was late and Linhona had cooked a meal to feed nine men his size. He was still trying to recover from it when Annaya came in from the small sitting area set aside from the kitchen.

"Tell us the story, Linhona."

"Sister," he warned.

The look she cast his way was scorching. "I like to hear it," she scowled.

"It's late." He shifted a quick glance to Scaja. "And it upsets your mother."

"Why's she keep telling it, then?"

That was an answer he did not have, except to say that storytelling was in Linhona's blood and perhaps telling such a terrible tale lessened the pain of it for her. She told a story better than anyone he ever knew, even the skilled bards in Morturii and the lads from the Hyacinth Court in Rusa, where the Flower Prince lives. Yet, no one ever benefited from Linhona's gift except her family, because she would not do it for anyone else, and her oldest story, her best story, was the reason why.

He sighed as Linhona got up and moved her chair until her back was to the fireplace. Annaya found a place at her feet. It was no use trying to talk Linhona out of it. Whether it upset her or not, her daughter had asked for a story. *The* story.

She always began the same way: "I was told by my father, who was a man much like your dad," and she smiled at Scaja as he sat in his overstuffed chair, teeth clamped around the stem of the pipe that filled the room with fragrant smoke, "that one must have a few words before a book to frame the story for the reader, much like a painting is framed. Consider this story as the words before my life began, for this is the thing that happened that shaped all the things yet to come."

Linhona clasped her hands loosely in her lap, and he marveled how beautiful her hair was, how pretty she remained for a woman thrice his age and then some. Her voice was steady and warm and familiar as she began to tell the story.

Linhona's words turned very formal as she shifted into the High Speech, the one used for prayers and prophecy and eulogies to the dead, and spoke softly of how there was still ice on all the roofs and spring was not yet in the frozen ground when the raiders of the Minh came out of the east, blown in like the last vengeful wind of winter. She told them of her infant daughter killed that day, and how they had taken Gedda, her strong, gray-eyed son, as a slave. Her voice became muted as she spoke of the rape of the village women and the murders of the Elder and the levyman and their families, and how her best friend, old Maba the baker, had been knifed in the breast because she cursed them fearlessly, and how one pretty Aralyrin woman had been set free because she had the mark of Om-Ret branded on her thigh. Last of all she spoke of Jorlen, her half-Hilurin husband who had tried and failed to defend them, and how she herself and only a handful of others had escaped with their lives.

The fire crackled and Linhona's hand stroked Annaya's hair steadily. Annaya leaned against her leg and was still, her eyes closed. Scarlet thought she might have fallen asleep, were it not for the wince she gave when Linhona mentioned the dead baby: how the squat, parchment-skinned Minh had put the infant into the town well with the others, and how Linhona had walked for days afterward not knowing where she was headed, only that she must keep moving or die.

Scarlet cast an uncomfortable glance at Scaja, because he never knew why Linhona must tell this part, or why she spoke of her own survival and freedom in such a tone, as if she had not deserved it. The raiders might have chosen otherwise and taken her with her son back to Minh, and then they would never have known her. Could she have regretted that? How could she possibly?

Scaja had tried to explain it once: "She thinks she brought it on them," he said in his stolid voice. "Bad luck from her reading and writing. Her husband allowed it. He was not of the blood," he always added, as if that explained everything. *Not of the blood* meant that Linhona's first husband was Aralyrin, that his Hilurin heritage was diluted, and so he did not have the Gift and could not kindle the fire by dropping a withy-thought into the sticks or make healing tea by breathing on the water or whistle fish up to the surface to be sang to sleep and caught in the hand. These things and much more Linhona taught her children of the Gift, which occurred only among Hilurin families and certainly not among everyone and was a closely guarded secret, but she had flatly refused to teach either Scarlet or Annaya how to read.

"The next morning it was over," Linhona continued. "We could see the Minh from our hiding place. They were a long line of straggling black against the purple hills. We went back to town, but it was ruined: the well polluted, the fountain shattered into bits of marble, and the mill and the grain barns in cinders. Half the houses were burned. I felt like I walked in a dream. You know how it is in dreams, Annaya? When you seem to move and walk but don't really get anywhere?"

Annaya nodded, mute with interest but also sleepy.

"I went home to our cottage. When I got there, I took things blindly and stuffed them into a sack: a cooking pot, a bowl, a blanket. I tried to leave the cloth doll that Gedda used to play with, but I could not. I put on Jorlen's new boots and took his coat and long-knife and whatever else I could find of value, and I left. I did not know which direction to go. It was cold and I could not think well. My head seemed to be wrapped in layers of wool that muffled my very thoughts. When I was many leagues outside of the village, I sat down by a tree and went to sleep, and during the night it snowed."

It was that image that haunted him the most from Linhona's story. The thought of her sleeping on the bare ground, dressed as a man, snow covering her in her weariness, like some doomed wanderer from a fairy tale who would soon be set upon by the Shining Ones and taken into the Otherworld. Scarlet shivered a little and Scaja patted his arm, the earlier argument between them already forgotten. It was not so easy for Scarlet.

"I had a fever when I woke," Linhona said, "but it

seemed to help me think. I found I was on the west road to the Channel. It was as good a road as any and less traveled, which was well with me. That night, I tried to burn Gedda's doll. I used my Gift to whisper up a fire and threw it in. I watched it catch and flare. The little yarn curls on its head began to smoke, and suddenly I had the thing out of the coals and was beating at the flames with my bare hands. I spent most of the night stitching the scorched cloth together with scraps torn from my hem, and my hands were blistered, but I was comforted when I laid my head on a bed of evergreen and held the doll to my breast. I did not turn east to follow Gedda, for he would have forgotten how to speak Bizye by the next spring, and would not know me when I saw him again. If I ever saw him again. Gedda would be forbidden to speak of his home, forbidden to utter our names, and we would be so long mute on his lips that our memories would turn to dust in his mind. Such are the methods of the Minh. This I told myself as I turned west, as Deva led my feet to Lysia."

With the dark part over, Scarlet could breathe again. Often, Linhona illustrated her tale with the many things that had happened to her on the western road, such as wolves and foul dreams of her baby crying out from the well, all rotted and green, but thankfully she left those out this time. Scaja passed his pipe over to him and he took a long puff of the sweet-smelling herb, holding it on his tongue to get the taste before blowing it out in a smooth line. Annaya was awake still, her eyes narrowed to slits and her body curled against Linhona's side.

"I came to Lysia," Linhona repeated, smiling at Scarlet, the darkness fading from her voice and her eyes glistening in the light. "At first, I did not believe a people could be so calm and happy. They knew of the Minh slaver ships, but seemed to know nothing of their bands of raiders. I learned later that the Minh warriors never journey this far in their land raids. It is the Nerit, you see. The Minh fear the mountain just as the Shining Ones feared it. I should have known about the raiders, for certainly there was no shadow on these people as there was on me. They seemed happy and well fed and unafraid of what tomorrow would bring. All the usual tragedies were here: misfortune, cold marriages, stillbirths, disease and old age. But there are no Minh with blood on their spears, and no children in the well. I should have been thanking Deva for her mercy, realizing that she tempers all things, but instead all I could do was resent these good people for their peace. There was no sense in my feelings, but it was the way I felt, and I told myself that I would not be able to live here."

Annaya stirred. "And then you met Scaja," she chimed in.

Linhona laughed and switched back to Bizye. "And *then*, I took a job at Rufa's *taberna* clearing tables and serving bitterbeer. One night, just about this time of year, a man walked in. He had shoulders like my father and was plainly of pure Hilurin blood. He had a boy with him, a little thing no bigger than my thumb!"

Annaya giggled and Scarlet rolled his eyes. "I wasn't *that* small."

"Oh, but you were, and loud, *and* demanding, kicking the table for attention. Your poor father was beside himself."

"So instead of bringing him ale..." Annaya coaxed. They all knew the story by heart, line for line. It never offended Linhona, and she seemed pleased.

"Instead of serving him, I went over to his table and picked up the struggling, fussy, thumb-sized boy, and gave him a big kiss."

"And he quieted right down," Scaja put in softly. Scarlet

had given him back the pipe and he clenched it between his teeth and looked on Linhona with gentle eyes. It warmed Scarlet to see it, their love, and he thought to himself of how seeing two people you love also love and care for each other is a kind of rare peace. The world makes sense, then.

"And I quieted right down," Scarlet added, joining the story at last. "And you helped Scaja carry me home that night."

"And you never left again," Annaya yawned, more asleep than awake.

"True as rain," Linhona said, ending the tale in the Byzan way.

Scarlet thought about that later as he went to his bed, sleepy with food and with the sureness of being safe and surrounded by familiar things. It was good to be loved in the world. He had never known a life without love, and hoped never to learn that lesson, having seen the folks who could not tell love from lichen, how their eyes were hard as bits of flint and their hearts like stones. He remembered all the times on the road when he had felt frightened, how many times he had almost been robbed or worse, or when the weather had turned so foul that he actually feared for his life. Through all of that, it was his memories that brought him through: Linhona in the kitchen or garden, her competent hands busy at whatever task, Annaya bouncing around, always so small, and Scaja's solemn face by the firelight. True as rain, they were his life.

A week and a day Scarlet stayed in the village. Then, on the eighth morning, a cold wind began to blow from the northeast and a light layer of frost crunched under his boots when he went to fetch water from the well. If he did not leave soon for Khurelen, he would have a hard time getting through the Snakepath into the lowlands. It was just as well. The soles of his feet had already begun to phantom-ache with the want for travel. The fence was fixed, the roof was patched, and he had helped Scaja put a new wheel on a freight carriage that broke down two leagues from the Salt Road. The night they returned from fixing the carriage, after a long dinner as Scaja lingered over his pipe, Scarlet told him he would be trying Whetstone Pass the next day.

Scaja looked at Scarlet through a wreath of smoke, his black eyes narrowed but soft, and he nodded. If he had objections, he knew well enough to keep them inside. Scaja left to tell Linhona that her son would be leaving.

Scarlet's bedroom was just a cot behind a curtain next to the kitchen, and later, as he packed and the smell of the waybread baking for his journey filled the house, Scaja pushed aside the curtain. There was a linen-wrapped bundle in his hands. He sat on Scarlet's bed, unfolded the linen, and began to carefully lay out the bundle's contents on the covers. Scarlet stared in astonishment, and Scaja gave him a small smile.

"Busy as bees, all of you!" Scarlet exclaimed. He touched the treasures that Scaja had presented: silver-plated pins and buckles, iron needles and tin spoons, and a handful of small, delicate buttons carved from bone. There was more: three linen lapels richly embroidered in blue and green by Annaya, and two lace collars stitched in a dragonfly pattern by Linhona, fully as good as any he had seen in the cities. He touched the buckles, admiring the light chasing of fine scrollwork Scaja had set into the metal.

"How did you ever...?"

Scaja shrugged. "Well, making a buckle is not so different from welding a wheel spoke. Easier, in some ways." He began gathering the wares up. "Work's been slow," he ended the subject brusquely. "I had the time."

"Scaja, is there anything—"

"Hush, lad, and let me help you pack."

Scarlet packed as carefully as he could without knowing how rapacious the Kasiri horde would be. Nothing too costly for a trip to Khurelen, except a small bottle of perfume he hid in his boot. The fine lace, the embroidery, and the better silver-plate he stowed under his bed, showing Scaja where it was for safekeeping. He wore his old gray woolen shirt, threadbare at the elbows but still warm, beneath the crimson leather coat and hood that denoted a pedlar throughout the world. It came down to his knees and the red dye was still bright after three years of use. He wrapped a length of faded wool around his neck and pulled on the storm-gray leather gloves that Masdren had crafted to fit his mismatched hands. Scaja nodded his approval at Scarlet's appearance and kept his doubts to himself.

"Just have a care," Scaja growled as they stood together in the yard before he set out.

"I always do," he answered, knowing that Scaja didn't believe him. He had half a mind to say that it was Scaja who being reckless now, but again held his temper and kept mute.

Scaja gave him a brief, fierce embrace and Annaya kissed his cheek. Linhona was pretending to be busy in the house, not ready to speak to him yet. She had sent the waybread –round, parched loaves rich with nuts and dry, tough grains that would not spoil so long as they were kept dry– through Annaya. She could be as stubborn as him, sometimes. He wished she would come out to bid him farewell and was angry and resentful over her refusal to see the truth, as well as Scaja's.

He pinched Annaya's cheek a last time. She was nearly as tall as him now. "I like your Shansi," he said.

She gave him a secretive smile. "So do I."

His eyebrows went up and he grinned. He tapped her nose. "Behave yourself while I'm gone."

Annaya snorted and tossed her glossy hair over her shoulder. "Take your own advice before handing it to me."

He left them reluctantly and started on the road that led through the village and up the mountain pass, where the perilous Kasiri and their Wolf-chief were encamped.

2.

Liall

Liall, the White Wolf of Omara, strove always for an atmosphere of calm to reign during his robberies. To meet an enemy in the dark is one thing, to challenge folk in the open, under the blue sky in the melting snow is quite another. There is a trick to keeping order on a highway: keep the road open and paying while preventing the rough and naturally-disorderly Kasiri from running wild through the women and the goods, spreading terror and mayhem. The woman who set up a strident screaming in the early afternoon threatened the fragile peace of the prosperous toll road, and that warranted Liall's attention.

He looked over his shoulder to check on Peysho's progress with the short line of journeyers waiting to take the well-tended pass through Nerit Mountain. Peysho Ar'sinu was his enforcer, a handsome, brawny bear of a man in his fortieth year or thereabouts. Whenever he approached, Liall invariably got the impression of a slow tide rolling toward him, but he was never fooled: Peysho had a mind like a precise clock, with never a detail forgotten or mislaid.

Though he kept them hidden by a gaudy Kasiri jacket, Peysho bore on both of his beefy upper arms the red tattoos of Om-Ret: a serpent devouring her own tail. He had recently shaved his hair down to dark brown stubble on his head, and Liall thought this vanity, since Peysho's hair had lately begun to turn gray from his years of living hard and fast in outlaw camps. His skin was the color of pale bronze and his one undamaged eye was a mirthful hazel.

Peysho's name suited him, as it meant *red-eye*. He had a small red star in his left eye from a Minh mace that had crushed his cheekbone twenty years ago, and the eye had filled with blood and never fully healed. He seemed to see well enough with it. On occasion, Liall wondered how he looked to Peysho through such an organ; if his amber skin and white hair was colored with a mist of bloody crimson when he gazed at him. It seemed fitting.

Peysho's one constant companion was his countryman, Kio, a fellow Morturii many years his younger, deceptively kind of face and slight of body, but an artist with a blade of any type. Kio had wide, tawny-gold eyes like a lion and wore his feathery chestnut hair to his shoulders. There was a scattering of beard on his cheeks that he refused to take off, believing it made him appear more masculine.

Alas, Liall thought, his face is as sweet as a girl's, and that soft beard only makes him that much prettier. These facts caused Kio a great deal of embarrassment, for he was as much a soldier as rough Peysho, with whom he had roamed untold cities and camps together before landing in Liall's tribe of Kasiri five years ago. The Longspur *krait* had been home to them ever since.

Like the Byzans, the Kasiri were a gaudy lot, but rather than show off their artistic inclinations in architecture and gardens, they expressed themselves through dress. Set against the stark landscape, they could blind one with their colors: purple and red and orange silks, black velvets, fine striped linens of blue and silver knotted with pearls. The men wore tasseled coats of satin and gold-cloth over mud-stained breeches and wide-topped, high-cut boots that were a Kasiri trademark. The women wore the boots, too, but under the long dresses of highborn ladies, dripping with rhinestones and ribbons. Their dresses were considerably more worn and patched than any noblewoman would be caught wearing, but Kasiri women took the fading and fraying in stride. When a dress finally fell apart, they simply tore it into rags for patching brilliant quilts or braiding into sleeping rugs. Kasiri girls wore their hair shorter than most, for it was a hard life and a long mane of hair would only complicate things. To compensate, they wove stunning headdresses out of long, brilliant threads of silk and decorated them with bits of semi-precious stones and flecks of gold and silver and copper. The headdresses were a few inches high, square with a long back that covered the neck, and from the hem hung long strings of faceted crystals and polished crimson beads. Women pinned their short locks under the headdress and swayed their strings of crystal as they walked, arching their necks and preening for the rough, handsome men of the krait.

In temperament they were like beasts that had been only lately domesticated. Kasiri men were simple for the most part; content to take their share of spoils and women and food and wine and mostly never thinking to ask for more. Power and intrigue did not interest them, and they were happy that Liall, the strange and powerful Northman, had challenged for the right to lead some twenty years ago. Since then, he had never failed to protect them or lead them wisely. *Wisely*, to a Kasiri, meant coin and meat and goods, and Liall knew that his authority was secure only as long as the Kasiri were well fed and warm. If they were not provided for, they would begin to roam and be dissatisfied, like dogs belonging to a careless master who thinks little of their welfare.

There was no rancor or bitterness in Liall when

he pondered these facts. Like many scholars of great intelligence, he believed he had learned that men are greedy, soulless beasts, intent only on what they can gain for themselves. There were few men in the camp he spoke to beyond the cursory words of command, and none he considered his true equal. Peysho was the closest thing he had to a friend.

The camp was deceptively scattered-looking and unkempt, but in fact the Kasiri were very well-organized, with wagons on the outer rim, armed toll posts at each road leading in, and yurts in the center. The mountain pass was a perfect place for a toll road: a high, clear promontory of wind-swept dirt and packed snow. At its center was a wide space of eighty paces or more, surrounded by rough monoliths of porous, rust-colored rock thickly veined with white quartz. Chipped into smooth blocks, the stone was excellent for sharpening knives, which was how the pass had derived its name. The stones also kept the worst of the wind from assailing the encampment.

The three roads leading down from the promontory —one to the Skein River that flowed into the Channel (the Sea Road, it was called), one to the road to Khurelen and the southern lands beyond, and one back to the village of Lysia, Skeld's Ferry and the Iron River— were clearly visible from every angle. It was just a high, flat space stuck like a shelf between two small mountains, but it was the shortest road through from north to south. The only other road was the old Salt Road, a lonely, meandering path through the sandy lowland valley between the riverbank and the Neriti hills that took three times longer to traverse than Whetstone Pass. It was also thick with slavers and cutthroats who were not above raping the occasional wife or carrying off a daughter or son to the Morturii slave markets.

Travelers would pay for safe passage through the

busier pass rather than risk the Salt Road, and old Dira the whoremaster, bless his black, lecherous heart, had remembered that the Kasiri had an ancient claim to a remote mountain road in Byzantur near Lysia. Dira had a yurt full of pretty male doves and winsome flowers to feed, slaves all, and the old man was anxious about the state of his purse. It had been a thin year for almost everyone in Byzantur, and the Longspur krait had no fodder stored up for their beasts or any amount of coin or goods they could trade to get through the cold season. They came to the pass in late summer, when all other Kasiri were heading back into Chrj and winter pastures. Whetstone pass was their last option before they must admit defeat and disband the Longspur krait to larger, more prosperous tribes. Disbandment meant not only the death of a krait, but of family ties as well, and all Kasiri feared such an end.

Today's travelers were quiet enough. Most had been warned of a well-armed Kasiri krait astride the road and had come prepared to sigh and pay as little as they could get away with. Others, it seemed, were less informed.

The screaming woman was a fat matron with a shock of iron-gray hair stuffed under a billowing yellow bonnet. She had locked hands with one of the Kasiri and was jerking and tugging at him and yowling so loud that several of the men had stepped back to jeer at the poor fellow. The other travelers were growing skittish at the noise and a few were longingly eyeing the western road they had recently ascended from the Channel.

Liall jerked his chin up at Peysho, and the man came to see what he wanted. "Aye, Wolf?"

"What's amiss? That shrieking will have them all fleeing off the side of the mountain like a horde of verrit."

"Oh, her?" Peysho jerked a thumb over his shoulder. "Her weddin' ring, I gather."

"Is it worth much?"

The enforcer shook his head and spat into the snow. His uncouth accent was Falx and grew heavier when he drank, so that at times Liall, himself not a native to this continent, could barely understand him. "Nowt but pewter with a shine o' gold painted on. I've got teeth in me head worth more."

Liall laughed and called out to the unfortunate Kasiri, who turned out to be cat-eyed Kio. Kio was actively trying to retreat from the shouting, scolding matron, but she had him in a limpet's grasp and would not let him go.

"Ho! You there! Let her keep her rusty ring."

Kio ducked a slap aimed at his head and tried to dance further away from her. She was on him like tick. "I'm trying, Atya, but she won't leave off!"

There was a scatter of laughter, old Torva and Eraph and a few others, and Peysho grinned and went to settle the fracas. Liall did not stay to watch. There was a smaller line of travelers coming up the southern road from Lysia, and that was his post for the day. Among Kasiri, even a chieftain was expected to do his share of work.

Lysia was the nearest village to the mountain, being nestled right up under the shadow of the Nerit's belly like a chick to a mother hen. It was not an opulent village by any means, but compared to the bedraggled traffic that drifted in on corked and tar-painted ships from Patra and trundled up the mountain in a steady trickle from the long Sea Road, they were at least prosperous. The travelers had been many of late, for there was much civil unrest in Byzantur and rumors of war on the horizon. Whether it was war with the Bled or civil war amongst themselves, no one seemed to know, but the traffic was heavier day by day as people deserted the virtually undefended northern reaches of Byzantur and headed south to the capital cities.

Liall settled himself in a wooden chair behind a stone bench that served for a bargaining board and began the day's work. He had dressed for the occasion in a thin, leather hunting jacket over black breeches and high boots with iron buckles up the side. His lean waist was cinched by a studded knife-belt with a pair of very fine Morturii long-knives hanging in their silver-capped sheaths. He wore no hat, and the whiteness of his close-cropped hair drew stares. His face was not the usual face one would see in Byzantur or Morturii or even in the wondrous city of Ajir, for not even the exotic slave markets of Minh had ever dared to hold a Rshani in captivity.

Liall's cheekbones were like carved shelves of stone and his skin was the color of deep amber. His expressive eyes, thickly lashed in silver, were a pale, washed-out blue, and his angular features were planed so sharply that they could have been carved from oak. His hands were large, long, and graceful. In Byzantur, among the dark-haired Aralyrin and the slight, beautiful Hilurin, who have skin like pearl and hair the color of blackest soot, he was as unusual as a green cat. He did not believe his face held any beauty, but he knew that very few in Byzantur had ever seen anyone like him. For that, they would have to travel beyond the continent to his home in the far, icy north, where all men live in darkness for half the year.

The air was chilly and the temperature dropping rapidly, but Liall had been raised in a far colder climate. He wore no cloak or overcoat, only a ruff made from the pelt of a white wolf to keep his neck warm, and (purely for vanity) a teardrop sapphire from one ear. He looked, he hoped, sufficiently imposing.

The first two travelers, a bard and a female dancer, were well acquainted with toll roads and Kasiri and paid what he asked without blinking. The third was a well-fed Sondek merchant who pled dire poverty until Peysho shook him by the neck until his teeth rattled, at which point he produced a half-bit of gold from the lining of his pocket, along with many a stuttered apology. Liall worked through the line of travelers and then waited for the next batch to come through, which they did in small groups broken up by the passing of an hour or half an hour. The day went by that way, and Liall was yawning by the time the last traveler approached.

The last in line was a Byzan pedlar, known by his knee-length leather coat dyed a shade of deepest red, the color of the migrating redbird that travels the entire circumference of Nemerl in one year. He was a slight, pure-blooded Hilurin lad of no more than twenty, with astonishing dark eyes, soot-black hair, and pale, fair skin like the petal of a white rose. Like all Hilurin males, his chin and face were naturally hairless, which often hid the age of Hilurin men and made them appear younger than they were. He also carried a sturdy stave with him, perhaps for walking or perhaps for fighting off bandits.

Liall stared until the young man shifted his booted feet and looked away in discomfort. How small he is, Liall thought. The top of his head would not reach my chin.

Although the pedlar was small, Liall knew better than to judge him by that. The Aralyrin army was the most determined fighting unit on the continent, and this young one before him was partly of that blood. He did not want to admit it, but Hilurins fascinated him. Their proud tenacity, their secretive, aloof nature, and the legends his own people had concerning their ancient origins captured Liall's enormous curiosity. His natural inquisitiveness stirred the latent scholar in his soul and made him yearn for the days once spent reading gilt-edged books and perusing ancient manuscripts.

As always, his memories prodded the dark places inside him that he habitually left undisturbed, and he was troubled and unaccountably annoyed at the innocent pedlar.

Elden, who used to be Lina's husband until she got fed up with him and joined another camp to the east in Chrj, moved to stand behind the handsome pedlar and looked him up and down like he was a piece of meat he had a mind to purchase, leering in a suggestive manner. Liall found this distasteful and he gave Elden a scowl until the man retreated.

"Well, red-coat, and what does a pedlar have for the Wolf?" Liall asked, giving the pedlar a warm look that was rewarded with a frown of suspicion and dislike.

"It's been a lean year, Atya," the pedlar began, dropping into the customary speech of a born haggler. Despite the frown, the lad addressed him respectfully enough and gave him his proper chieftain's title. His voice was low and pleasant to the ear.

More than pleasant, Liall admitted privately, to look at as well as to hear. He studied the pedlar's face and decided the Hilurin was exceptionally attractive, despite the smallness.

"So I hear, but luckily we have had good trade this week," Liall said. "My krait is fed and warmed by city garments, and my needs are not what they were a month ago. Otherwise, you would not get through for less than everything you carry and what is on your back besides."

"And then I'd freeze in the snow," the pedlar said resentfully. "A real wolf wouldn't be that cruel. He'd kill me quickly and be done with it."

Liall did not care for his tone, too haughty for a mere pedlar and clever besides, and the young man was staring at him with frank scorn. Though Liall was used to sensing the ever-present disdain from village folk, most took more care to hide it than this one. Byzans were coldly disapproving, but passive and distant. This one before him was different. He was fire to their water.

"There are wolves and then there are *wolves*," Liall said. "Either way, fast or slow, you would be just as dead. Do you really want that?"

The pedlar's eyes flickered a little. It might have been fear. Liall waved his hand and laughed. He did not enjoy frightening youngsters, even youngsters who disliked him. "My fangs are whetted enough for one day. Let me see your wares."

The pedlar slipped the ratty, well-padded pack off his shoulder and carefully emptied its contents onto the stone as a few more of the krait, having gleaned what they could from the Sea Road, gathered round to watch. Liall waited as the young man neatly stacked all the items and made a tidy pile of them.

"Is this all?"

"All, bandit-wolf."

Liall gazed at him evenly. It was on the tip of his tongue to inform the pedlar that the Kasiri had an ancient claim to this pass that made the toll legal in their eyes, but he closed his mouth firmly. Why was he contemplating explaining himself to a mere peasant boy? Being a thief had never bothered him before.

"I ask you again: is this all?"

The pedlar would not meet his eyes.

"I could have you searched."

The pedlar shrugged, apparently unaffected.

"Searched like a Minh would," he added. "In places no gentleman would think to look."

The pedlar hesitated before he reached down and produced a little gilded bottle of perfume from his boot, placing it like a crown on the pile. Liall saw then that the pedlar's left glove looked strange, too narrow in some way, and he realized that this one carried a rare genetic marker of the Hilurin: a four-fingered hand. The young man saw the direction of Liall's gaze and looked uncomfortable, but made no move to hide his deformity.

Liall picked up the scent and sniffed it. Blue poppy and probably the best item he had. Beside it was placed a little metal and glass compass, which is another trademark of the pedlar's profession. Few traveled without at least a compass and a hand-map of Byzantur. Kio moved to stand behind Liall and fixed the pedlar with his aureate gaze, his delicate features turning down in disapproval.

"I see you've met the Minh," Liall said wryly, which provoked a volley of fresh laughter.

He looked resigned. "Take what you will, I can't stop you."

"Just so, you cannot."

Liall's long fingers dug through his little pile of cheap wares and tin silver-plate, splaying them over the stone. It was not much. There was little to provoke desire or greed on the part of anyone but the most desperate of thieves. In the Byzantur tradition, this pedlar traveled light and poor. Probably a wise habit, since he also traveled alone, unarmed, and was young and pretty enough to tempt men to acts other than thievery. Perhaps that was his true profession? But no, Lysia was a Hilurin village and there would be no street of doves and flowers there, no ivory-walled bhoros or ghilan houses to tempt a virtuous people to carnal lust. Dira the whoremaster had hoped this would mean more traffic for his trade, but alas, most Hilurin males seemed to be prudes.

The pedlar caught him staring at him and met his eyes boldly. "Perhaps we could make a trade," Liall offered. He slowly dropped his gaze to rake across the lithe body before him, and the high color rose in the pedlar's cheeks. Not so innocent after all, he thought. He takes my meaning quickly enough.

The pedlar backed up a step, alarm crossing his

features.

Kio frowned. "These stuffy, milk-faced Hilurin," he sneered. "They should all wear masks so a man isn't tempted to waste his time courting cold stone."

Liall threw Kio an annoyed glance, and the Morturii's face went sheepish. "Sorry, Atya," he muttered.

Liall shrugged and gave the anxious pedlar a rueful smile. "Relax, boy. The nights are long in these mountains, but I am not yet reduced to forcing my bedmates."

The pedlar bared his teeth as if he were the wolf and not Liall. "I'm not your boy."

There goes that bit of folly, he thought. Liall realized that this young man did not fear him; he loathed him. Not having much experience with Hilurin, Liall had had a passing thought to delay the handsome pedlar, to coax him alone among the yurts and wagons and perhaps ply him with a drink or five until his muscles lost that tense set of danger. The way the pedlar refused him outright, as if Liall were beneath his notice, offended Liall gravely. The atya was a man who often claimed to have no pride and no honor, yet, when the pedlar snarled and showed Liall his pretty teeth, Liall's pride was goaded.

"And you are as close to Khurelen as you will get by this road."

"Then I'll go by the Salt Road, damn you."

"Go right ahead. I suppose your folk will see you once or twice by next spring, but don't expect to make much of a living when you spend half your working days traveling an empty road. You know," he lowered his voice and leaned forward, folding his hands on the stone, "despite my good manners, I *could* just take what I want."

The pedlar stared right back, black eyes as merciless as a snow bear's. "Yes, but you'd have to kill me to get it, and that wouldn't be very good for business, would it? The army doesn't like Hilurin, but they like Kasiri even less. They could send in troops, burn you out. Rape is still a hanging crime in Byzantur."

All true, but Liall meant none of what he threatened and was oddly confounded and insulted when the pedlar believed him capable of it anyway. He settled back in the chair, his mood soured. Around him the air turned colder and he smelled snow skirling down from the heights. There would be a storm before morning. He motioned to Peysho.

"Batten the wagons down and get the supplies inside," he said in Falx, assuming that the pedlar would not understand him. "There's wind and snow headed our way."

"Aye, Wolf."

The pedlar looked up at the sky, and Liall realized that the boy understood him quite well. So, he mused, he is quick of mind as well as brave.

Few Byzan pedlars, Hilurin or Aralyrin, cared to journey outside of their own country, but this one had obviously been to Morturii enough times to necessitate learning the language.

The boy made a noticeable attempt to calm himself. "Take what you want," he offered, pointing at the pile of wares. He was visibly eager to have this unpleasant exchange with ruffians over and be well below the snow line while the light lasted.

Liall regarded him narrowly, taking in the shabby, red-dyed coat, the patched shirt, and the boots that would need mending before the month was out. He felt a familiar but unpleasant stirring beneath his skin: pride, his old enemy. Once, years ago, he would have disdained even to exchange words with this commoner. Who did he think he was? An illiterate country chapman with patches on his elbows and his hair freshly cut with his mother's kitchen scissors, a seller of cheap cloth and soaps, and he thought himself *superior*. This one sneered and looked away as if Liall were an offense to his eyes, a sick dog or town drunk, an object of scorn or pity.

He felt a familiar heat rising in his chest, and he forced it away in haste, shocked at his reaction. The volatile and unpredictable tempers of northern warriors had long been an asset in battle, and their enemies feared it even as they derided it, calling it *berserker* rage. But why would arguing with a mere pedlar ignite his temper so?

Liall shook his head slowly. "I'm not interested in perfume and sewing needles. I want something else from you."

The pedlar's red mouth grew tight and pinched like a pursed rose, and he glared. Far from fueling Liall's anger, the look stirred him. He had always liked fire in his women. In men, he liked it even more.

The pedlar made a noise of impatience. "I am prepared to pay you a fair price, you... what is your name?"

"Liall."

"*Li*-all," he grated, getting the pronunciation wrong.

"Lee-*all*."

He said it aright. "Liall, I'm willing to pay you fairly, but there are some things I will not *trade*."

The Wolf suddenly rose from his chair, watching with amusement at how quickly the pedlar retreated from him. His smile was predatory. "You may find, little redbird, that there are many wicked things a man will do, just as soon as he realizes he has no other choice. Now take your buttons and go back to chaste Lysia, for you won't take this road today, or any other day, so long as the White Wolf holds this pass. Not until you pay my toll."

"Which is what, exactly?" the pedlar asked tightly, his hands curling into fists.

Liall leaned close, resting one palm on the cold stone, and motioned for him to come closer. After a moment, the pedlar took a few cautious steps forward so that Liall could whisper in his ear. Just as quickly, the pedlar recoiled and shook his head.

"No," he vowed, one word with a weight of scorn behind it.

Liall shrugged. "Then have a safe trip home, pedlar." He motioned to the armed Kasiri and they pressed forward, smirking, with their arms crossed over their chests.

After a moment of hard silence, the pedlar gathered his wares and shoved them into his pack. All the while, Liall watched him. Without a word, the pedlar turned and trudged back to the edge of the camp. Liall saw him pull up his hood and draw his long red coat closer about him before starting down the path. The wind was growing teeth by then, but it was not a long journey back to Lysia, perhaps two leagues, and the pedlar would be sheltered from the wind by the trees lining the high banks on either side of the path. The Kasiri would have no such protection on the first promontory that spanned the Nerit, and his men knew it. He could see it in the way they scrambled to get the animals and their own possessions, including their women, into safe shelter.

Liall sighed. The pedlar was just a dot of red on the path now. He dispensed with the last of the travelers and signaled to Kio to follow him.

Peysho's loyal companion was scrappy as a gutter rat and quick with his hands. The serpent-worshipping Morturii were famous for two things: the making of weapons and the making of magic. The latter Liall discounted, having no belief in magic and having seen too many charlatans in Morturii passing themselves off as sorcerers, but he had seen the truth of the former. Morturii have the knack of handling blades, even their females, and Kio was an artist with them. Liall had seen him launch a dagger at an insect with casual ease and hit a target he might have made once in a lifetime. In Kio's hands, a kitchen knife became a whirling circle of death. The housewife had not known her peril.

Peysho's yurt was warm, and his women, two Minh half-bloods and an ample-bosomed, tattooed Chrj, were busy arranging furs and serving him wine and hot soup. When Kio entered behind Liall, the women finished their work quickly and left, knowing Peysho was in good hands and probably relieved of the fact. Truly, there was not much more for women to do in a Kasiri camp than cook and clean and please a man in other ways. As atya, Liall would have welcomed the chance to increase the Longspur krait's number by taking in a woman or two from Lysia, but Hilurin women tended not to stray far from either home or convention, which was a pity.

He settled down on a heap of furs and Kio poured a mug of bitterbeer for Liall and one of wine for Peysho. Kio shivered as he threw off his cloak and gloves and huddled near the iron brazier, rubbing his hands over the small flames. Liall caught Peysho watching his lover, Kio, and noted with some interest how Kio's eyes were glittering gold in the light, and how the fire pulled reddish sparks from his oak-leaf hair.

"Take a cup for yerself," Peysho scolded Kio. "Get some heat in yer blood 'fore yer lungs take a chill."

Kio, never a man of many words, rolled his eyes and reached to help himself to Peysho's own cup. Peysho grinned at the familiarity, for though the two had shared a yurt for as long as Liall had known them, Kio was invariably aloof to Peysho in public: a matter of upbringing, perhaps. Morturii held strange notions regarding men and their habits. There was little shame attached to physical affection between Morturii males, but for the one who took on the passive role in that relationship, the man who allowed himself to be penetrated and otherwise treated as a woman, there could be grave consequences. They had never spoken of it, but Liall was shrewd enough to recognize that Peysho and Kio were fleeing from something in their shared past.

Ah well, matters were different everywhere. As in Byzantur, so in Morturii, and in Minh and in the north continent where he had been born and which common men still believe is a fairy tale, for no land could be locked in ice and darkness for half the year and its people still survive. Surely only beasts lived there and not men, if it was real at all.

Kio handed him a mug of soup. It was a thick broth with chunks of meat and tubers, savory with some expensive spice, probably taken in trade for a toll. Peysho's six women, who he dubbed his *ehgli*, or wives, were diligent with the quality of his food and often lavishly extravagant of Peysho's care. They would do well to, since he was a generous husband as far as Kasiri went, and he treated them with detached kindness and his demands were few and he had no other use for them. Morturii men took only one wife at a time, but Kasiri had no such law, and Peysho seemed to take delight in seeing how far he could stretch the privilege.

Liall sipped at his mug and mused how it was ill that the approaching storm would keep his camp indoors and separate. Not that he had ever been especially sociable with his nomads, but he liked to watch them drink around the campfire until they were cross-eyed, laughing their fool heads off at whatever filthy song was being roared to the scraping of a poorly-tuned tal vielle or a warped box harp. It was a matter of endless amusement to him that he would finally find some measure of comfort in the company of illiterate peasants, escaped convicts, felons, mercenaries, horse-thieves, and pickpockets.

After such an evening, the remainder of his night

would be highly predictable: he would recline in his bed in his chieftain's yurt, watching the brazier cast patterns and shadows on the walls until sleep claimed him. Occasionally, Dira would send him a woman. Less frequently, there would be a beardless, silken dove or a rough-handed soldier fresh to the krait, and he enjoyed their company and their eager touches more than the women, for his tastes ran that way. He never allowed them to sleep in his bed, though, and he rarely sought the same body twice. To do so would be to invite intimacy, and above all, Liall guarded his heart. Like most cynics who have been shattered by love, he openly scoffed the concept of it while often finding himself in profound awe at the power it could wield over people. There was no place for love in his life. Barring everything else – his fear, his past, and his uncertain future – he was unconsciously certain he did not deserve it.

After his bedmates were dismissed, his thoughts would invariably turn to home. Even though it brought him pain, he could not stop thinking about it, like a man who keeps poking a sore tooth with his tongue to see if it still hurts. He would think about his family left behind and wonder how they fared, and whether or not there had been famine or plague in his land, or if they had gone again to war. Sometimes he longed only to hear the sound of his own language, and then he would speak words in his native tongue to the walls of his yurt: snatches of poetry, bits of song, or jokes he had learned as a boy.

He knew that it was not wise to dwell too long on home. Byzans had a saying that the gods loved to play tricks on mortals, and eavesdropped on human wishes and daydreams to plot their pranks. Perhaps they were right.

One morning about three weeks ago, it had snowed early and he had gone out to take his post watching the Sea

Road. Snow usually fell only on the heights in that land of amber and gold, on mountaintops and the high passes of the Zun mountain range between Minh and Morturii, in the Nerit, and of course in Lysia, which was in the mountain foothills itself and higher up than most villages. As he stood watch among the swirling white flakes, Liall spied a tall, cloaked man trudging through the camp, escorted by Kio. The traveler's head was uncovered, and Liall saw that his hair was pure white. His heart beat faster at the sight, but it was only a well-traveled old man in good health, a tinker returning to his home in Arbyss, and not one of his own northern people at all. He was bitterly disappointed and let the man pass down to the Sea Road for a copper and a row of tin buttons in the shape of beetles, and he shouted at Kio for no reason. Peysho watched Liall shrewdly and would have spoken, but Liall growled and Peysho pulled Kio away. No, it was not wise to remember too much.

Seeing he was again brooding, Peysho pushed Liall's leg with the toe of his boot. "Copper for yer thoughts," he ventured in his atrocious accent, slurping a mouthful of hot soup. He spilled some on his chin and wiped it away on his sleeve.

Liall shook his head. "Nothing. Only wondering how bad the weather will get up here."

Peysho snorted. "Well, ye can't be worried for yerself, not with that ice water ye call blood in yer veins, so that worry must be fer us."

He chuckled. Kio and Peysho were often aghast at how little he wore on a snowy morning, when the rest of the krait were piled high with fur cloaks over their leather and deer-hide jackets. It put them in awe of him a little, which is not a bad thing for a man who leads.

"Don't fret over us," Kio put in. He was better bred than Peysho and had finer manners and speech, yet they made an odd kind of sense together. "The weather's harsher in Morturii than it is here."

Most of the Longspur krait —named after the brown bird that makes its nest in the flat plains— were from Chrj and had the look of that people, being lean and sharp-faced, their hair ruddy or brown or even a dark gold. Their eyes tended to be green or hazel: unique colors in this land of black-eyed people. Many bore bluish-black tattoos rendered boldly in complex interlocking patterns, the symbolism of which was known only to them. The rest of the krait were Morturii or a mix of swarthy Bledlands outlaws and half-Minh Aralyrin, the spawn of captured slaves, whom the Hilurin would have absolutely nothing to do with. The Hilurin were a little more accepting of their people who had married into Chrj and Morturii families, which made up the greatest part of the Aralyrin population of Byzantur, but they stubbornly lived apart from them in their chaste little villages. A pity, since it made them much easier for their enemies to find, and they had many. One hundred percent of the power in the official government of Byzantur was held by Hilurin politicians and nobles, whose people comprised perhaps two percent of the population. Ancient tradition and religion alone held this status quo together, but it was fraying more every day. The Hilurin power structure could not last much longer, and villages like Lysia would bear the worst of it when it fell.

"Still," Liall answered, "I think it best to stock up on staples and firewood. As long as the krait is fed and warm, we'll have no trouble from within our ranks."

"And none from without, so long as we keep our knives sharp. I've seen to that," Kio put in with a touch of smugness, He had been training several of the youths in dagger-play for months. He also taught long-knives, daggers to the men, and the short, stabbing rapier called a *sperret*, which is wielded in tandem with a small shield for very swift, in-and-out fighting. Very few fighters carried swords in the Southern Continent, and the long-knife was preferred for close work. Byzans in particular, small as they were, never used swords. The standard weapon throughout the Southern Continent was a pair of long-knives, the blade perhaps as long a man's forearm from his elbow to the tips of his fingers, with a short, slightly-curved wooden haft and no hand guard. The Morturii made such blades from the black ore of the Byzan hills, and they were prized all over the world.

Liall finished his soup and handed the cup back to Peysho with a nod of thanks. "Well then, it's back to my cold bed."

Peysho waved his arm expansively in the general direction of his women's yurt. "Why go to bed cold, Atya? Ye can have yer pick."

He grinned. "I might, if you ever acquire a woman younger than yourself."

Peysho laughed. "My wives're exactly the right age to know how ta take care of a man. What would I do with a young woman?"

"Not the same thing I'd do with her, I venture."

Peysho shrugged good-naturedly. "Go see old Dira, then. He still has a dove or two ye haven't plucked."

Every krait has its prostitutes, but being the atya, Liall was leery of visiting the same girl or boy too many times. Misunderstandings could occur. He would just have to wait until their travels led the krait close to a larger city, one without so many prudish Hilurin.

"A pox on Dira's stable of skinny birds and on your wizened hags," he pronounced, which sent Peysho into more laughter. "But offer again when you get yourself a pretty boy-wife or two."

Kio muttered darkly under his breath and poked up the

fire with a stick, and Liall laughed and clapped him on the shoulder. "I'm teasing, Kio. Peysho only has eyes for you."

Peysho caught Kio's eye and winked, and the younger man subsided, mollified.

"Right, then." He waved at them, embarrassed at himself. The attempt to stir jealousy in Peysho's contented yurt was motivated solely by his own bitterness. He did not desire Kio, or not very much, but he did envy them their happiness. "Sleep well."

3.

A Restless Night

Liall dreamed of the pedlar that night. They were not in Byzantur, but in Rshan, and it surprised him to see the pedlar in his home country, dressed in hunting silks with silver threaded through his black hair. It must have been a snow bear hunt, for the riders were dressed splendidly in much finery and jewels, not the usual type of hunt at all. Sharpened stakes were strapped to their horse's flanks, but no swords or bows. The snow bear is a quick beast that hunters find difficult to bring down from a distance, even with a crossbow. The white-furred bear blended in well with his surroundings, and even well-seasoned hunters with a ready supply of bolts had the occasional accident. A horse would sometimes trip and snap a foreleg in the ice, and the downed man and his mount would become meat for the bear instead of the other way around. Or they could get caught in a small boat crossing a river or lake that had not yet frozen, which also meant death. The hulking snow bear became an otter in the sea, an agile beast armed with eight-inch claws and fangs the size of fingers. Liall had seen it happen before, and it was not a memory he cared to recall.

In his dream, the pedlar was smiling, happy to be going on an adventure. It made his chest ache to watch the beautiful youth as he waved and laughed, calling Liall by his right name, his old name, and telling him not to be a want-wit.

Then the dream shifted. They were racing their horses

over a snowy field, hot on the trail of the bear, hounds baying ahead of them, the rest of the hunting party shouting and whipping past. Suddenly, the snow bear was there. They had stumbled right into his lair and he was among them, slashing and tearing and biting. Men and horses were screaming and someone was yelling in a high, wild voice for the spears. Liall looked frantically for the pedlar and saw that his horse was down and he was in the center of a massacre, hunters and mounts and dogs torn to bloody chunks around him, the ravening snow bear in the thick of it. Liall locked eyes with the pedlar before the bear took him. The boy vanished beneath a mountain of white fur and claws, and one of the last things Liall saw before he woke up was Scarlet's slender body covered in blood from head to toe.

Liall woke with a gasp, his heart banging against his ribs. Yet it was not the dream that caused him to close his eyes on a spasm of pain, but what he saw in the instant before waking. The haughty pedlar lay in the snow with blood spilled over his body, but his face...

For a second, the face Liall saw was not the beautiful pedlar's. It was another he recognized, but could not name: a visage from his earliest childhood dreams. The face was cold and proud, with a clear, high brow and eyes so black they were like living night.

Who is this pedlar? he wondered as he lay staring at the rough walls of his yurt. How does he manage to affect me so?

He shivered in sudden cold that had nothing to do with the weather and pulled the fur closer around his body. Could the pedlar be his *t'aishka,* his immortal one? If so, it would not be the first time in Rshani history that it had happened between a Byzan and one of his folk, but in all cases the reunion of souls had proved disastrous for everyone involved. Byzans had not been welcome in

Rshan for thousands of years.

Liall started when he heard a scratching sound outside his yurt. It was Peysho rubbing his thumbnail on the canvas wall.

"A messenger, Atya," Peysho called.

He glanced at the marked candle burning on a stone pedestal by his bedside. Perhaps two hours had passed since he left Peysho's yurt. The wind had died down outside, but now it was much colder. He sighed at the feel of the warm furs around his body, briefly wishing he had taken Peysho up on his offer.

"Ye might want to see this one, Wolf."

He got up. There were few people who would send him a formal message. Somehow, he knew it was coming.

The messenger was an aging Minh lately from Volkovoi, and with the look of that people, being squat and yellow-skinned with wise, narrow eyes and clipped speech. Volkovoi was a harbor city across the Channel in Khet. It was one of the last open ports north before the sea.

The Minh wore the traditional blue-striped cloak and the silver badge of his office, and he insisted on being paid before he spoke. He was, he said, on his way back to his homeland and had agreed to make a brief, hazardous stop on the shores of Byzantur. He carried a message to the White Wolf of the Longspur krait from a certain Captain Lanak of the merchant ship *dal Ostre Nadir*.

The Minh held a small box out to Liall, and he signaled Peysho to pay the man yet again.

"For your silence," Liall said meaningfully, with a hard look at the Minh. Liall was surprised that the Minh had agreed to carry the message at all. If the man was caught on land in Byzantur, he would be killed on the spot. The Minh were deadly enemies to the Byzans.

Curious but knowing better than to press, Peysho did as he was told and dismissed the messenger, who hurried back down the Sea Road to his waiting ship. Peysho went back to his warm bed and the even warmer Kio as Liall stood frozen in place with his hands locked around the box. He did not open it right away, but set it aside in his yurt until his nerves stopped jangling. The box was wooden and plain enough, but the case was stamped with Sinha letters, the language of Rshan.

When the great eye of the moon hung over the mountain pass, looking close enough to touch, he opened the box and looked inside. He sat and looked at it for a long time.

I tried to run from it, he thought. A man can try, at the least.

He had lost so much of himself in Byzantur, drowning his memories in the lonely blue shadows thrown by the crags of cliffs and the jutting shelves of rock, in the last red gleam of the sun before nightfall, or in the first wink of a silver star in the deep, open sky. The weight of all that came before and the chiaroscuro contrast of the life he had now seemed to him like two ships bent on an unwavering course to collision. Now that he was about to lose it, his second life was suddenly very dear to him. The past had come seeking him like a persistent hound.

It has not all been sweet, he reminded himself. This life could cradle him gently or rend him to ribbons of flesh with its claws. It depended on the day, and how drunk he was the night before, and whether or not the tide that pulled at his mind in an endless crosscurrent of guilt had battered and eroded him enough to weaken his resolve, his promise to himself not to dwell on the past. Not to think at all, if possible. His dreams were not so easily commanded, and they knew no master.

"I tried to run, Nadei," he said aloud. "I told you I never wanted it."

"Atya?"

Liall turned, startled. Peysho had not gone back to his bed, but stood on the wooden steps just outside his yurt. Liall rose and thrust back the thick flap. "What are you doing?"

Peysho shrugged.

Liall shook his head. "Come in, then. I have no che or anything warm. Will bitterbeer do?"

Peysho nodded and accepted the cup without comment, sinking down onto a padded ottoman as Liall returned to his place on his bed. Several minutes crawled by, wherein Liall would not speak of the messenger and Peysho would not ask.

"Kio will be annoyed with me," Liall observed.

"With me, more like." Peysho supped his beer. "He's not used to sleeping alone."

"You should go back to him."

Peysho nodded agreeably but made no move to get up.

Liall looked at his knotted fist resting on his knee. "Do you have dreams, Peysho?"

Peysho shook his head. "Nah. Not that I remember, anyways. What's the use of 'em? I got everythin' I want right here."

He probably means that, Liall realized. "Well, I do dream," he sighed out. "No one knows who I am here, my *aman,*" he said, naming Peysho *friend* for the first time, for he had become aware of a deep sense of loneliness surrounding his spirit. "Not even you know, and you would not believe me if I told you. I never thought I would be in this rustic place, chieftain of a krait of unwashed bandit Kasiri. I am the foreigner here, with not a single soul knowing my true name. In my dreams, they do not call me Liall."

"What do they call ye?" Peysho asked, but Liall only closed his eyes, recalling how deeply it had wounded him to give up his name. It was a pain he had long suppressed.

Nazheradei, echoed a boy's voice in his mind, entreating, and he could never answer for the shame that clung to his skin. The crime that he committed in that other life haunted every step of his feet, every breath, every word spoken or promise uttered.

I will never be clean of it, Liall confessed silently as he watched the embers of the brazier dying down to pale ash. Never clean, nor free.

"It is of no consequence," he answered. "All that matters is who calls me. His name is... is Nadei," he stuttered, faltering over it. "Every night in my dreams, Nadei calls me, but not to his arms. When I go to him, I see that he carries a knife. I am not frightened of him or the promise of ending in his hand, and that is a great comfort to me. I go willingly, because in death there are no dreams."

Peysho was regarding him with grave worry, and for a moment Liall believed he had been very foolish to confide his flaws to a subordinate who would be justified in presenting his doubts before the krait warriors. In accordance with krait law, weakness was not tolerated in a Kasiri atya.

But when Peysho reached out and covered Liall's clenched hand with his own, Liall felt ashamed. Among the curiosity and doubt, there was genuine sympathy in Peysho's eyes.

"What c'n I do? Just name it and I'm yer man."

"Do?" he echoed. He smiled very sadly. "Go to bed, Peysho. This is the past I speak of. There is nothing anyone can do."

Peysho hesitated. "The pretty pedlar," he said. "Does he remind ye of this Nadei?"

Liall regarded him with surprise. That was too astute, he thought. And then: He knows me better than I realized. He tried to recall how many years he had known Peysho.

Kio had been barely a man when they joined his camp and began traveling with them. That was five summers ago.

"Perhaps," he allowed. "He has the same fire in him, the same temper and pride. But I do not wish to speak of it. The pedlar is gone."

"He'll be back," Peysho said, very certain.

"That will be an interesting meeting."

Peysho clucked his tongue, shaking his head. "Watch out ye don't regret him, too, Wolf. The past has a way of playin' over when ye least expect it."

Liall paled. "Good night, Peysho."

After Peysho had taken his leave, Liall put the box away. Sometime in the night, he took the two items from it, dumped the box into the campfire, and walked away so that he would not have to watch it burn. There was no one on the path to the Sea Road and no yurts camped that far over. It was a good place to stand and clear his head, where he could just make out the glimmer of waves in the distance.

Liall folded his arms in his cloak and watched the moon traverse the sky in the hushed silence of the heights. Beside him was a shattered pine that was perhaps a thousand years old, yet still carried a few straggling needles on one crooked limb. When the moon trespassed on the limb outlined against the indigo sky, the twisted hand of the pine seemed to reach beyond her to trawl for a handful of stars. The wind chattered through the dry branches like laughter. Liall closed his eyes and felt a pang of longing he had not allowed himself to feel in half a century.

In the dark places, the dream-boy called his name again, and he turned his mind away quickly before the sound could break him. *You cannot haunt me forever, Nadei.*

Liall could almost see Nadei smiling that cold smile of his, his hair like frost, his eyes the exact shape of Liall's own. *Oh, can I not? The more you run from me, the closer I draw near.* The knife he held never wavered, though there was blood on his feet.

Liall shuddered and looked at his hands as if searching for meaning in their lines. There was no written message within the box, only two tokens: a ring made of rare platinum and precious *filiri* sapphire, and the single white feather of a swan. The ring was for his safe passage, to prove who he was and to open doors. The feather was different. In the folk tales of his people, a white swan feather had only one meaning.

Come home.

Liall woke to Peysho scratching at the wall of the yurt again, then the flap moved aside and Peysho thrust his head in. The angle of the moon behind him told Liall it had been only an hour or so since he had fallen back asleep. The feather and the ring were tucked safely under his mattress.

"There's a matter, Atya. Ye'd best come."

Grumbling, he pushed aside his blankets and furs as Peysho retreated. So much for sleep. There were few reasons he tolerated being roused twice from his bed: raid, flood, fire, or the soft skin of another nuzzling his side. None of those were in sight when he exited the yurt and stepped close to the circle of warriors huddling close to the campfire. Then the circle opened up and Kio flung the black-haired pedlar at his feet.

The pedlar's hands were tied behind his back and his white skin was dirtied with ash. His dark eyes blazed with fury as he struggled uselessly with the ropes binding him. "Let me go, damn you! Kasiri dogs!"

Liall laughed and drew his cloak closer around him. This, at least, was a happy diversion. The wind was frigid. Inwardly, he felt a tinge of admiration toward the youth for venturing out into the dark, cold forest in an attempt to sneak past his men. He watched as the pedlar attempted to rise and Peysho grabbed him by the neck and flung him back to his knees in the snow and dirt. The boy looked fierce as a wolf, squatting on his heels and baring his teeth in the orange light of the campfire.

"What's this?" Liall flowed down to one knee and took the pedlar's chin in his hand, just barely retrieving his fingers before the pedlar snarled and snapped. He contemplated his whole digits, and then the boy, more thoughtfully and with less humor.

"You have the temper of a Minh," he said, which was more of an insult among Byzans. "Perhaps they should call you the wolf instead of me. Speaking of which." He reached for him more swiftly this time, dodging his dangerous teeth and seizing his smooth jaw in his hand. "You did not give me your name before, though I gave you mine. I will have it now."

The pedlar only narrowed his eyes at him and closed his mouth more firmly.

"You're stubborn, I'll give you that," Liall said, greatly impressed. "And you have courage, if not the brains to back it up. Did you not know we would patrol the forest?"

"I knew."

"Hark, he speaks at last." Liall released him. Standing up, he motioned for Peysho to slash the bindings on the boy's hands. "So you thought you could slip past the Kasiri, did you? Whence comes such confidence?"

The pedlar stood and stripped the severed-leather laces from his hands before he angrily kicked them toward

Liall with the toe of his boot. "I'm not confident. I have to get to the other side of this mountain and you won't let me by. That's all."

"Ah, but I will... for a price."

"I don't like your stinkin' mucked price," he snapped. Behind the pedlar, Peysho chuckled, then prudently coughed and looked away.

Liall dropped his voice and moved a little closer to the irate youth. "The price, or me?"

The pedlar met his eyes unflinchingly but did not answer immediately, and Liall saw that he was struggling with his answer. The atya fought down a surge of irritation. Princes had knelt at his feet once. Who was this illiterate merchant to refuse him? Who did he think he was?

"Come now," he coaxed. "You will not injure my feelings. I am no charming prince, this I know. But still, am I an ogre?"

"No," the pedlar judged after a moment, studying him. "You're a wolf."

"And you do not like wolves?"

"I like wolves fine, so long as they stay clear of my path. Wolves and men don't mix."

Or men and men, Liall supposed he would have liked to say. Peysho had shooed the tribesmen off and taken himself away with them, leaving Liall with the pedlar, the campfire, and the soft-snowing night around them.

"What about wolves and pedlars?" Liall asked softly, daring another step.

"I don't..." the pedlar began. He stopped and swallowed hard, looking up at Liall. There was no fear in his eyes. "I don't see why you're vexin' yourself, is all."

"Vexin'?" Local dialects often threw him. He waited for the boy to explain.

"Why are you going to so much trouble on my account? I can't be worth this much bother."

Liall began to suspect that this one was not terribly experienced with the desires of men.

"Are there no mirrors in Lysia? Give me your name," he urged.

"I–" he closed his mouth. "Let me pass."

Liall shook his head slowly. It made the pedlar angry again.

"Damn you, why not?"

"Because I'm not through vexin' myself, I suppose."

Snowflakes drifted slowly down and settled on the pedlar's black hair as he glared at Liall in loathing. Then, he abruptly dropped his gaze to his boots and his shoulders slumped. "All right," he muttered.

"What?"

The boy clenched his hands into fists and yelled it at him in a rush; "I said *all right*, I'll meet your gods-be-buggered price!"

Liall cocked his head as he regarded the pedlar. This capitulation was unexpected. Now that the youth had consented, Liall discovered that he had not asked enough. The pedlar would scrub the kiss from his mouth and walk away: still hating him, still believing himself superior, and Liall would have won a hollow victory.

Liall noted the stance of the pedlar's feet and the position of his fists before he spoke his next words. After all, this one had already mortgaged his precious pride. He would not enjoy what he heard next.

"The price has changed, red-coat."

The pedlar gaped. "What?"

"Today, it was a kiss. Tonight, since you have disturbed my sleep crashing about in the woods, it is one hour."

"An hour... what?"

He would have to be more blunt. "One hour," he said with a smile he hoped was gentle. "With me. Alone."

The pedlar's eyes widened. "If you think I'm going to...

just to cross your stupid..." he sputtered.

"Peace, I am a fair man. If my price has gone up then so must your reward."

"Reward?"

"One hour with me, and in return you will use the road freely for one-half turn of the season."

"You're a bastard!"

He nodded. "There are many bastards where I come from, figuratively and literally. And it's not always an insult in my homeland to be called such."

The boy mouthed an earthier epithet at him in Bizye, one that involved his mother and stables and a probable liaison with a diseased horse. There was a limit to how much insult he would endure, even from such an alluring mouth. He stepped forward and the pedlar gulped and withdrew hastily.

"Have a care, pretty one."

"Don't call me—"

"I will call you whatever I please, since you deny me your name. Amend your lapse in manners and I'll amend mine. Our business is done here." He snapped his fingers and Peysho, who had only retreated behind a nearby wagon, came into the firelight. "Return his weapons and pack to him and escort him down the path to Lysia," he commanded, his eyes were still locked with the pedlar's, sky-topaz meeting midnight.

The pedlar opened his mouth to answer, but Peysho put a hand on his am. The boy jerked away from him.

"Come, lad," Peysho soothed. "Well-played, but enough fer one night."

The pedlar left, sending a final, furious glower in Liall's direction. Liall winked slyly, which did nothing to ingratiate him further. Then the pedlar was gone with Peysho, their soft footfalls muted by the crackle of the fire, his crimson coat swallowed by the night. Only then did Liall realize that he still had not gotten the red-coat's name.

"Damn," he swore softly, standing alone in the firelight. He had won the round again, with no more pleasure than the last time.

4.

Soldier of the Vine

This Wolf is putting me off balance, Scarlet fumed. He had never seen a man so tall, so pale of hair and dark of skin, and with such long, large hands. The atya dressed like a lord in silver and black, his speech was learned and fine, but his behavior was more suited to a bhoros house than a bargaining table. Scarlet trudged down the mountain path in the dark, so livid he could barely think, but cautious not to tread too close to the edges of the path and to keep his ears open for prowlers in the evergreen forest.

First he charges me a toll to a road that I've been crossing for free since I was fourteen, now he denies me fair passage at all! What gives him the right? Of course I tried to sneak by!

He had thought the soot on his face –applied from an abandoned hearth as he waited for dark on the edge of the village– was a nice touch, but he had felt silly for it after he was caught and fully expected the Kasiri to beat him or worse. The atya's reaction confused him. Liall had been amused instead of angry, and had mocked him instead of setting his men on him, calling him *pretty one* as if he were a girl.

Thinking on that left him flushed and furious all the way back to Lysia. Scaja was awake and tending the fire when he crept back into the house. His father watched him enter without comment, taking in the sight of his smudged face and shamed expression. He then went to the cupboard and came back holding a pewter flask and mug.

"You look frozen. And you're filthy."

Scarlet hung his head. He would have to get water from the well and heat it if he did not want Linhona to scold him for the soot on his sheets.

Scaja read his mind. "Go and get the water," he advised, "and I'll pour us one."

Scarlet hauled in a bucket of water, icy-cold from the well and set it on the iron plate above the fire to heat. He thought about using his Gift to whisper the water to be just a tad warmer, or dropping a withy-thought into the fireplace to brighten the coals, but Scaja disapproved of using Deva's Gift so casually. The water would heat in its own time.

"Tried to sneak by him, did you?" Scaja asked in an offhanded manner.

He nodded shortly.

"Didn't work?"

"What does it look like?"

Scaja paused for a long moment. "He didn't hurt you, did he? If he—"

"No, Scaja," he responded quickly. "I was hurt more by the thorns in the forest."

"Ah." Scaja subsided.

They lapsed into silence as they waited for the water to heat.

"Have you thought that just paying his toll might be the easiest way to get through?" Scaja asked, handing him a mug half-full of pale green *anguisange*. Scarlet was surprised, for anguisange, or serpent's blood, as it was called commonly, was Scaja's favorite. The price was dear, so he almost never had any. He must have been saving it.

"I can't," he hedged, taking a drink. The potent wine

burned him all the way to his toes.

Scaja shrugged. "I don't approve of tolling, but the man's been fair enough from the talk I've heard. He's never taken more than a body can afford and there's not been anyone hurt or killed, although a few wore shredded pride when they stumbled back. Like you."

Scarlet took off his shirt, knelt by the fire to lift the bucket off the plate, and set it on the well-scrubbed stone hearth. He cupped his hands and splashed water on his face. It was still cold, but anything was better than facing Scaja when he told him the rest.

"He doesn't want goods or coin from me."

Scaja frowned. "No?"

"No."

A moment passed. "Well, are you going to tell me?"

"First, he wanted a kiss," he stuttered, and Scaja's brow clouded with anger. "And now he wants me for an hour."

Scaja's jaw dropped and they avoided looking at each other for a moment. "Oh." He cleared his throat. Shock was evident on his face. "Well." He coughed. "I see."

"I'd have given him his damned kiss tonight," Scarlet blurted, reaching for a cloth to wipe his face. "But he changed his damned price."

Scaja coughed again. "A man does not sell himself to anyone," he cautioned firmly. "Lying with another for pleasure or love is one thing; this is quite another. I'll put my fist to yon Wolf if he ever stirs from his mountain, and to you if you ever let such fish-rot get to you." Scaja's black brows knitted together until there was a deep, angry groove in his forehead. "We'll see if he acts the rapist after I set his boots on fire. I can send a withy to kindle a fire in Jerivet's hearth all the way from here, you know."

He knew. Scarlet was afraid his father was angered enough to go out seeking Liall, but Scaja shook his head.

"I'm too old to go picking fights. I don't blame him for his desire, only that he sought to force it on you." He chewed his lip for a moment. "He hasn't threatened you, has he?"

Scarlet thought back. "No. Not seriously."

Scaja nodded. "You take after your birth-mother, you know. She was a beauty, like you."

He scowled and splashed water as he washed his arms, not wanting to be reminded of what the Wolf had called him, even if Scaja meant to compliment. His pride had taken enough of a beating for one day.

"Perhaps it would be best if you took the Salt Road for a while until his fancy lessens. He'll find someone else to catch his eye and you'll see he's no longer interested."

"And if that doesn't work?"

"If that doesn't work, then maybe his fancy isn't a passing thing," Scaja mused, stoking the fire with another split of wood. "Do you think him handsome, this Wolf?"

Scarlet was beginning to think he was in the wrong house. Scaja had never been so plain with him before. His heart sped up a little. "Why would that matter to me?"

Scaja shrugged. "Beauty always matters to youth, and I no longer know what interests you in a mate. You don't talk to me anymore." Hurt bled into his words. "Scarlet, I've been wanting to ask you if—"

"No." The denial was out before he could stop it.

"It is not common among Hilurin men," Scaja went on, "but no one would take it ill if you—"

"I said *no!*" he exclaimed, shocked and frightened for no reason that he could name. I can't tell him, he thought as his heart slammed against his ribs in sudden panic. I can't!

"Shush!" Scaja scolded. "You'll wake the house." He pushed at the embers with the poker and waited a minute before speaking again. "I'm not accusing you, and I'm not suggesting you give in to him. No such thing," he said low and forcefully. "I'm just... I've noted that no girl has ever caught your eye in Lysia. Not since you were old enough to think about such things."

Scarlet waited, feeling very cold, as if dread was ice and it was seeping into his marrow. After a long moment, Scaja poked the fire a bit more and looked briefly at his son. Scarlet looked away. His heart felt like a lump of glass in his chest.

"Well, then," Scaja said cheerlessly, taking his silence for meaning. "I'd hoped we could talk about this like men, but I see you're not keen on it. You're grown now and master of your own life, I suppose."

They sat in silence for a long moment. "I'm worried about you," Scaja confessed. "Your spirit isn't here in Lysia and it never has been. When you took to wandering, I was happy for you. I thought you'd found what you were looking for, because every time you came back, you were so eager to be off again. I guess I thought you must have been hurrying back to someone you loved, though why you'd hide that from me..." his words trailed off and he shook his head as if clearing it of evil thoughts. "Now I know there's no one, and I begin to think your travels are less about wanderlust than just plain being lost."

"I'm not lost," Scarlet finally got out, wondering what spell was on his tongue that he could not talk about *this* with Scaja, when they could talk about everything else. This odd, tangled thing that would not allow his blood to warm when a pretty girl gave him an admiring eye, but made him feel jumpy and sick and turned his belly to knots of confusion when it was a handsome man. He had seen the slender youths for sale in the Morturii souks. Unfortunate, underfed young men with painted lips and cheeks patted with red powder, stripped to the skin and wriggling to show off their bodies to the crowd, hoping some rich jeweler or lonely widower would buy them. More often than not it was a rough soldier from some encampment, or a silk-clad Minh trader who did not haggle, but only inspected their bodies as if they were cattle, making them turn and pose for his probing fingers. The boys made doe-eyes at the prosperous buyers, lowering their eyelashes and pursing their mouths into pouts, but at the soldiers and the rogues they showed contempt and subtle defiance and generally tried to make it known, by silences and ill-looks and other ways that were not openly rebellious, that they would not make for a good purchase. Often, when a particularly pretty, high-priced youth was being offered, there would be a public display of his talents to entice the crowd and drive his cost up.

Scarlet thought of the cheers and catcalls rising from the crowd when the slave knelt before some hired actor or handsome servant, and how sick he felt to realize that he shared an affinity with those sweating men who watched the most avidly.

I'm not like that, he thought fiercely. I have to be in the souk, I'm a pedlar! And I wouldn't do any of those... things.

"I'm just not sure where I'm supposed to be," he confessed, skirting the other issue. That much was true. It was what drove his wandering feet: the desire to find out where he belonged and, honestly, with whom. He loved his family, but ever since his childhood, he knew there was someone out in the world waiting to be found. Someone meant for *him*. He just had to keep looking.

"Well, either road, it won't hurt you to cool your heels at home for a bit," Scaja said heavily, putting the poker away and facing him. "Until you know what it is you're looking for, don't be in such a hurry to run off and find it. Sometimes the answer's right in front of us. We're just moving too fast to see it."

Scarlet nodded. It was only good sense his father was talking. He finished washing and dried off before taking up his drink again.

Scarlet was still edgy when he went to bed, and sleep was a long time finding him. Linhona was glad to see him in the morning, which dawned cold but crystal clear. The mild winter season was nearly upon them and it seemed wisest, if he must take the longer Salt Road, to stay until the weather shifted again. It would only snow in the mountain and high passes anyway, but the copper weather-witch on the roof promised it would come down hard and nothing was guaranteed in Nemerl, so he stayed in Lysia.

True to prediction, the snow came and lingered for four days. There was not much in the house to occupy his time, and Scaja's workshop was only big enough for one craftsman. Two days of a young, energetic man underfoot, one who was used to being busy from dawn to sunset, and Scaja started growling, so Scarlet spent some time visiting Shansi, the blacksmith's apprentice who was to marry Annaya. Shansi seemed like a likely enough lad, solemn, not overly handsome, and serious about his trade. The apprentice spent a good hour showing his potential brother-in-law around his uncle's smithy before Scarlet began yawning and bid him good night. It was dark when he stopped by Rufa's for bitterbeer and pipes.

At first, he had hoped to find some travelers who could tell him the condition of the Salt Road, but there were few guests at the inn. He played darts and stars for a bit before he got bored, then took his bitterbeer to sit nursing it by the fire, watching the snow falling past the one window and thinking about what Scaja said about wanderlust and being lost. Behind him, a man tuned up his tal vielle and began to play a slow melody, joined a moment later by a farmer strumming a dittern. Scarlet vaguely knew the men for Hilurin free-holders who worked the land north below Lysia, but he was in no mood for music or talking.

He had nearly finished his drink when a lean-faced Aralyrin soldier clad in the red and brown colors of the regular Byzan army sauntered over to stand by his table. The soldier wore a crimson bindweed vine embroidered on his sleeve –the badge of the Flower Prince– and had a single green stripe on his collar that denoted his middle rank of captain. Scarlet knew all the ranks, and he was on talking terms with several of the soldiers stationed at the Patra garrison, which he had to pass on each and every one of his trips to Ankar.

"No luck sneaking by the Wolf, eh?"

It was said with dripping sympathy, an oily tone that whispered dark alleys and bad bargains. Scarlet studied the seasoned warrior and noted that, for all the shabby appearance of his uniform, he had a fine fighting axe hanging at his belt, and his boots and the metal-studded leather armor he wore on his wrists and legs were sound.

"No," he returned shortly. "And how did you get wind of my business?"

"The village Watch."

Old Kev, who had been the first to greet him home. Scaja must have told him what happened on the Pass, which meant everyone in Lysia knew. The soldier took a seat beside him without being asked.

Now that the soldier was nearer to the fire, Scarlet

saw that his face was scarred: two long slashes on either cheek, which looked to be deliberately done. A punishment, perhaps. He had the black eyes of a Hilurin, but he was too tall and hairy to have much of the blood. His face had the plain, weather-worn look of the north: high cheekbones, a scattering of short brown beard on his chin, a lank scrawl of shoulder-length hair halfway between black and brown with reddish tints, and a long, thin nose that spoke of his Morturii ancestry.

"Pity," the soldier said, and lifted his mug. "Not quite clever enough."

"Perhaps not," he allowed. Scarlet wondered what the soldier wanted with him. He still wore his long pedlar's coat, so perhaps the man just wanted news of the road. In a moment more, the soldier asked.

"Nothing unusual. There's a fever in Zarabek, but that's no news this time of year. Nantua has a new mayor and he's thinking of putting a tax on pedlar's goods, the puffed-up prick. Good luck to him, since the trade in Natua is already so poor that only good-hearted chapmen bother to stop."

The soldier nodded and grinned, the long scars giving his face a sardonic cast. He was older than Scarlet first estimated. Now that the man was close, Scarlet realized that something about the soldier disturbed his traveler's sense, warning him to beware. His eyes were drawn again to the crimson vine on the soldier's sleeve, and he reminded himself that this one served the Flower Prince and had sworn an oath to uphold justice and rule in Byzantur. Perhaps they were both just having a cross night.

"And are you a good-hearted chapman?"

He shrugged. "That depends."

"On what, son?"

He did not like to be named a boy. He disliked it even more that night and that was no fault of the soldier's, but he glared anyway. "I'm a man grown and not your son, soldier."

The scarred man laughed, throwing his head back. Scarlet saw that he had one chipped canine tooth and the rest white and strong. His eyes twinkled at Scarlet in false good humor. "Fair enough. Your pardon, sir, and may I freshen your cup in apology?"

Scarlet was simmering but mollified. His pride had taken a thrashing from Liall, and he was short-tempered and sore.

Mirilee had been the alewife at Rufa's taberna since before Scarlet was born. She came to pour their cups full and the soldier passed her a coin. When she had gone, the soldier looked at Scarlet pensively and pursed his lips in thought. "I hear that a farmer named Kellun is taking a cartload of wool to be washed and dyed over the pass. Perhaps you can travel with him." His white teeth flashed in the lamplight. "Inside the wool."

The thought of traveling inside a cartload of greasy, unwashed wool was unpleasant. Scarlet grimaced and took a sip, wishing the soldier would leave him alone. Then he remembered Jerivet the potter, Scaja's old friend. Jerivet was planning to go over the pass with goods meant for the Bledlands market, and he loaded his cart with straw to cushion his wares, packing it around the plates and cups to prevent breakage. If he gave the potter a few copper slips to pay toward whatever toll the Kasiri charged, he might agree to help him.

The soldier leaned forward. "You've thought of something," he said genially. "I can see it in your eyes."

"Perhaps," he answered and shrugged. He was coming to dislike this soldier with a long nose too interested in his business. "Good evening." He rose and left his drink half-finished.

Scarlet did not see the soldier's eyes follow him as he

drew the collar of his red coat tighter and went out into the snowy night, nor did he see the calculating smile that crossed the soldier's face as he picked up the abandoned mug and slowly drank.

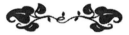

Scaja seemed resigned when he revealed his plan, but did not try to forbid it. He only put on his cap and went to speak to Jerivet. Jerivet said it was the foolishness of youth and seemed to think it was a grand adventure, and was patiently disposed with Scarlet when the next bright, snow-free dawn arrived and the pedlar showed up on his doorstep wearing a sheepish look.

"I hope this works out the way you want, Scarlet." Jerivet grinned as he covered him with straw, delighted to be part of some mischief at his age. "Your dad says you're a stubborn one."

Scarlet tried to find a comfortable position in the back of the cart amid the piles of crockery. "Thank you, Jerivet," he told him sincerely, just before the old man dropped another bundle of straw on his head and spread it over him. He sneezed and they struck out for the pass.

He had never realized before how rocky the road to the pass was. Riding in the back of a cart surrounded by pottery and covered in straw was not the most comfortable way to travel, and he hoped there were no insects in the straw. He consoled himself that the wool would have been a worse situation.

As they drew closer to the pass, Scarlet heard voices being raised: traveler's complaints, Kasiri calling back and forth, and one voice he recognized immediately. He recalled Liall as he stood before the campfire, how the bald enforcer, Peysho, had thrown him at Liall's feet like a gift. The atya had been surprised, but there had also been amusement in his gaze and some other emotion Scarlet could not recognize.

"Well, well, gran'ther, what have ye here?"

He recognized that rough voice, too. It was Peysho, who had seemed curiously sympathetic when he pushed him back down the road last time.

"Load of pottery, meant for market," Jerivet told him happily.

"Let's have a look at it, then," Peysho said, and there was rustling in the straw not far from his feet.

Scarlet froze and held his breath.

"Good wares," said a voice, startlingly near. It was Liall. "Not fancywork. Plain, strong, crockery. A silver bit, old man, to see it safely to market."

"Aye," Jerivet said pleasantly. He heard a clinking sound. "I've not a silver bit, but I've five coppers. Will it do?"

Liall's voice was just as agreeable. "As good as. Or, if you will, a set of plates."

"One only?" Jerivet returned quickly, and the haggling began in earnest.

He should have known. Jerivet could dicker the skin off a Minh and make him like it. Scarlet sighed inwardly and held very still as Jerivet pulled out saucers and bowls to extol their value. Jerivet's rummaging shifted the straw, and the end of Scarlet's nose began to tickle, then someone else reached in near his face and pulled out a bowl. A shower of very fine dust fell on his cheek.

He sneezed. There was a moment of silence before an iron hand reached in and clamped around his wrist, and then he was hauled bodily out of the cart, covered in scattered hay. His pack followed, tossed at his feet, and he was mortally glad he had left the bottle of blue poppy scent behind.

Liall truly looked like a robber prince today, with a small sapphire earring dangling over the white fur around his neck, and a fine blue woolen cloak with a polished silver brooch. Both his pale eyebrows climbed as he studied the pedlar. "Well, old man, it seems pottery is not all you carry," he said smilingly to Jerivet.

"He didn't know," Scarlet said hastily, afraid they would punish Jerivet.

Jerivet's expression went briefly startled before smoothing out again.

"And you are a poor liar," Liall told him. He turned to Jerivet. "Let you and I be done, old man, two of everything and two copper bits, and you are paid for the journey." He laid his hand on Scarlet's shoulder for an instant before Scarlet threw it off. "This one we will not charge you for, but he will not cross with you either."

"This boy is son to an old friend," Jerivet admitted. "I can't leave him here if you mean to harm him." His whiskered jaw tightened. "I'll fight you if I have to."

"Have I hurt any of your people yet? Do not fear for him, old father. One of everything and one copper bit, and I am paid," he said, dropping his price even lower.

"Done," Jerivet declared, and promptly began piling glazed crockery into Peysho's arms.

"You, on the other hand, have not paid at all," Liall murmured aside to Scarlet.

Scarlet glared, wanting to hit him.

Jerivet finished with the crockery and dropped the promised copper coin into the bowl on the top of the pile. Jerivet gave him a sad, sympathetic look before climbing back onto his cart, and Scarlet was a little sorry for having ruined the old man's adventure.

"I'll see you when I get back, lad. I will," Jerivet shot a look at Liall, "or there'll be pure hell to pay." Jerivet clicked his tongue and the old dray horse moved forward over the rutted road that led through the pass and down to Khurelen.

"Well!" Liall slapped his hands together and turned to look down on Scarlet. "The toll has risen for you again, redbird." He was smiling broadly.

Peysho gave them both an arch look and muttered an order to the Kasiri hanging about. They scattered and Peysho trudged toward a round red tent on a raised wooden pavilion, balancing crockery on his arms with little grace. It was the largest and richest tent in the camp, and Scarlet suspected it was Liall's own dwelling.

Though Scarlet had no fondness for Peysho, he was dismayed when the man was gone because it left him alone with Liall.

"I admire your resourcefulness," Liall said as he plucked a hay straw from Scarlet's hair. "But I fear I cannot reward it." He put the end of the straw in his mouth and chewed it thoughtfully as Scarlet stood there embarrassed and uncertain what to do next. "However, since you are so determined, I will offer you another bargain: stay with me tonight and you will have free passage for a full turning of the year."

"No."

"You are so swift to refuse," Liall complained. "Am I that ugly?"

Scarlet clamped his lips shut. *No, you're that handsome.* It was truth, but it was *his* truth, not to be forced out of him.

"Very well." Liall crushed the straw and cast it aside. "If you will not be moved by desire, perhaps I can trust in the natural parsimony of Byzans. Stay the night and I will pay you a hundred sellivar."

Scarlet's first reaction was to gape at him. Not only had he already been told *no* twice, but... one night worth a hundred silver coins? A full year's pay? The man was clearly mad. "You have no sense!"

"You value yourself too cheaply, pretty one."

His face went hot. "Scarlet," he announced in defense. "My name is Scarlet."

Liall tilted his head back. "A fair name for a fair lad, and it suits you, if I understand the meaning. Tell me, Scarlet; do you lie awake at night dreaming up these tricks?"

"If I did, I would succeed better."

Liall laughed. "You wrong me to think me less clever."

"I can't take the whole blame for this," he muttered. He was already resigned to being sent back to Lysia. "The soldier did suggest wool, but raw wool has fleas."

Liall took a step toward him. Before he could step back at this new intrusion, Liall had fitted his hand under Scarlet's chin. The chieftain studied his face intently.

"A soldier?" he echoed, his nearly colorless eyes glittering. "Give me his name."

"I... I can't, for he never gave it."

"And like a true Byzan, you never asked. What does he look like? Perhaps I know him."

"Lean, with a chipped tooth and scars on both sides of his face," he said without thinking, and winced when Liall's fingers tightened. He did not like the soldier's manners, but he had no reason to wish him ill or bring the atya's wrath down on him. Also, the soldier wore the Flower Prince's badge and so was sworn to uphold the law in Byzantur. "He meant nothing, I'm sure. He was teasing me for my failure."

"Your failure?" That white brow arched again. "Ah, your stealth in the forest, or lack of it. He sounds an unkind fellow at the very least, taking his pleasure in misfortune."

"It's an unkind world," he informed, very aware of Liall's hand on him.

"Indeed, but not everyone who mocks you means you ill, just as everyone who lays a hand on you is not necessarily your enemy. Tell me more of this soldier."

"There's nothing to tell."

"What was his rank?"

"Captain. He wore the crimson vine on his sleeve." He tried to pull away, but Liall was not letting go. "What does it matter?"

"Perhaps I'm merely jealous." Liall leaned close again, and for a moment Scarlet believed he was going to claim the kiss.

"Consider it; a single night for a hundred coins."

Liall's breath was warm on his skin, scented of spice and cloves, his voice deep and compelling. There were lines of sorrow or pain around Liall's eyes, a trace of bitterness or grief perhaps, and it took him by surprise to see it so clearly. Liall smelled clean, like the herbs his mother put in the clothes press, and that surprised him, too. He expected a Kasiri to smell of leather and sweat and horse. Pale eyes held his searchingly, and for one heartbeat, he nearly leaned into Liall. He caught himself an inch away and jerked back.

"N-no," he stammered, appalled at himself and embarrassed by the awareness in Liall's gaze. Was this magic, had he been bewitched by some Kasiri sorcery? No, not a spell, only fascination, and an ill one at that. What was he thinking? Liall had offered nothing but shameful bargains, and would bring him nothing but harm. He was behaving like a fool.

"No," he said more strongly.

Liall shrugged. He dropped his hand and Scarlet took a step back. "As you wish, pretty Scarlet."

He ground his teeth together. "Have I leave to go?"

"Down to the village," Liall agreed.

Damn him. He shouldered his pack and turned to trudge

back down the long road, cursing under his breath.

"Scarlet," Liall called out when he was several paces away. "Wait one moment."

He paused and looked over his shoulder.

Liall was waiting with one hand on his hip and a look of honest questioning on his face. "I do not intend to harm you. Despite what you may think of me, I am not in the habit of brutalizing my bedmates. It is also my suspicion that you and I are alike in our tastes, and that you would take much pleasure in my touch. Why not just give me what I want and be on your way?"

Scarlet took a deep breath and resisted the impulse to hurl his pack at the atya's head. If the bastard was puzzled, it was no fault of his. "If you must ask, then you wouldn't understand my answer."

5.

Peysho's Story

When the pedlar left the second time, Liall had little hope of seeing him again. There was enough trade north to Patra and Sondek to keep an industrious pedlar busy, so there was no need for him to come through the pass if he knew there was trouble waiting. In all likelihood, he reasoned, the pedlar would decide that the toll road was too much trouble, and would either take his business north or go south by another way.

And then he had tried his latest trick. When Liall hauled the hay-covered pedlar out of the wagon, he wisely resisted the urge to double over in laughter, for the pedlar's pride was already dented. The youth reminded him of someone he used to know: a hot-tempered boy who never took no for an answer and did precisely what everyone told him he could not do. A boy who had no respect for authority and no inkling of how much his reckless nature kept his mother up at night.

You lost that boy, Liall reminded himself, and wondered if that was the real reason he pressed the pedlar to accept his invitation. There was an Rshani legend of an enchanted mirror that showed only the past and ensnared all who gazed within, until one day a young man with no memory looked into the mirror and broke the charm. Truly, he thought, a man without memory might count himself blessed. Regret is a persistent hound.

The pedlar –no, *Scarlet*– had swayed into Liall at the last, closed his eyes like he wanted that kiss after all, but then he recalled his pride and withdrew. Liall was in favor of pride, until having it did a man more ill than good. Scarlet worried him. Liall believed the boy was putting up a bold front to show that he would not be intimidated, and was not really as intemperate or impetuous as he appeared. He had mentioned a man: the soldier of the crimson vine. Perhaps it was the soldier who put him up to it?

He whistled for Peysho as he continued to watch Scarlet stride down the mountain path, and the big man came jogging up and winked at him with his crimson eye. Liall did not give him a chance to speak: Peysho could be an unmerciful tease.

"What was the last news we had of Cadan?"

Peysho blinked. "Cadan? I heard that rotted bastard got himself killed down in the Bled. Why?"

"Just a hunch," he said absently, watching the slender line of Scarlet's body.

Peysho's sudden grin was wide and eager. "Fucker used to jibe me for my bloody eye. Bet he's jibing at himself, now, eh?"

Liall frowned. He did not like to be reminded of how he had scarred Cadan's face, or of how he disposed of the bodies of the three women Cadan had murdered. That is in the past, he told himself uneasily, and the past never changes. "It was not a thing I enjoyed," he said. "He had to be punished, so I punished him. Nothing more."

Peysho shrugged. "No argument from me on that account. Never did see a man who liked to hurt as much as him. I was glad to see the back of him. Ye did right, Wolf."

He nodded slowly as the bright smudge of Scarlet's red hood disappeared below the ridge. "I know, but I should have settled it better."

"What, ye mean go easy on him?"

"No," he sighed. "I should have finished him." He thought for a moment. "Maybe you should send Kio down to Lysia tomorrow, have him sniff around for news of a scarred officer in the Byzan army."

"Officer? Couldn't be him," Peysho scoffed. "He ent that smart."

"It's the regular Aralyrin army, not the royal one. You don't have to be smart to get a commission there, just brutal and clever at hiding it, and he was that."

"Well, I have my doubts, but I'll do as y'say. And if it's him?"

"If it is him, I won't make the same mistake twice. But forget him for now. I need to speak with you about a matter." Liall regarded Peysho with a calculating eye. "Not here. I'll meet you in my yurt at dusk."

"Why not mine?"

"Kio is there."

Peysho was shrewd enough to take his meaning. Liall knew the man would make his appearance early and alone. Peysho left uneasily.

True to Liall's expectations, just as the rim of the sun dipped under the peak of the Nerit, Peysho's boots were on the mat outside his yurt. Liall offered him wine and Peysho sat heavily on a pile of pillows and tried not to look as uncomfortable as he felt.

Peysho took the silver cup from his host –treasure from some passing merchant– and glanced around him in an effort at courtesy. "Nice rug," he said, deadpan.

"A fine weave," Liall agreed. "Try the wine."

He set the cup aside. "The wine is fuckin' lovely, I'm sure. Now, what in all Deva's bleeding hells is this about?"

Liall smiled. "You took the long way around the river to say *that*, I see." Peysho glowered at him and Liall chuckled. "Forgive me for having fun with you, old friend. It's not easy, what I have to say, and so I thought…" he shrugged. "I've been told I have no tact."

Unexpectedly, Peysho's gaze went long and he stared resolutely at the wall of the tent. "Ye will be askin' me and Kio to move on, then?"

Liall was genuinely shocked. "What makes you say that?"

"I thought," Peysho began. "Well, and not every man in the krait is happy that ye've put Kio in charge of the fighters. Ye remember when ye put me in charge of runnin' the line, and the men had to answer to me fer any tolls or treasure? I had to fight five men that week."

So that was it. According to krait law, any man could be deposed from his position if he was not strong enough to hold it. Promoting Peysho to enforcer had been a risky move, but the man had acquitted himself well and earned great respect among the Kasiri. Putting Kio in as captain over the fighters had not yet caused any great amount of trouble, but Liall suspected this was because most of the men were afraid of Peysho and knew of the bond the two men shared.

Liall took a sip of wine to stall. This would want a delicate hand. "And you're aware that it's not so much you they object to as Kio?" Liall had heard the pointed grumblings about Kio and ignored them, for his word was law in the krait, but only so far. The Kasiri could like his choice or not, but if any man decided to challenge Kio, that would be Kio's business alone.

So that is why he looked so alarmed when I ordered him to come alone, Liall thought. He assumed I wanted to spare him the shame of being banished from the krait in front of Kio.

"Forgive me," Liall said slowly. "Even after all these years, I sometimes forget that I am not in my own country." He set his wine cup down and chose his words carefully. "A man's bed is his concern and no one else's. Where you love is your own business. In my land, no one would give your choice a second thought."

The enforcer brightened a little. "Fer true?"

"Truly."

Peysho looked deep into his cup for a long moment and then drank thoughtfully. The fire popped lazily and the smell of wood smoke grew stronger before the vent carried it away. Liall knew that Peysho must have been rethinking the future plans he had been making all afternoon. He was saddened that he had put his friend through misery without need. At last, Peysho sighed and set his drink aside.

"We ent got it so easy in Morturii. Things are different there. I could almost envy yer land, cold an' all."

"Is this," Liall made a vague gesture, "why you had to leave Morturii?"

"Not me, but Kio. He was a soldier once, same as me. I was his commandin' officer. Fool lad got caught on his knees in the barracks one night. Civilians are one thing, and what's done in town ent spoken of in the field, but soldiers are forbidden to know each other like that. *Morale* and all that, they say. The generals believe it weakens the ranks." He snorted to show his disdain of that notion and went on: "Well, they sent the other lad to a floggin', but Kio's from a good family, poor but thought well of, so they sent word up t' the headquarters, askin' what should be done about him. We waited two days to hear back, and in that time the other lad took fever in his wounds and died of it. Kio was scared to death, thinkin' he was bound for the same fate, and me... I was too close to the matter to see clear."

Peysho shrugged his broad shoulders uncomfortably, and Liall recalled he had scars there; old ones faded almost silver with long age.

"We got the word back, and it was bad. Not only floggin', but a brand as well. Right 'ere." Peysho touched the center of his forehead. "Turned out Kio's family has an enemy in the army, and they saw their opportunity and took it. I went straight to his cell and knocked his guards out with a stone. Broke one o' their pates, I found out later, and he died from it, so I was a marked man, too, after that. No matter, we were both done for. The Morturii army takes a dim view of *sekeche*."

It was a crude insult, taken from the lowest of brothels; a word for a man who puts his mouth on another man.

"Do not say such things."

"Oh, I claim the title," Peysho said, showing Liall his rough grin, "if not the shame. Kio's a good man. He's a devil with a knife, he is, but when we're alone he's so... he's gentle and true and... and t'think someone would *punish* him for..." He broke off in disgust and reached for his cup again. His other big hand rested on his knee, clenched into a tight fist. Liall was quiet in respect, filling Peysho's cup as he calmed himself. Liall refilled his own cup and took a long drink before he spoke again.

"Listen to me, Peysho. I have had news from the north."

That perked him up. "Yer own people? Deva's hells!"

Liall reminded him of the Minh messenger and the box he had carried over so many leagues. "There was a swan feather inside. Among my people, this is a message to return at once."

"But ye ent heard from yer family for years," he scoffed. "Ye don't mean to desert the krait?"

There was fear there, the wolf cub's dread that the pack was not strong enough to meet its enemies on even ground, or the soldier's worry for a missing general.

"I do not mean to abandon them right away," Liall assured. "Yet, I must go eventually. I have no choice. And so, I plan to leave the krait in your care, Peysho. You will be atya in my place."

Peysho set his wine down quickly before he spilled it. *"Me?"*

"It is my right under krait law, is it not? The men will not be shocked, even if you are. As for Kio, well, we all have our hurdles. There will be words, I'm sure, and some of the men may challenge you or him or both, so think carefully before you agree."

Peysho was a seasoned soldier and accustomed to abrupt shifts in fortune. Liall saw him absorb the facts and weigh them soundlessly in his head.

"When will ye come back?"

Liall shrugged and wondered at the feel of his own body, the weight of it, like one millstone had been shifted off him and another put on.

"It is doubtful I will even reach Norl Udur alive, much less be able to return," he said, switching the true name of his land for the more common one his country was known by in Morturii. "A single journey there and straight back would take almost a year, and I have many old and powerful enemies who will try very hard to make sure that I never set foot on my own soil. Also, if I am fortunate enough to survive, I do not know how long I will be required to stay. It could be years before I return to Byzantur. Most likely, it will be never."

Peysho nodded slowly, accepting that truth as well. His rugged face was pinched with sadness. "Ye have my blessing, and the blessin' of any gods I've ever prayed to. Ye're the best man I've ever known, Wolf. The fairest and the most noble."

Liall pushed his arm. "Stop that. You'll have me wailing like an old grandfather in his cups."

He grinned. "Want some salt t' go with those tears?"

Crying in the beer, he meant. They laughed together and then wandered out onto the platform outside, both to escape the smoky interior of the yurt and to watch the jeweled stars emerge from the red curtain of dusk.

There was much to do, many plans to be made. Liall rested his palm on the ball of Peysho's shoulder as they silently watched the changeable sky shift hues into night.

6.

Grandma Goes Up the Mountain

Scaja opted to spare his feelings and said nothing when Scarlet showed up on the doorstep, slapping snow from his boots. Linhona quietly set another plate at the table and went to hang out laundry. Scarlet was too unsettled to dwell on what anyone else thought, being consumed with thoughts of his own.

Liall might be a wolf, but he was not the common bandit Scarlet had taken him for. There was something strange about him and his Kasiri, something strange in all of them, even in Peysho, who looked as fearsome as a Bled warrior but carried crockery without complaint. Or perhaps, he thought sullenly, you just never knew a Kasiri before.

Scarlet could not help remembering how Liall had looked when he was hauled out of the wagon to face the atya: tall and imposing and clearly expecting even the trees to bow down to him, and the sun and moon to rise and set at his orders. Despite Liall's accent, his speech was cultured and clear. Even when he was behaving like a villain, he draped that veil of manners over the whole lot, just like the court dandies at Rusa were trained to do. Not for the first time, Scarlet wondered where Liall was from. Nemerl was a large world, he knew, and Byzantur only a small part of it, but what people had such dark coloring of skin and such dead-white hair? None he had ever heard of. He marveled that such a strange man had decided to dwell in Byzantur.

He put his questions to Scaja that night as they brought in the wood before supper. "You've seen him. What did you think?"

Scaja gave his son a sharp look, then shook his head and stacked another split onto the armload Scarlet held. "Think? You mean with my head, or with my Gift?"

Scarlet looked at his boots. "Your Gift, if you please." Scaja could see much about men that was hidden.

"I'm not sure you want to go down this path, son."

"I'm just–"

"Wondering. So you've said. Well, you're old enough to pay the price for your curiosity. This Wolf is not a simple man; I'll say that for him. There's a shadow and a secret on his heart, and he guards it well. Even my grandmother couldn't have seen into it; it's that closed and locked. Like an iron gate hung with chains." Scaja paused in his work and squeezed his eyes shut. When he spoke next, it was in the formal, stilted words of prophecy. "An old pain, but still red and raw as the day it was made. He would savage the one who breached his fortress to approach that wound, or kill him dead."

Scaja opened his eyes and sighed, dropping the High Speech for common Bizye. "I'm sorry, lad, but your Wolf *is* a killer. Whatever he's told you, whatever he's filled your head with, he's got blood on his hands. Keep away from him. Go back to Ankar or Patra even to Volstland, if you're so sweet on danger, but stay clear of the Nerit until he's long gone."

"Is he proud?" Scarlet asked. It occurred to him that perhaps he had wounded Liall's pride when he refused him so bluntly, and maybe he could apologize and so settle matters that way. He was still thinking of ways to get around Liall, unwilling to see what his father was plainly telling him.

"Is snow cold?" Scaja countered gruffly. He obviously

considered the matter closed. "Why ask what you already know?"

He pondered that as he carried his burden in and knelt before the firebox to arrange the wood splits in a pattern, a deep frown digging a furrow between his brows.

"*Scarlet,*" Scaja snapped. "Stop mooning and get the wood stacked."

Mooning! He ducked his head and obeyed. Linhona said something to Scaja, too softly for him to hear.

"What?" Scarlet demanded.

Scaja shook his head, gently pushing Linhona into the kitchen. "Naught, boy. Go. Get your work done."

Scarlet sighed and went back for another armful of wood, trying to dismiss all the wondering from his brain.

It did not stay gone for long, and when it came back, it irritated him greatly. After brooding around the house for a full day, he spent the next afternoon working with Scaja to repair a wagon wheel at Tradepoint. He wore his fine new Morturii long-knives at his waist, and that put Scaja in a bad temper.

"What Hilurin goes armed to a friend's house?" Scaja demanded.

"A pedlar," he answered back smartly.

Scaja continued to mumble darkly under his breath as they worked in the cold air with Deni and Zsu looking on, casting pointed looks between his son and Zsu before shaking his head and muttering about cats and curiosity and the world-wild. Scarlet shook hands with Deni and promised Zsu a set of ribbons from Khurelen, whenever he managed to get there, which prompted another round of black looks. When night fell, Scarlet wandered over to the taberna rather than stay home and confront Scaja about what was bothering him.

Scarlet sipped bitterbeer in the comfy noise of Rufa's

place and thought dark things into his cup. There had to be a way to win this Kasiri chieftain over without losing more pride than he had left. However, even the idea of paying Liall's price made him angry. And besides, he found himself thinking, he'd know I was not granting him his demand out of desire. I'd be giving him what he wanted to get what I wanted in return, like a whore.

That thought made him livid and embarrassed all over again, so he paid for another beer to wash it out of his head and was drinking it too quickly when the soldier of the vine appeared beside him. The soldier helped himself to a chair at Scarlet's table and flicked him a mocking smile.

"I hear they caught you again!" he crowed. His scars wrinkled.

Scarlet silently wished him away. "My own doing," he retorted, wiping foam from his lip. "At least they didn't punish Jerivet."

"That must have been a pretty moment," the soldier laughed. "I'm surprised you still have your head on your shoulders. The Wolf isn't known to be forgiving."

He shrugged irritably, conveniently forgetting that this echoed, more or less, what Scaja had told him about Liall. "What do you know of him? You've been in the army for some time, by the look of your uniform. When have you faced him?"

The soldier eased back and studied his face. "Oh, I haven't," he said casually. "But I've heard tales. Women raped and strangled, men branded or beheaded."

Despite the soldier's words and even Scaja's warning, Scarlet found that difficult to believe. The first day he had seen Liall, he had witnessed him ordering his tribesman to unhand a woman. It had been easier ordered than done, for the woman was beating the Kasiri boy about his skull.

He had me in his camp, he thought, alone, at night, with armed men all around, and he let me go. Would a murderer spare a woman who defied him? Would he dicker over crockery and the price of tolls, or would he just take what he wanted, no excuses?

Scarlet eyed the solider. What was his aim? Was he here to assess the threat of the krait before reporting back to the Flower Prince, or was he just an idle soldier on his rounds of the villages, looking for a bit of company on the road? The kind of company that one pays for, he thought sourly, and was glad there were no bhoros houses in Lysia. He decided the soldier was a liar and a gossip, and that the Gift had whispered false to Scaja. Liall could not be a killer.

"Well, he's left my head alone."

"You must have a charming tongue in your head, despite your lack of cunning. Or perhaps he's heard of your pretty sister and hopes to curry favor with you and your father." He leaned forward and Scarlet's nose wrinkled. The soldier's humid breath was musty with stale bitterbeer. "Perhaps that's what you should do, boy. Dress in your sister's clothes and let him steal a kiss or two and he'll let you cross over."

"Keep your own tongue in your head before I cut it out," he warned as calmly as he could, resisting the urge to throw his mug at the soldier's face. He was unsettled by how wide the soldier's shot had gone and yet how close it had come. "And don't speak of my sister."

"Oh, of a certainty, young sir. I beg your pardon." The soldier shrugged the threat off. "The name's Cadan," he informed. "Lately of Patra. I'm newly assigned there, you might say."

"Scarlet," he replied brusquely, rising. He left his mug on the table and left Rufa's, not looking back to see if Cadan was watching him.

Scarlet thought a walk in the night air might cool his temper, but his hands ached with the need to hit something. Reaching the stone well —named Second Well, the first being near the village gate— in the center of the village square, he crossed his arms and stood shivering as a light, dusty snow began to fall. The snow was little more than a mist and nearly magical in the moonlight. He sighed deeply and allowed the feathery snowfall to calm him.

Why did I defend Liall? he asked himself. It's stupid to be attracted to him, naïve beyond excuse. The man has no honor and can offer me nothing beyond a single night of pleasure, bought at a shameful price.

Even Scaja knew that, and Scarlet ruefully thought that his father would be more accepting even of the loud and uncouth soldier, rather than a Kasiri robber wolf. At least the soldier was partially Hilurin.

He was quiet coming in, not wanting to wake anyone. As he took off his wet gloves and laid them near the smoldering hearth, he caught sight of his face in the little mirror above the mantle, and it stopped him cold.

The light snow was threaded through his hair like cobwebs, dusting it with white. The snowflakes were melting rapidly, but he saw the plan then as clearly and whole as if sent by a dream. Not his sister's clothing, but his mother's: flour in his hair, padding underneath to give him a matronly figure, and one of Linhona's gowns. He spared a moment to wish his Gift extended to illusion, as his grandmother had been said to be able to do. No one he knew had ever been able to use their Gift like that, or at least, none would admit to it. Linhona would have his ears when she found out, but oh, it was a splendid idea!

He grinned into the mirror. So, a bandit thought he could keep a pedlar from traveling the roads, did he? The Wolf was about to be proved very wrong. No one penned him in.

He woke with a start in the small hours of morning, sticky with sweat from the lingering images of a smoky dream. Scarlet pushed his damp hair back from his face with a shaking hand. There were horses; that much he remembered. Not like Byzan horses. These were huge beasts with short tails and curling, wooly coats. He had never seen such creatures, not even in his travels to Taim and Merkit that had taken him dangerously close to the borders of Minh. Much of the dream had been hazy, like looking through fogged glass, but he was unnerved to remember that Liall had been there, and he had not been a gaudy Kasiri in the dream, but clothed in rich fabrics and sitting astride a silver-caparisoned horse. He, too, had been clad in rich furs and velvet, and he remembered his dream-self shouting and spurring his horse to Liall's side, and all the while he was filled with a sinking, awful feeling in the pit of his stomach that he was too late.

He fumbled to light a candle and then washed his face at the basin before sliding back under the covers. Even with the candle out, it was hard to sleep again. Liall would not leave his thoughts. Who was he, anyway? Was he truly from Norl Udur, the northern kingdom so far away that no Byzan in living memory had taken the journey? Why did he dream about him? He truly did not like the man or what he was trying to force him to do at all. There was nothing alluring about Liall's methods, nothing noble about his krait. The whole source of fascination was the man himself, his long hands, his lofty height, his strange, pale hair, and the knowing looks that felt like intimate caresses.

Scarlet shivered in bed and pulled the covers higher,

cursing himself. Stupid boy, he thought morosely. Are you that pained for company that you'll take the first flea-bitten rag-tag who smiles at you?

Yes, Liall was a handsome man, but a detestable one, and as compelling as he was, Scarlet would not be pressured or pushed. He would not be treated as he had seen the male slaves treated on the block in Morturii, preening and debasing themselves for a bit of attention and the hope of a better future. In part, it was those memories that made him reject Liall so fiercely. Had his sneering refusal set the present in motion? Had he scratched Liall's pride as much as Liall had wounded his own? If he had only laughed and said no, would Liall have treated it all as a joke and let him pass?

Scarlet rolled on his side and sighed. He had no wish to be Liall's friend, but there was no telling how long the krait would hold the southern pass, and he needed to be on good terms with their leader to be able to get through.

Two hours before dawn, Scarlet rolled out of bed in the darkness and set about gathering what he needed. First he dressed in his own clothes: his gray wool sweater and his leather breeches and boots and his red pedlar's coat. The gown and cloak would hide it all anyway and would give him a matron's girth. He would *not* walk out of the village in a gown, but he could stop in the woods and dress there, comb the flour into his hair and put on the matron's cap. He had to fumble around his house in the dark to keep Linhona from catching him rifling through her clothes press with the intention of borrowing her gown and bodice and her good green cloak, but he hoped to have it back to her within a month. He lingered over his long-knives, wanting to take them but fearing they would give him away or that he would trip over them if he hid them under the gown. At length, he decided the roads to Khurelen were safer than the roads north and to leave his weapons at home. It would be a decision he would regret.

Khurelen, the first village over the pass, was several days away, but if he left quickly and made a good start down the Snakepath, he could manage it. He could not take his own pack –Liall would recognize it by now– so he took Scaja's, intending to tie some of the goods into his shirt and fasten some under the wide skirt as well. He would just keep his four-fingered hand hidden in his sleeve as best he could. Last, he tugged on an old pair of brown gloves and filched two apples from the bin before sneaking quietly out of the house. The moon was full and riding high, outlining long swaths of clean snow interspersed with patches of dark earth as he walked out of Lysia. An owl hooted in the treetops and Scarlet looked up to see the wide shadow of her wings ghosting across the white face of the moon.

He climbed the long trail in the moonlight and reached the woods below the pass only a half-hour before dawn. There, in a wide, cleared circle near a deep ravine, he hung a small brass mirror on the low branch of a young juniper. Almost too much time was spent carefully combing the white flour through his hair before putting on the linen cap, but at last he was done. He peered at himself in the mirror he intended to sell to a steading family on the road to Khurelen, and frowned in disappointment. The disguise did not look half as well as he had thought it might. If anyone got a look at him in broad daylight, the ruse would be over. He tugged the starched cap down tighter and began to put on the gown and the overlapping bodice. It was harder to do than he imagined. Scarlet cursed when an apple fell out of his half-laced bodice and he had to chase it before it rolled into the ravine, wondering how in the world Linhona and Annaya managed this every day. Finally, he threw the green cloak over all and started up the final stretch of road.

Even if he was not confident in his appearance, he was sure he could mimic an old woman's gait and posture. He remembered to slow his pace and hobble as if his knees pained him as he drew nearer to the wooden fence the Kasiri had set up as a roadblock. It was not difficult to limp up to the loitering men, but walking with everything tied under his skirt was.

"'Tis early for a grandmother to be out traveling," called one of the Kasiri from his watchpost.

Remembering Linhona's oft-told story and her imitation of an old crone, Scarlet tuned up the pitch of his voice and added a quaver. "What can't be helped must be endured."

The man nodded genially, turned, and whistled a piercing note. Scarlet continued to toil up the hill as Peysho came, followed by Liall, both of them looking mildly surprised. Neither of the men were conspicuously armed, and Scarlet realized they must just have risen from bed. His heart began to beat faster.

"Well, gran'ther," Peysho sang out, "it's a cold day fer a woman yer age." He looked at Liall. "Shall the ache in her bones be toll enough for 'er?"

Liall took another step forward and looked keenly at Scarlet as he hunched in his cloak and kept his eyes cast down. His heart thudded too hard, too fast, and he was afraid Liall could hear it. When he risked a peek from under the cap's brim and saw Liall's mouth twitch, he knew he had lost.

7.

The Wolf's Clothing

M y, my," Liall drawled. "What big eyes you have, granny." Though Liall marveled at Scarlet's bravery and again admired his stubbornness, it was a serious effort not to bray laughter like a donkey.

"The better to see the road, gypsy-king," Scarlet croaked out in an excellent imitation of an old woman's bleat. He had obviously decided to play this to the hilt.

Liall struggled to keep a straight expression. Peysho was not faring much better, but had stifled his giggles by gnawing on his lower lip and glaring, which gave him a truly frightening aspect.

"And such a lovely dark color, too."

Scarlet cast his gaze down quickly, but there was no hiding those liquid-dark eyes without a trace of age about them. The rosy alpenglow that suffused the mountain at dawn had aided his disguise from a distance, but this near there could be no mistake.

"What strong, white teeth you have, granny!" Liall grabbed Scarlet's hand, the left one with the missing fifth finger, and stripped off its glove, holding it to his breast as if he were a smitten lover. He was enjoying himself immensely. "And what fine hands, so smooth and young."

"The better to bash your smirking face in!"

Peysho gave up the fight and guffawed. Liall laughed lightly and struggled to hold on, for "granny" had turned surprisingly strong. Scarlet aimed a punch at his nose.

Liall dodged it and grabbed Scarlet's wrist to drag him closer, trying to pin his arms in a bear-hug.

"You're a violent old woman," he chided casually.

"Don't pretend you were fooled!" Scarlet shouted up into his face, aiming a kick at his shins. "Let me go!"

Peysho howled with laughter and fell down into the snow, holding his sides, convulsed with helpless glee. On the other side of the camp, heads were turning to see what the commotion was about. Kio saw Liall struggling with "granny" and he nudged old Dira and they and a few others ran over to see what was amiss, though they could tell even from a distance that there was no danger. Soon, a knot of grinning Kasiri surrounded them. Scarlet's fair face colored with shame now that they had an audience. He struggled wildly and aimed another kick at Liall's knee, but the older man was a head taller and outweighed him by a hundred pounds. Liall laughed and hugged Scarlet closer, and perhaps he grew too confident, for the hard toe of Scarlet's boot connected with his kneecap and he yelped and hopped. Still, he was not angry. Not yet.

"Ow! You've maimed me. Now I shall have to claim damages from you, granny-boy!" Liall seized Scarlet's shoulders, jerked him forward, and smothered his lips under a kiss.

The elation he felt at finally settling that fetching mouth under his was short-lived. Scarlet's teeth sank hard into his lower lip.

"*Ah!*" Liall jerked his head back and tasted the salty warmth of fresh blood flowing over his tongue. "You bit me!"

"Let go or I'll stab you!"

Scarlet's forehead butted his nose. Liall felt his anger rising and he grew rougher with the pedlar as the Kasiri watched and laughed. "Calm down, it's only a game, lad!"

Scarlet threw Liall off, wiping his mouth on his sleeve, and stood several paces away, his chest heaving and his eyes spitting hate. The silly cap had fallen off and revealed his midnight hair underneath, though his bangs and the fringe of disheveled hair around his face were grimed with the flour he had combed into it. With his legs tangling in the wide skirt and his padded bosom jiggling, he looked ludicrous, which only made the men laugh harder.

"No!" Scarlet shouted over them. "It's only a game to *you*! I've lost work on your account. It may mean nothing to you if I go back to my family empty-handed, but I'm only a pedlar. If I don't work, I don't eat, and my parents are getting old. They depend on me. Unlike you and your kind, I can't just steal whenever I need something!"

Liall wiped the blood from his chin and shrugged. Well, perhaps the pedlar was right. He had taken matters a bit far, and he had not cared that it made trouble for Scarlet at home. Hell's Teeth, he had not even known the brat *had* a family until he said so. How was he to blame for the boy's scrawny kin?

"It was just a game," he repeated sullenly. One that was now over, he supposed.

"Then it follows that my life is a game to you. Should I be flattered? You've been trying to force yourself on me since the moment we met. That's not a game, that's rape, and you're a pig of a common thief and a raping villain."

Peysho had arisen and was wiping tears from his eyes. "Atya," he called, but Liall ignored him.

Smarting under Scarlet's insults, Liall scowled blackly. "Watch your tongue, boy, no one calls me that."

"Villain!" Scarlet accused. "Despoiler and brigand and robber!"

"That's enough," he said tightly. The Kasiri men stopped laughing. From the corner of his vision, Liall saw Peysho take a step toward Scarlet, all mirth gone, his hand outstretched.

"Lad," he tried to caution.

Scarlet seemed to be beyond listening. "Murderer!" he threw as a last shot.

Liall had never been able to fully tame the violence in his blood, the rage that was known to overtake Rshani males in battle and conflict and sometimes even in love, but he could often make peace with it for years at a time. *Berserker* rage, their enemies called it, and the elders trained youths to control the blind, unreasoning ferocity they inherited from an ancestral race so distant and implausible that they had become myth to their descendants.

As atya, Liall wielded brutality like a sensible whip. He never resorted to it unless a lesson was needed or there was no other way, and yet, with one word, Scarlet swept aside his control.

It was more than just the accusation. Perhaps it was also his bruised pride: being refused by a beggaring pedlar when he had once been accustomed to pampered princes and great ladies plying for his attention. Or perhaps it was because he had misjudged how much he wanted this plainspoken youth to think better of him, and finally realized that he had gone about it so wrong that it could never be amended. Whatever the reason, Scarlet's taunt shattered Liall's restraint and roused his temper to the boiling point. Liall went after him.

"Liall!" Peysho shouted, but stayed where he was.

Liall was beyond listening. His dark face was suffused with blood, skin gone nearly black with fury. His lips drew up in a snarl.

Scarlet saw Liall coming and backed up a few steps, as if he were too surprised to do anything else. Liall shoved hard, both palms planted in the center of Scarlet's chest, and Scarlet went down with a surprised *oof,* landing on his back in the snow. Liall knelt and put his knee in the pedlar's chest while his fingers delved in his boot for the short dagger he always kept hidden there. Scarlet's eyes went wide when he saw the dagger, and he twisted, trying to push Liall's leg off him. Liall moved to straddle Scarlet's sides, his knees on either side of Scarlet's hips, and grabbed the neckline of the dress.

He slashed at it, cutting through the laces of the bodice and the underlying gown until he had the garment open to reveal Scarlet's familiar red coat beneath, and the Kasiri found their mirth again and roared with laughter when Scarlet's "bosom" –a pair of cloth-wrapped apples– rolled over the snow. A few more slashes had the dress off him and Liall threw the pieces aside. Scarlet had stopped fighting, perhaps because he realized that flailing about when Liall's dagger was busy was more dangerous than lying still.

"A miracle!" Liall called to the watchers. His mouth twisted in a cruel smile. "We've cut open grandmother and found she's swallowed a boy, and here he is!"

Liall looked down at his prisoner as the howls and taunts washed over them, and then turned the dagger in front of Scarlet's eyes so the dawning red glow of the sunrise caught it, bathing the blade with crimson. He leaned over Scarlet, keeping the boy pinned, and with the tip of his blade he gently traced the outline of Scarlet's lower lip.

"Now," he said lowly, for Scarlet's ears alone, "if I cut your clothes off, boy, will I find a girl under there?"

Liall saw then that Scarlet was trembling and that there was real fear in his gaze. Fear of *him*, of what he would do.

"Don't," Scarlet got out, his voice shaking. "Please."

Liall's blood turned cold in his veins. How it must cost him to beg, he thought suddenly, appalled at his own actions. It is not often that a man can see himself through another's gaze. Too much stands in the way of it. He saw himself in Scarlet's eyes all too clearly, and saw what he was: a bloody-minded thief on top of him in the snow, armed men all around, a blade pointed at his throat. He was a brigand, a thug, a felon bent on rape and murder.

This is what you have become, he thought in despair and revulsion. This is how far you have fallen. You are Liall, a degenerate Kasiri bastard brutalizing a boy half your size because he insulted your pride and refused to give you his body. Are you proud?

Liall got to his feet and backed away. He stood sweating and chilled as the pass filled with the red light of dawn, so sick he thought he would vomit. Peysho was watching Liall with a sad, knowing look on his face. Liall would not meet Peysho's eyes.

"Get up," he ordered Scarlet in a ragged voice. "Get out."

Scarlet fled.

8.

Shadow of the Past

Scarlet abandoned what little pride he had left and ran. A mourning dove trilled from the trees as he loped down the mountain path, and it sounded like mockery to him: *foooooooool fool fool!*

A game, Liall said. If waving his knife around was a game, what was he like when he played for true? It seemed incredible that he had ever found anything attractive about such a brute. He was angry at himself for ever thinking it.

At the bottom of the path was the little circle he had hidden in to dress, ringed in by a row of tall junipers laced with snow. He stopped there, his breath like fire in his lungs, and stripped off the slashed remains of the bodice. It was ruined. He would have that to explain at home and bruises besides. His heart thudded as he leaned his shoulder against a scraggly evergreen and strove for calm. The wind sighed through the thick branches.

You've got only yourself to blame, he thought reproachfully. You insisted on having your way and challenging him instead of doing as Scaja advised and taking the Salt Road for a while. Well, you called him out. How do you like his answer?

His chest ached where Liall had pressed down with his knee. He rubbed the bruised flesh there and tried to think what to do next. All of his goods had been left on the mountain. He could not even continue on by the Salt

Road, and would have to go home empty-handed and shamed after being pawed at and stripped by a Kasiri. The thought of Scaja's eyes staring him down in silent disapproval made him feel faintly ill. He shivered in humiliation and covered his face with his hands.

"No better luck?"

Scarlet whirled around to see Cadan step out from behind the broad trunk of a tree, his fighting axe casually slung over his shoulder. The birds were suddenly silent.

"What are you doing here?" he demanded, shaken. He had not heard anyone creep up.

The soldier was staring at him with an odd intensity. He took a step closer. "If I'd known you liked to dress as a woman, I would have said fairer words to you when we met. Yes, and paid for your beer besides."

Cadan gave him a bone-thin smile, and Scarlet was abruptly very aware that they were alone here, that he had left his long-knives at home, and that no one would hear him in the village if he should call for help. He suddenly wished he had never met Cadan or Liall at all.

Kev would say this is what I get for talking to strangers, he thought. "Go away," he commanded weakly, and Cadan laughed.

"Your mouth is bruised," Cadan said, taking yet another step. "Did the Wolf steal a kiss? Ah, I see he did. He always fancied his boys pretty and stupid."

Scarlet stepped forward, meaning to step around the soldier, but Cadan moved to block his path. "Where do you think you're going?"

"Home."

"In a little while. Maybe."

Scarlet's eyes flashed to the crimson vine on Cadan's sleeve uncertainly. Surely an officer had more honor than this, or at least better wits? The sense of danger in the air was palpable, and he suddenly knew beyond all doubt that Cadan meant him harm.

"Let me pass."

Cadan's arm shot out and shoved Scarlet back. Scarlet stumbled but recovered quickly and curled his hands into his fists. "What do you want?"

The scars on Cadan's cheeks writhed as he smiled, and his eyes glittered with a strange, hungry light. "I've seen the look on your face when you talk about the Wolf." His gaze raked Scarlet's body. "You could look at me that way. I wouldn't mind."

"You're mad. I despise that bandit."

"But you don't. You want him."

Scarlet's throat had gone dry. "You're wrong." He wanted to say more, to declare that he had never been attracted to any man, ever, but his instincts told him his denial would be met with more of the same derisive amusement.

Cadan's smile turned knowing. "Stay a while," he invited. "I will treat you better than he did." He made a grab for Scarlet's wrist.

Scarlet twisted aside and threw a punch aimed at Cadan's eye. It landed solid and Cadan's head snapped back. A small gash opened up on the soldier's left eyebrow and began to bleed freely. Cadan swiped at the blood with the back of his sleeve. His smile turned predatory as he raised his fists.

"You want to fight me, hill-brat?"

Scarlet dodged the first punch. The second impacted squarely on his chin and made his knees wobble.

"Hilurin whore," Cadan jeered. "There are easier ways to get on your back."

Scarlet tried to hit him again, but Cadan swayed and ducked, evading the thrown punches easily. Cadan jabbed thrice with his right fist and connected all three times: hard, painful blows that made Scarlet's teeth click and his eyes water and his brain feel like it was a bean rattling in an empty gourd. One or two more and he would be unconscious.

He was not even trying to land a blow now, only trying to guard and stay on his feet as Cadan circled him with catlike steps.

Scarlet forced himself to face the facts: Cadan was bigger, stronger, and a far more skilled fighter than he was. He was not going to win this battle with his bare hands. There was only one chance.

Scarlet turned and bolted for the edge of the woods. He did not see Cadan's expression change, shifting into a fierce mask of hate like the were-beast in the tales of shapechangers, nor did he see the soldier sling the axe from his shoulder in a blur of movement and hurl it at his back.

The blunt side of the axe-head smashed high into the back of Scarlet's right shoulder, careening off the bone and leaving his arm numb and useless. He fell to his knees, a wave of excruciating pain forcing a cry from him, and then Cadan was on him. A strong arm wrapped around his neck, hauling him to his feet. The soldier's breath was hot on his throat.

"Don't make me run after you," Cadan panted in his ear. "I've got a long day planned for us, wouldn't want to use up all my strength at once."

He struggled, slamming his boot-heel down on Cadan's instep, and the man released him with a roar and threw him down. Scarlet tried to scramble up and run. Cadan was there again, using his greater weight to force Scarlet back to the ground. Scarlet writhed under him, turning onto his back where he could throw a punch, but Cadan's hands were suddenly around his throat, cutting off his wind.

He could not get a good breath in his lungs. His knee

sought to come up between Cadan's legs ineffectually, blocked by a sudden twist of Cadan's body. The fingers of his good hand clawed at Cadan's wrists, trying to tear the choking grip from his neck as the soldier straddled his waist. Cadan leaned his weight on his arms, his thumbs digging deep into soft tissue.

Scarlet was aware of wet snow trickling into his collar, the dull wave of agony that was his shoulder, and the panicked feeling of drowning. Air, he had to get air! Desperately, he clawed for the little dagger he kept in his belt, but it had not cleared the sheath when it was torn from his fingers. Cadan hurled it away, allowing Scarlet one loud, tortured breath before the life was being choked from him again. The soldier's body ground against him, and Scarlet was overwhelmed with disgust to feel the hard outline of Cadan's rigid phallus pressed against his hip.

His strength was ebbing. The world darkened at the edges little by little until the dawn began to fade like the last images of a dream. There was nothing but the cold and his own evaporating sense of fear. The last breath in his throat was like a spike of frost, but he felt calm, at peace, and wondered for a fleeting instant if the Otherworld would be anything like this one.

Then a bizarre sound intruded, an enraged roar like the baying of a wolf, and something crashed into them with the force of a storm, knocking Cadan off him. Scarlet rolled to his right, his injured shoulder taking the brunt of his weight, and a jolt of pain went through him like a hammer. He blacked out.

"Get up," Liall ordered Scarlet, his voice raw. "Get out."

Scarlet fled.

Liall watched Scarlet run, the mountain air rasping in his lungs like sand. He knew he would not see Scarlet again. If the pedlar ever chanced this road again, he would send Peysho to wave the pedlar through. Or even, he thought desperately, go down to the village myself and beg his pardon.

It was a silly thought. He knew he would do no such thing. The lad was right. Liall had abused Scarlet's pride and dismissed his way of life as worthless. All the slights he was angry at Scarlet for sending his way, Liall had committed first.

The tribesmen dispersed, muttering among themselves, but Peysho remained. He approached the atya warily.

"Liall?" he called, as a man will call a dog who had been acting strangely of late, while keeping a sharp axe behind his back against rabies or worse.

"Stop looking at me like the bride on her wedding night to the ogre," Liall growled. "I am myself." He began to sheath the dagger in his boot and halted, gazing at the blade that had frightened Scarlet so. He made a face of disgust and tossed it into a thicket of winter-bare bracken near some rocks. That was one blade he would not want to look at again.

"Ye should follow the lad down the path. Just to see him safe and all," Peysho said.

He waved that away. "He'll be fine."

"Ye could've hurt him," Peysho persisted. "The way ye were slashin' at him… ye could've cut 'im bad and not even know it."

"He ran like he was healthy enough."

"All the same," Peysho began stubbornly, and Liall could see the burly enforcer had the matter in his teeth.

Liall scowled at him, unaccountably annoyed. What business was it of his? "You have one pretty lad to worry about, don't take on another."

"Here, now!" Kio sang out, and Liall knew he had offended Kio as well.

"Deva's shrieking hell, I'll go!" Liall snapped.

"Give me a minute to fetch my knives," Peysho stalled.

"Stay here," Liall ordered. "We've wasted enough time on this nonsense."

Liall strode cursing toward the path to Lysia, leaving Peysho to scratch his chin and look after his chieftain worriedly.

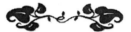

Scarlet, grandson of Herec, son of Scaja, of the blood of Lyr.

Scarlet roused enough to wonder who called his name, but saw only flashes of light, a whirling dance of butterfly colors, and through them, like a veil of shining gauze, Byzan faces in the void beyond, many faces of men and women of his race. Never had he seen so many Hilurin people in one place. They stretched out their white hands to him.

Scarlet of Lysia.

Who calls? Who is that? He felt irritated at being woken from the cocoon of syrupy warmth that rocked him like a babe in a cradle, carrying him to the Otherworld. Linhona and Scaja would miss him, true, but he would see them again. If only those voices would go away and let him rest.

Wake, Scarlet. Not for you the longsleep, the rest

without dreams. This is not your time. Not now, not on the long voyage across the deep, cold sea, nor even when you come at last to the first home of the Shining Ones. Wake, O Anlyrabeth.

Anlyrabeth? He wondered what the strange word was, and why it should sing through his mind like ripples on a pond, circles that touched him with a sting like iron.

How sad that even the name of our race has vanished among you. So far fallen, the Anlyrabeth. So far. But wake now, Scarlet. Wake and live longer than memory.

Longer than memory? He felt like laughing, but he was too tired. The Byzan faces, men and women with deep black eyes and dark hair like his, faded back into the fluttering bits of color, and he fell dreamless into the dark.

Liall saw Cadan's hands knotted around Scarlet's throat. The pedlar was glassy-eyed and he hung from Cadan's hands as if dead.

He shouted and threw himself at Cadan, tearing the brute's hands away. Liall grabbed the soldier's arms, lifted him, and flung him bodily into the bole of a tree, where he crashed face-first. Few had ever seen Liall use the full extent of his strength, and he was stronger than any Byzan or Minh or Morturii alive. He fully intended not to leave Cadan alive to speak of it.

Cadan scrabbled and came up on his knees. His chipped tooth had split his lip. He leered and spat blood. "You're too late. Just like the last time, eh, Liall? Too late to save them, too late to save him."

It was true. Even by moonlight, Liall could see how still

Scarlet lay, how his white neck was marred with bruises and his chest was unmoving. Cadan laughed again, his bloodied mouth twisting up into a cruel, familiar sneer. Liall reached into his boot for his dagger, found it gone and remembered why he had thrown it away.

Oh, lad, it was just a game. I'm sorry, so sorry...

A silvery glimmer caught the sunlight beside Scarlet's still body, and Liall could make out the angular shape of an axe-head and the short curve of a wooden handle denting the snow.

Liall picked up the axe. Cadan limped backwards, holding his thigh. Bright blood dripped between his fingers.

"Did I hurt you, then?" Liall asked. His voice was dangerously soft. "Looks broken to me."

Cadan chuckled. "I'll live."

"You will not." He declined to question Cadan about what the man had planned to do with Scarlet's body. The petty details of revenge –whether he intended to plant the corpse outside of the village with the Kasiri mark cut into his skin, or whether he planned to have what was left of Scarlet delivered to the camp– mattered little. Most likely, the folk of Lysia would conclude that the Kasiri had murdered Scarlet for defying them, and rumors of a violent Kasiri band would spread. Tolling and robbery was common everywhere, but the Kasiri were only barely tolerated this far north in Byzantur. The regular army would be glad of a solid reason to brave the wrath of the Bled lords and wipe the Kasiri out. Cadan must have been planning this for a long time.

Liall hefted the axe. His own thoughtlessness had cost Scarlet his life, and that made him cruel. "You're a soldier now," he said slowly, soft as a cat's paw. "An officer. How did you manage that, I wonder?"

"Leading soldiers and leading Kasiri isn't so different."

Cadan again spat a thin stream of blood at him and tried to put his weight on his bad leg. It crumpled under him. "Men are animals. You're the one who taught me that."

Liall glanced at Scarlet, who sprawled so still in the snow. "Not all men. In that, I lessoned you wrong. I would feel badly about that, if I thought I had anything to do with the forging of you. But no, you were already a brute when you found your way into my camp."

"You were right," Cadan insisted. "I treat 'em like dogs and they lick it up. I'm good at it."

"I don't doubt it. Like most sadists, you have a knack for brutality," Liall said in a low, terrible tone. "The army must be getting desperate, to raise a cur to rank." Liall advanced on Cadan, swinging the axe deftly back and forth, just to show him what was to come.

Cadan hobbled back from him in alarm. "If I'm a cur, what are you? You're the biggest thief I ever knew!"

"Possibly."

"You maimed me!!" Cadan shouted, pointing to the scars on his face. "You bastard whelp of a she-bitch! One day I was your right hand in the krait, your enforcer, and the next you cut me off from the Kasiri forever! After the famous Wolf drove me out, every atya from here to Minh spit at the sound of my name. No one would take me in or let me join their krait. And over what? Nothing!"

Liall's jaw clenched. "Over two Byzan girls and their mother."

Cadan wiped blood from his face. "Scant fun, they were, screaming and crying the whole time. What are filthy peasant dirt-diggers to you, anyway, eh? Why do you care?"

Liall's hands curled tight around the axe-haft. "Because I am not a murderer."

Cadan's eyes were tar-black holes of hatred as Liall raised the axe over his head, intending to hurl it and cleave that visage in two, but he should have remembered that a rat is most dangerous when cornered.

"Hah!" Cadan shouted, at the same time, his right hand came up and flung a dagger at Liall. It was a little thing, more suited for a woman's purse than a warrior's belt, but Cadan aimed for his eyes and Liall instinctively took the time to bat the projectile away with the axe. Another little dagger flew at Liall, lodging deeply in the upper part of his right thigh, and he staggered. The axe lowered.

In the stolen moment, Cadan was gone, whirling and throwing himself over the snow-slicked embankment and into the concealing brush of the deep ravine below. Liall jerked the knife out and ran to the edge of the junipers, cursing. There were only trees and brush. The sun was not yet high enough in the sky to touch the bottom of the ravine, and there was a thick layer of mist rising from the dim gloom. Cadan had taken a last chance at life, but there was no possible way he could climb out of that gorge with a broken leg, much less make the journey to a friendly village. He was as good as dead.

Liall spat and threw the axe down, sick with unsatisfied rage. He turned back to look at the crumpled figured lying very still in the snow. His feet moved and he knelt beside Scarlet. The pedlar's eyes remained closed as Liall gathered him in his arms and held him.

"I did not intend this," he whispered. His eyes stung and he swallowed hard. "I swear I did not."

He pressed a kiss to Scarlet's temple. The pedlar's slender neck, laced with black bruises, lolled over Liall's arm. Liall gave a moan of distress and his hand went instinctively to support. Then he saw the artery beating in Scarlet's throat.

"*Oh,*" he breathed. A thread of hope touched him. His fingers pressed to be sure. Yes, the heart still drummed, but there was no breath in the lungs and Scarlet's chest did not rise.

Any man who has spent time at sea knows the mariner's trick of reviving those with water in the lungs, or whose breath has stopped while there is still life in the body. Liall placed Scarlet back on the ground, tilted his chin up, pinched his nose shut and fitted his mouth over his, praying that Scarlet's throat had not swelled and his airway closed up from Cadan's grip.

He had wanted to kiss him, but not like this. Scarlet's mouth was cold under his. Liall blew a long, steady breath into Scarlet's throat and stopped, waited a moment, and then placed his hand firmly in the center of Scarlet's chest, pressing down hard until he heard the air coming back out. Nothing. He did it again, giving his breath, his hands shaking and sweaty.

Breathe, he prayed.

A third time, Liall forced air into Scarlet's lungs, but this time, Scarlet hiccupped and Liall felt his lips move. Liall drew back and gave a shout of relief, laughing aloud in pure joy when Scarlet coughed and his eyes opened.

"Liall?" Scarlet choked, his voice raw and thin. "What happened?"

"Hush. Just breathe, Scarlet. You're safe."

"Safe," Scarlet murmured. "Help me up."

Liall grasped his arm to help him stand, but Scarlet gasped and fell back.

"My shoulder," he moaned. "Oh, it hurts..."

Liall moved his coat and shirt aside and hissed at the purpling bruise that was forming. "Does it feel broken?" he asked.

Scarlet winced. "I don't know," he said in a rasping voice. "I've never... broken anything before."

"Let me." He slipped his hand inside the fabric and tried to feel around the raised flesh for blood or splinters of bone, but Scarlet gasped and moaned loudly the moment

Liall's fingers probed the egg-sized lump. Liall readjusted Scarlet's shirt tenderly, leaving the injury alone. There was nothing he could do here.

"You need a *curae*," he said. "I think he knocked a chip out of the bone."

Scarlet nodded and Liall saw the bluish-white ring around his pale mouth. He was close to fainting again. "Stay awake!" he commanded, harsher than he wanted to be. "I do not know the village. You must show me where you live."

"Wainwright's Lane," Scarlet whispered. "Have you seen my dagger? I lost it..."

Liall helped him to stand, but Scarlet swayed even as he got his feet under him. "Forget the dagger, where is the lane?"

"Third cottage... on the right... past the..."

And then his eyes rolled up in his head and he fainted. Liall caught Scarlet before he fell and hauled the pedlar up in his arms, carrying him through the snow like a child.

9.

Two Coins

"Hello in the house! Open up, for Deva's sake!"

The door was thrown open and a middle-aged man stood there. He had a shock of dark hair gone steel gray at the temples and he clutched an iron fire poker in his hand. The man opened his mouth to speak, then he saw what Liall carried and his jaw dropped. Behind him were a black-haired woman and a slip of a girl with features very like Scarlet's, and Liall knew he was at the right house.

"A brigand," Liall explained hastily when the older man hefted the poker menacingly. "I found him on the road. Let me in, old man, your son is injured!"

"Scaja!" the wife flailed at his shoulder. "Open the door!"

Scaja backed down and swung the door wider, though he did not put the poker down. Linhona darted to the back of the small dwelling and moved aside a heavy woolen curtain. There was a narrow bed behind it and Liall moved to lie Scarlet down. He settled Scarlet on the covers and turned to her. "Have you a healer in the village?"

Linhona shook her head, white-lipped with fear, her eyes all for her son.

"He may be badly hurt," Liall said.

Linhona pinched the staring girl. "Annaya, get the midwife!"

"Midwife!" he exclaimed.

"There is no other," Linhona snapped at him, her eyes filling with tears as she took in Scarlet's state. She moved aside the blanket to examine the bruises on his throat and leaned her head near to listen to his breathing. "We are lucky to have even her."

Annaya raced out the door. Liall frowned. It was true that no trained curae would spend years of his life learning medicine only to go hungry in a poor tradesman settlement, but he doubted a midwife would be of much use with broken bones. He moved the blankets around, settling the warm fabric up to Scarlet's chin. Behind him, he could feel the eyes of the man and woman on him. When he turned back to them, Linhona nodded to her husband in silent consent. Scaja looked suspicious and eyed Liall up and down. Scaja still had the poker in his hand.

"There's blood on you," Scaja stated, looking at Liall's leg.

"A knife throw," he answered, "from the man who tried to kill Scarlet."

"A brigand, you say. Not one of your people?"

Liall shook his head. "No." Scaja looked doubtful. "I swear to you, no."

"And where would this bastard be now?"

"In hell, if there's any justice."

Scaja's lips thinned and he nodded in satisfaction, and Liall saw that his words had pleased the old man. This rough Byzan would not pretend a gentility he did not possess, not when it came to his own flesh and blood. Now Liall knew where Scarlet had come by his plain speech and honest manner. These people were devoid of guile. No wonder their son was so poor a trickster.

The father sighed and reluctantly replaced the fire poker by the hearth. He drew himself up to his full height, which was only a few inches more than Scarlet's. "My name is Scaja," he said formally. "My wife is Linhona."

"Liall," he returned simply.

Scaja sighed, dropping his pose. "Well, *Liall,* let us get you cleaned up before old Hipola comes. She's already going to be nosier than a hound, no sense giving her more to gab about."

Linhona tended to Scarlet while Scaja led Liall to the pump near the small, winter-stripped garden outside the little cottage. It was a real iron pump, costly and a nuisance, for in the cold months its iron base would freeze the water inside and burst if it were not kept warm and primed. The pump looked old but well tended. These were people accustomed to work and making do.

Scaja pumped the handle and Liall splashed water cold as needles of ice onto his face and over his bloodied hands. The leg wound had bled freely and he scrubbed at his breeches with the thin towel Scaja handed him before rinsing his hands a last time. The wound could wait to be cleaned and bandaged. Through all this, the father said nothing, only handed him another towel when he was done. It was threadbare but clean, and Liall thanked the man courteously when he handed it back.

Scaja took the cloth and looked at him for several moments, saying nothing. Liall began to speak and then decided that, as every man is a monarch in his own house and he was in another kingdom now, Scaja should have the first say.

"So," Scaja said at last. "You're the Kasiri who tried to make a whore of my child."

Liall bowed his head. It had been a long time since he

felt shame. This deliberate man had taken his game with Scarlet, the very one he had covered with excuses and laughter, and shown him for the mean, squalid thing it was.

"I crave your pardon, sir," Liall said lowly. It was all he could say.

Scaja shrugged. "It's not my pardon you need. Scarlet's a forgiving lad, even when it's not deserved. For me, I can't see the back of you quick enough."

Scaja's words cut deep, as truth often does. He had been nothing but trouble to Scarlet since they met. There was no reason to believe that would change. "Would you like me to leave?" he asked.

Scaja thought about it for a moment. "I would, but it's not my decision. Come inside, then, if you're set on this." Scaja turned and left Liall standing in the bare garden with a forlorn look on his face.

The ancient midwife pronounced Scarlet's shoulder unbroken and Liall had to accept her verdict, there being no other. Scarlet had awakened and he watched with a bemused expression while Liall fidgeted nervously under the hard looks of his parents and the midwife.

Hipola, the midwife, fed Scarlet an herbal sedative and bound his shoulder tightly, forbidding him to move from the bed for two days and from the village for two weeks. Liall could see the last command irked Scarlet, but the pedlar did not argue with her, for his throat had swelled and it pained him to do more than whisper. Liall attempted to pay Hipola, but she shoved the silver sellivar coins back at him and took the copper bit offered by Scaja instead. Liall was very aware of Scarlet's eyes on him when she did this, and of how it made him feel.

Hipola shoved the slip deep into her apron and threw Liall a wizened glare of dislike. She smoothed her fuzzy, iron-gray hair about her face. "There is a wolf in your house, Scaja," she announced loudly to the walls. "Beware his fleas."

She left and Linhona went to make a healing tea. Scaja drew a chair for Liall next to Scarlet's bed, for it was obvious he was not leaving, and sent the girl to a neighbor's for the day. With a last look at his son, who smiled wanly and nodded in reassurance, Scaja drew the woolen curtain closed and went into the outer room, leaving them alone.

Liall did not know what to say. Scarlet looked at him for a long time, seeming to study every feature.

"You saved my life," Scarlet got out, his voice so hoarse and small that Liall winced. "How am I supposed to pay the toll for that?"

"You should not try to speak."

"I'll speak if I like," he growled, then wheezed in a breath. "Answer my question."

Liall spread his hands. "Your life was in danger only because of me. Cadan is... used to be... a Kasiri. And a friend, but he became my enemy and sought vengeance on me through you. You owe me nothing for my interference with that outcome," Liall said. He cleared his throat in sympathy. It must have been agony for Scarlet to talk.

"Why does he hate you?"

"Perhaps because I finally saw him for what he was and rejected him. Men do not forgive that easily. It matters not. I only wish you to know that there will be no toll for you as long as my krait holds the pass. It is a scant offering, but something tells me you would not accept more."

"I would, but not for the reasons you think," Scarlet said in that cracked voice. He moved and shifted in the bed, sitting up as he began to search his pockets with his good hand. "Here."

Scarlet opened his palm, showing Liall two copper bits. They were round, medium-sized coins of pure copper with a square hole stamped in the middle; a fair price for a poor chapman to buy his crossing.

"This is to pay my way," Scarlet said, watching him. "However I came to be in danger, you saved my life. I owe you a debt, and you know how Byzans feel about debts."

Liall felt shame eating at his conscience, that a peasant pedlar should know more of honor than him. He took the two flat coins and closed his hand over them. "I thank you," he said formally.

"And you'll send payment to my family for the wages I've lost and two weeks hence that I would've earned."

He bowed his head to cover his surprise. "Consider it done."

"A *prosperous* pedlar," Scarlet pressed.

It would have been unforgivable to laugh. "Indeed. Most prosperous and wise, is Scarlet of Lysia."

Scarlet smiled a little, though his eyes were beginning to droop. The pain draught the midwife had given him was working. He sank back to the pillows with a sigh. "I pay my debts," he said faintly, already falling into sleep. "Goodbye, Wolf."

"I wish it were not," Liall said before he could stop himself.

Scarlet did not answer as he drifted off to sleep. Liall looked down at the coins in his hand.

I am a great fool, he thought. He settled back in the chair to keep watch over him, but two hours later, when Linhona came in and confirmed Scarlet was breathing properly, he knew it was time for him to go. Scaja let him out.

Standing on the little cobblestone walkway, Liall made to say something to Scaja, perhaps to offer his apology again or promise to send herbs and medicines for healing, but Scaja shook his head before Liall could speak.

"It's not me you need to make it up to," he said stiffly.

Hospitality can be stretched only so far. "Please send for me if there's anything I can do," Liall murmured. Scaja regarded him with narrow hostility, saying nothing, and Liall bowed and left.

The trip back up the mountain path was lonely and cold, and halfway up, about noon or so, Liall met Peysho and a knot of fighting men. Peysho looked relieved.

"Well, now. Are ye forgiven?" Peysho grinned, obviously believing Liall's long absence meant he had finally won his desire, but Liall strode past him. Then Peysho saw the blood on him. "Ah, Deva, what happened?" he asked anxiously.

Liall wondered if Peysho thought he had killed Scarlet. *Probably.* "It was him," he answered wearily. "Cadan. He attacked Scarlet, hoping to pin the murder on us, I think."

Peysho fell in beside him. "The bastard's dead, then," he said with great satisfaction.

"I wish he were. He threw himself down a gulch. I think I broke his leg for him. He won't be soldiering for a while, at any rate."

"And little red-hood?"

"Home, where his mother can nurse him."

Peysho pulled on his chin as he matched Liall's long strides. "Kasiri are happiest on the move," he quoted. Perhaps it was meant to suggest that they had overstayed their welcome on the Nerit. Peysho had a point, but Liall's pride was battered enough for one day.

"Don't tell me how to rule the krait," he snarled. The two copper coins were clasped so tight in his hand that the edges were cutting him. They seemed much heavier than they should be.

"Aye," Peysho said, ducking his head and submitting. "Is the lad well?"

"He will be, I suppose," Liall muttered. "He won't be traveling for weeks, but he'll heal."

Peysho cast another look at him. "Liall..."

"I did not harm him," Liall answered, goaded by the worry in Peysho's eyes. "Yet... it is still my fault. You were right, Peysho: I do regret my jest. Whatever role I have played in this, I am heartily sorry for it."

Peysho fell silent as they climbed the path, and Liall did not confide the rest: that regret was only a small part of it. There was also loss and guilt and the deep sense of shame that clung to his skin. For a moment, he bitterly wished he had never met the pedlar.

I had almost forgotten who I was, he thought. How can he remind me so much of my past, when he knows nothing about me?

"He will be well," he repeated. Be well, Scarlet, he sent silently back to the village. It felt like goodbye.

Later, as he sat in his yurt in front of the smoking brazier, he rolled the pair of copper coins between his fingers, deep in thought. Eventually, he found a bit of leather lacing and threaded the pierced coins with it to make a necklace. He did not believe in talismans, but the power of memory has a magic of its own. The coins would serve to remind him that, for all his intelligence and learning, he could look as deeply as he was capable at anyone, man or woman, and still not be able to see them at all.

10.

Fate Dealer

Spring, the Month of Kings.

Fate was pitched beneath the fluttering, blood-red banner of Om-Ret, in a saffron tent inside the dusty souk of Ankar, somewhere between the cloth racks and the slave stalls.

The Fate dealer was not what Scarlet expected. Most Fates were crones, withered and wise and quite revered in both Morturii and Byzantur. This one removed his beaded veil and revealed he was a young man with a sharp, fox-like face. His ruddy hair was the color of dead oak leaves, and he kept it bound away in a long braid down his back, like men wore across the Channel in Khet. His hands looked older than his face and were covered with many small scars. There was a noticeable tremor in them, though he dealt his cards with swift snaps of his fingers, not a movement wasted.

The Fate reminded Scarlet a little of Rannon, the trim and competent *karwaneer* who had led his first caravan, but Fate's voice was pure Minh.

"Choose your fortune, redbird," Fate said, the edges of his words clipped and fierce, a true marker that he had learned to speak Bizye later in life.

Behind the Fate was a carved wooden bust, dark with age, resting on a little pedestal. Scarlet saw with a thrill of fear that it was a carving of a Shining One. Like all such rendering of the ancients, the statue was bald and had heavy, aquiline features. Pale chips of stone were his eyes, and his gaze was fearsome and unknowable.

Scarlet resisted the urge to make the sign against bad luck. Byzans generally shunned all images of the Shining Ones because of the dire legends surrounding them, and the Morturii were no less suspicious. It was odd that a Fate would display something like this. Scarlet tried to keep the curiosity from his face as he tapped one of the two piles of cards that Fate laid out on the table before him.

Fate pushed the abandoned pile aside and brought the other deck to the center. "Ask your question," he said, placing one hand palm down on the small stack, "and put your hand on mine."

Scarlet thought for a moment. "I've had some trouble back home," he said, settling his hand over the warm skin of the Fate dealer. "I'm leaving for Byzantur tomorrow; what will I find?"

In the back of his mind, unvoiced, was another question: Will I ever find what I seek in my own land, or should I start looking further away?

The continent of Khet was a possibility, though he had never been there. Crossing the Channel was a hazardous undertaking, and Scarlet knew of no pedlar who had ever tried it. He also thought of venturing further north in Morturii, having heard that the renegade soldiers in Volstland had been tamed by the southern troops of regulars, and that trade was good there. A shrewd merchant might make something of his life in such a place.

Scarlet's sudden discontent was natural. He had learned much about himself in the past few months, thanks to Scaja and Liall, and the questions the experience stirred up in his soul would not leave him. Liall would not fade and vanish from his memory like the bruises on his neck.

Instead, the Kasiri's presence in his thoughts only grew stronger.

Beyond the curtain, the great souk buzzed with activity. Fate retrieved his hand and shuffled the cards again, cut them, and had Scarlet choose a last time. There were only a dozen or so left in the deck now.

Fate slipped three cards from the top of the pile Scarlet had chosen and laid two side-by-side, faces down. He then placed the third crossways at the foot of the two, and flipped the first card over. "Signet card," Fate intoned. "This is you."

Scarlet peered at it. It was a thick piece of paper about the size of his hand, stiff with paint and the many layers of varnish the artist had applied. The background was black, like all Fate cards, with the design executed in thick white lines. It was a man standing on the crest of a hill, facing out over a barren landscape. Angry clouds swirled over his head, but the man stood proudly.

"What does it mean?"

Fate shrugged. "They are your cards. Only you can say what it truly means, but this is the card of changes. You are being influenced by those you love, yet your will pulls you in another direction, one not usually taken. Ah," he shook his head, "it is a hard road, if you choose it."

"But should I choose it at all?"

"Let us see." Fate turned the second card up, the Shield card, which is the one that reveals what quality the questioner is using as a foil. A fish swam under moving waters while a growing reed pushed into the sky, and above it all the sun blazed and the stars wheeled. "Motion," he said, with an eye to the color of Scarlet's coat.

"That takes no reading to see."

Fate made a seesaw gesture with his hand. "We are all in motion, but these are your cards. You chose them."

He had a point there. "So I did." Scarlet was already missing the four copper bits he had paid for this silliness and was beginning to feel like a fool in the silk-lined tent with its candles and incense. Most Byzans believe in such things and he was no exception, yet after Cadan and the near miss he had experienced on the mountain path, he felt older and more cynical.

The Fate turned over the Scythe card, the card of recommended actions to cure the situation. "Stasis," said the Fate. It was a plain card: a mountain and an empty valley with a calm night sky overhead, and a shooting star speaking portents. "If you would have peace in your life, do nothing. When events come, let them flow around you, but do not engage them."

Scarlet felt a prickle of irritation. What kind of advice was that? "I can't ignore being alive."

"Some can, but I see you cannot." Fate's smile was gentle. "Now we will see what the Gods will for you." He chose one card from the bottom of the deck, the Fate card, and laid it face up above the trio of other cards. His face did not change. "Kinesis."

Lightning hewed a sky of black, and below it the earth cracked open and flood waters rushed by in a welter of change, motion, and chaos. Scarlet leaned back in his chair. "A strange reading," he said, noncommittal.

The Fate nodded. "Especially for a Byzan. Your cards are always so dull." He began to gather them up and put them back in the deck, but when his fingers touched the Fate card and shifted it aside, Scarlet saw there was one more card beneath it.

"Now that *is* odd," Fate remarked, picking it up. "That never happens. These old cards," he flicked one to show Scarlet how stiff and slick they were "they never stick together, yet this one was hidden beneath your fate."

Scarlet leaned forward, intrigued in spite of himself.

"What is it?"

The Fate held it a little away from him teasingly, like one does with a child. "Are you sure you want to see? Little Byzans should not be too curious."

Scarlet reached for it and the Fate grabbed his wrist. The Morturii's sharp eyes fixed on Scarlet's missing fifth finger and the unnatural slenderness of his hand.

"Fourth card, four fingers," Fate murmured. "You have the mark of Deva's favor. Do you also have Deva's Gift?"

No Morturii should know of such things. He tried to retrieve his hand and the fortune dealer held onto it, tugging until Scarlet turned his palm over and let the man see the lines crossing his skin. The tremulous pads of the Fate's fingers felt warm and buzzing as bees as he traced those lines.

"A strange Byzan indeed." Abruptly, he released Scarlet's hand and pushed the hidden card over.

It was more cryptic than the others: a bare window set in a field of stars, a moon in eclipse above, and inside the window was the moon in quarter phase with no stars at all. "What is it?"

"Deception," Fate said. "Be on your guard. You will be told a lie or you will fall in love with one, and you will follow it to the ends of the earth."

"That doesn't sound like me."

"Oh." Fate put the card neatly back in the deck. "And I suppose you know yourself well, do you?"

Fate's eyes were prettily sly, and Scarlet felt the heat creeping over his face. Those eyes saw too much.

"Good day, Fate," he said as politely as he could. He could almost feel the rigid countenance of the statue watching him.

"Good day, little Byzan with the Mark," Fate called out, but he was already gone, out of the sweet-smelling tent and into the brassy market, with its noise and dust and smell. Scarlet inhaled deeply to clear his head of the odor of incense and beeswax. He hefted his pack a little higher on his shoulder, though it slipped down again immediately. There was a broken strap on the right side that needed to be picked apart and mended properly instead of tied up with string, but he had been too restless to just sit and do it.

This last trip had been tiring. He had caught a fever in the wake of his narrow escape in the woods and had been confined to bed for several weeks through the short winter. Linhona nursed him and he was well by the time the snow began melting on the Nerit, though Hipola disagreed and declared him still unfit for travel. The promised money had arrived from the Kasiri camp, with a little extra silver tucked in besides, but Scarlet knew it was not nearly enough to sustain them through the summer. He had to go back to work.

Scaja worried darkly and Linhona fretted until she nearly made herself sick. He started out for Ankar on the second day of the month of Kings, a lucky day that heralded the true birth of spring.

Annaya was more optimistic. "The warm air will do you well," she told him briskly, sounding very grown-up as she officiously handed him a wrapped bundle of dried fruit and waybread.

Scarlet sensed it would be unforgivable to laugh. Annaya would be married soon and have her own house and family to look after, but to him, she would always be his little sister. He stowed the food in his satchel. "Thank you, love."

She gave him a sly look. "Time was, in Scaja's grandfather's day, when the whole village would catch the wilding at once and dance naked under the spring moon."

"Oh, no doubt," he agreed expansively. "And every baby born that year was born in winter and the sires were anyone's guess." He smiled a little. "I've heard the stories."

"Scaja says they're true."

"What does Shansi say?"

Her black eyes glimmered. "Not much. We have better ways to spend our time."

He hummed a little and refused to ruin the day by arguing with her. Annaya was one of the few people who never tried to pen him in, but she dearly loved to tease. All his life, wherever he went, he had always felt like there were walls around him, and lately, even with Annaya's betrothal happiness brimming over and Linhona's flowers blooming in the garden, Lysia had begun to feel suffocating. Even if money had not been an issue, he would still have gone. Of Liall, there was no word. The men of the krait now never came further than the upper gate, and after the promised repayment of wages had been kept, Liall seemed to forget he ever existed. When he felt better, Scarlet ventured up the mountain to thank Liall, but he was dismissed by Kio with a vague excuse that Liall was disinclined to receive visitors that day.

Since this lack of interest was precisely what Scarlet had claimed he wanted, he could find no logical objection to it.

Scarlet lingered outside the Fate Dealer's tent for a few moments more and then made his way back to Masdren's stall. On the way, he had to pass the Street of Doves and Flowers, known by its colorful banners and by the pretty women and handsome youths who stood in the blue-painted doorways of each ghilan and bhoros. In Ankar, even whoredom had its hierarchy. At the very top were the khuri: the exquiste, devoted pleasure slaves of the very rich, owned for life and never sold, the shining jewels of great Houses. Doves and flowers were usually slaves owned by some rich merchant and put to use as whores in common brothels. The bhoros and ghilan were better educated and trained, and were sponsored by nobles and the wealthy. Some were also artists or musicians, and there were several bhoros in Ankar who were quite famous for their skill and beauty. Scrats –street prostitutes attached to no House or distinguished name– were the lowest of the low. In Ankar, connections were everything.

There were other ways to get back to Masdren's, but this route was shorter, so he braved the soft catcalls and obscene invitations, keeping his head down and his eyes on his boots. He heard the word *Hilurin* spoken in scorn, and looked up to see a boy, surely no older than Annaya, standing under the arch of a bhoros house entryway. The boy was Morturii to the bone, brown-haired and golden skinned, with eyes like yellow topaz.

He regarded Scarlet with narrow contempt. One hand lazed on his hip, and with his thumb and index finger he shot Scarlet a gesture not commonly seen in public. "Care to give it a ride, Byzan?" He moved his wrist back and forth.

Scarlet looked quickly away, suddenly ashamed for no reason he could figure. He quickened his steps and hurried off. Behind him, he heard the boy's lilting laughter joined by several other voices, both sweet and scornful. It made him angry to be laughed at, especially for such a reason, but there was no remedy for it. It was either let it go or stop and make a fight of it, and he knew that behind the delicate gilt and blue doorways of the bhoros lurked the eunuchs and watchmen under the orders of their House Marus or House Majess. These guards were always ready with a club in their hands to tame a brutal customer or a drunken soldier who had decided he would not pay. He supposed a pedlar brawling in the street with one of their whores would also be cause for a broken head. No, that would not do. Scarlet breathed easier when he reached the turn in the lane and was out of the district.

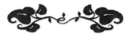

Leather shops always had the cloying tang of the tannery about them, and Scarlet could have found Masdren's counter by smell alone. Masdren kept a clean stall, chivvying his four small children with brooms and pails, and again Scarlet felt sorry for him. Ever since Masdren's wife had absconded with the scarf-merchant, the leathersmith's life had been harried with the added burdens of all the work and no help with his children. It was a wonder he still had all his wits.

"Back so soon from the Fate?" Masdren asked, giving Scarlet his weather-worn smile. Behind Masdren were his children, freed from their work for the day. They made mayhem of his little shop, careening into tables, chasing and hooting at childish games only they understood.

Scarlet shrugged. "It was a waste of coin."

Masdren nodded his agreement. "You're sure you won't think about staying on another week or so?" he asked hopefully.

"They're expecting me," Scarlet said shortly, dodging one of the little tots who seemed determined to bash his head in on something. "I promised Linhona I'd make it a quick trip this time."

"But you'll be back?"

"Yes, of course. In fact," Scarlet hesitated, and then drew in a deep, readying breath, "I was thinking of staying on in Ankar after the summer is over. When autumn comes, maybe I can find a house inside the walls."

Masdren was overjoyed. He clasped Scarlet's hand. "And your family? They're coming too?"

"I don't know," Scarlet lied. Scaja would never leave Lysia. "Perhaps."

"He will!" Masdren said in rare good spirits. "He will, and then, Scarlet-lad, he and I will make a proper Hilurin of you."

Scarlet smiled back weakly, knowing what that meant: Enough wandering for you, boy. Time for you to settle down, get children, grow old. Do what is expected of you. Be normal.

Masdren shook Scarlet's hand again and then he was off chasing his little daughter, who had tipped over a tray of riding gloves. Scarlet sighed and leaned his hip against the stall, looking out and resting his eyes on the mild blue sky crowning the bright colors of the souk.

He should have been rejoicing that he had made a shrewd financial decision. Masdren could undoubtedly teach him more of leather-working than Scaja ever had, assuring him a good living in Morturii, where the army always had need of tack and saddles. He could already repair several such items on his own and he was no stranger to horses, being a wainwright's son. He would be able to send money home to Scaja and take care of the family, and there would be no more worrying over them.

Why, then, did he feel so awful?

Fourteen days later, Scarlet crossed the Iron River from the Morturii side and he was in Patra again. He had to wait a full day for the ferry to be fixed, but he did not ride it all the way down to Lysia. Instead, he picked a landing about a half-day's march from Tradepoint so he could hit a last few steadings before home. Everything he did now had the air of finality about it, and he was savoring this journey. A farmer's wife offered him supper and he lingered until it was dark, when she exchanged a weary look with her husband before politely offering him a pallet beside their fire. The next morning saw him walking down the long, rocky slope that led into the grassy yellow valley below Lysia.

Walking out of the valley, he came upon a migrating redbird in a weathered oak with a trunk as wide as the grist stone at Jerivet's mill. He stopped to admire the song and dropped the last few crumbs of his hard waybread (purchased before setting out from Ankar) as a payment.

The bird hopped down and pecked at the morsels. A symbol for travelers everywhere, the well-traveled redbird was also represented by the crimson color of the traditional pedlar's coat. Perhaps this was a lucky omen.

"You must like waybread more than me," he said lowly, careful not to startle the animal.

The bird abruptly flew off to the north and Scarlet sighed. Scaja often spoke of his mother and how she had been able to charm eagles out of trees, but his own Gift was not so strong and all he could do was convince smaller birds and beasts to allow him to approach.

The sun was bright and it was unseasonably warm, and everywhere there were signs of the new spring greening the land. Stopping a league further up the road, beside Ferryman's Rock, he ate the last of the dried apples and smoked fish he had picked up in Patra. The water was icy for washing, but he rolled up his sleeves and held his breath as he splashed his face and arms. With a last rueful look at his tattered pack, he tightened the straps for the last haul home. On this route, he would not pass Tradepoint or Skeld's Ferry, and he was secretly happy not to have to pretend a smile for Zsu and Deni, or turn aside Kev's snide remarks with one of his own.

There was no sense of foreboding or darkness, and nothing ominous stirred in the back of his brain. He did not even remember the card reader's predictions in Patra, having put that episode out of his mind completely. Walking steadily, his mind was occupied with thoughts of Linhona's cooking and the petty sense of gratitude that tonight he would be in a soft, warm bed. Patra had been cold and unwelcoming.

About two leagues from the village gate, on the Owl's Road, he smelled smoke. Everyone had a fireplace in Lysia, naturally, but the smell was too strong for such a warm day. He cast his gaze to the sky above the mountains and saw the tall columns of smoke rising like black pillars from the hills.

Lysia was on fire.

He hurried his steps, hoping that it was only a barn that had caught ablaze or perhaps a grain store near the mill. He even took time to wish that it was not *their* barn, but then a new smell hit him and he lost all caution and broke out into a run. The mended strap that he had nursed all the way from Patra finally broke and he let it fall to the ground and began running faster than he had ever run in his life. So fast that his legs felt like wings and the ground was like air beneath him, but the road seemed to be longer than ever before. He ran, the air in his lungs like fire, all the way to the village gate.

Too fast. When he was in sight of the gate, the toe of his boot caught on a rut in the path and he went sprawling face-first into the dirt. He must have hit his head on a rock, for when he rose shakily to his feet, his vision was fuzzy and blurred. His face felt wet, and he wiped it away on the back of his hand and saw red. Ears ringing, he stumbled into Lysia in a daze of noise and pain. The building nearest the gate, Kerry's forge, was engulfed in flame, but no one was at First Well trying to put it out. Shocked, he tried to clear his eyes of blood and gaped around him. He was alone, and the village was... gone. Simply gone.

Scarlet had been born in Lysia, now he did not recognize it. He stumbled into the village square. Here was the stone circle of Second Well, and here the baker's, and here the horse trough outside of what had been Rufa's taberna, no more than glowing cinders and charred beams collapsed into a heap.

The first corpse he saw was Hipola the midwife. She was lying in the street, her gray hair a tangled veil cast across her face. Her throat was cut.

Scarlet back away from her, horrified and coughing on the black smoke, only to have his heel bump against the crushed skull of another body. He turned and saw it was Jerivet.

He stumbled away from them and tried to get his bearings from the well, finally gathering his wits enough to turn his face north. Staggering, he lurched toward the pond until he could see the water, and then turned left to Wainwright's Lane, where he saw more bodies. Two Kasiri men, known only by their bright jackets, lay sprawled in the lane, hacked and bloody.

"Deva," he whispered in horror. He began to run down the lane, looking for the house he was born in.

Three jagged, charred heaps of ash he passed, until he stood in front of what was left of his own house. The ashes were cooling. Only the large oak beams that had supported the dome were still smoking. Perhaps he wept, though he did not remember doing so later. He must have, for his life was under those ashes, lost.

He started forward, his hands outstretched, but there was nothing to save. The central brick pillar was still standing, blackened with fire and soot. Scaja's paved walkway, laid so lovingly with flat stones he gathered from the river himself, was still there, and the hearth and chimney made from rock. Somehow, he made it to the hearth. The little mirror he had combed his hair in so many times was shattered. As he approached, his fragmented reflection flowed over the sharp edges in a hundred shattered pieces.

His mouth moved in the broken mirror. "You told me true, Dad. There was an end to it."

"Scarlet."

Someone was calling his name. He was on his knees in the ash. He lifted his head, only then realizing that he was surrounded by Kasiri.

"*You,*" he snarled. His hands found the curved hafts of the Morturii long-knives at his belt. "Scavengers! You and your vermin couldn't wait until the ashes were cold before they began picking our bones? Get out!"

Liall stood with several of his men, among them Peysho and the tawny-eyed Morturii man with the brown hair and girlish face who shadowed Peysho's steps like a faithful dog: Kio. The Wolf's face was dirty with grime and he wore a faded leather jacket that made him look not at all like an atya. Kio had a wide, bloodied bandage around his upper arm and streaks of crimson ran down his wrist. They were all filthy with ash and soot.

From sacking my village as it burned, Scarlet thought, and his vision went hazy in anger.

"We are not looting," Liall said. "We were–"

"You're a filthy Kasiri thief!" Scarlet accused, far past caring. "Why else would you be here?"

Liall closed his mouth and would not answer, only stared at Scarlet with his cold and disapproving eyes. With a snarl, Scarlet slid the long-knives from their sheaths and in one swift movement flowed to his feet. He raised the weapon to slash at Liall's face.

He found his stroke parried by Kio, who had leapt in the way with his own knife drawn. Liall had not moved.

Scarlet batted Kio's weapon aside. "Stand away!"

The other Kasiri were moving back to give them room to fight. Scarlet lunged forward, eager to drive past Kio's defense, and Kio again deflected his attack. They exchanged a rapid series of feints and countermoves. On the final clash, the tip of Scarlet's knife slid past Kio's defense and narrowly sliced his cheek.

Kio snapped the hilt of his knife up, impacting with Scarlet's wrist, making the bone sing briefly in pain. Scarlet swore and retreated.

Kio backed away as well, shaking his head as Scarlet stood trembling with fury. Kio swiped blood away from his cheek and stared at his reddened fingers, and then at Scarlet, with considerable respect.

"If we continue," Kio said to Liall. "I may have to kill him."

"Oh, that won't do," Peysho said easily. He drew a knife from his belt and motioned for the other Kasiri to do the same. "Drop it, lad. Ye can't fight us all."

Scarlet spat at him. Peysho took it well, calmly wiping spittle from his jaw. Liall pushed Kio aside and stepped forward, well within range of Scarlet's knives.

"Enough," he commanded. "We are not stealing. We're looking for survivors."

"Liar!"

"Why would I bother lying to you?" Liall asked frigidly. "What need do I have? If we were bent on sacking this place, do you think you could stop us? We could murder you just as easy as the Aralyrin murdered your people." He motioned and Peysho obediently lowered his knife. The rest of the Kasiri followed.

A great, hot mantle of misery blazed up around Scarlet.

He was burning in it, like Scaja and Linhona in the house, ashes and red cinders. He was not even aware that his hands were lowered and he was defenseless.

"Your sister lives."

"Annaya?" he muttered from the fire. It seemed a miracle that he could still speak. "She's–"

"She's alive. She'd been hiding until the Aralyrin left, but some of them found her after their riders had gone. We came upon them and killed them all." He pointed to a charred area behind the ruins, and only then did Scarlet see the body of a tall Byzan there, much too tall to be Hilurin. His face was frozen into a furious death-mask, lips drawn away from his teeth in a snarl.

"Where is she?"

"In our camp, what's left of it. They attacked us as well, though not with as much enthusiasm as Lysia."

"If you've harmed her…"

Liall looked down on him with scorn and pity. "I told you. We saved her. I'll take you to her now."

Liall held out his hand to Scarlet, but he thrust it away. "Is she all right?"

"She's in shock, but not hurt." He looked at the blood on Scarlet's face. "I cannot speak for her mind."

Scarlet glanced back at the ruins of Scaja's house, the little domed dwelling his father had built with his own hands for Scarlet's first mother. "My parents… they were inside, weren't they?"

Liall's mouth tightened. "They were. Your sister saw everything. She told me."

His heart clutched. Little Annaya. Oh Deva, please… "Take me to her." He took a step and staggered. Peysho caught him.

"Ye've hurt yerself, lad," he said.

"It's nothing," Scarlet mumbled. "Take me to my sister."

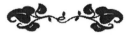

The pitying looks from the Kasiri as they entered the camp seemed to burn him as hot as the fire that consumed Lysia.

"Who else?" Scarlet asked as he trudged beside Liall on the path. Who else is left? he wondered in the deepest sorrow he had ever known. Who survived? Is anyone I grew up with still alive?

"None," Liall said.

Scarlet was thankful that Liall kept his face averted. He did not want the atya's pity.

They arrived at a green yurt on the far edge of the camp. Annaya sat by a small brazier in the interior, a flowered blanket draped around her shoulders. With Liall watching in the entrance, Scarlet knelt beside her, painfully aware of how vacant her eyes were. She stared unseeing into the little licks of flame. Her fingers were knotted so hard in the blanket's ragged ends that her nails had turned blue.

"Annaya?" He kept his voice low and moved very slowly, the way he had seen Scaja do with mistreated horses. "Annaya love. It's me, Scarlet."

Her lips twitched and her hands unfurled from the blanket. "Scarlet?"

"Yes, love."

"I saw them burn the house." Her black eyes were wide. "They burned it with Mum and Dad inside."

"I know. Hush, I know."

Her voice was so wobbly that it reminded him of a newborn colt trying out its legs. "This is like Mum and the Raiders... isn't it?"

It took him a moment to answer. "Yes."

She sounded like a child. "Only I'm not left alone with

no one." She reached for his hand. He did not flinch, not even when she dug her nails into his skin. "I still have you."

Her eyes brimmed over and Scarlet nearly wept himself with relief. She would not sink into the tearless grief that had nearly driven Linhona to madness when she lost her first family. She was Linhona's daughter, surely, but she was also Scaja's.

Annaya swayed forward and pitched into her brother's arms. Liall quietly left them alone to mourn.

Scarlet closed the flap of the yurt and tied it tight to keep out the mountain chill. The wind was kicking up again after the long silence it had kept all day. An old woman had come earlier bearing a pot of che for Annaya. Scarlet recognized the woman's office as being the same as old Hipola's in Lysia, and the che smelled of healing herbs. Annaya drank and fell asleep and the woman waved him out of the interior, assuring him with signs that she would watch over his sister.

Standing on the platform, he could see the columns of smoke and drifting ash to the north, and he deliberately turned away from them and crossed his arms over his shivering body. He stood there for half an hour or more, staring blindly out over stone and scrub, and jumped when a hearth-warmed blanket was dropped over his shoulders. Liall pushed a pottery cup into his hands.

"Drink."

"I don't–"

"Drink, boy."

Scarlet was exhausted and shaky and Liall's command

was the one certain voice he had heard in a day of nightmares. Tipping the cup to his lips, he drank. The liquid was clear and fiery, but he was numb and barely tasted it.

"How is she?"

"She'll heal," he heard himself say.

"I have no doubt of it." Liall shook his head. "You Byzans. What an amazement you are."

He glared at Liall for a moment, unsure of his meaning.

"I only meant that Byzan strength is vastly underestimated."

Scarlet was feeling anything but strong. All he understood was that Liall was not making less of his parent's murder and the massacre of his home. "Why do they do these things to us?" he demanded weakly. "Don't they know we're helpless, that we're no threat to them? We're not their enemies, the Hilurin nobles in Rusa are!"

Liall shrugged. "Why does any predator prey on the weak?"

"But they didn't have to kill *everyone*," he said plaintively. "What are they trying to do, wipe us all out?"

"That is a possibility."

The whole world felt unreal. Even the colors of the mountain he had seen a thousand times before looked too bright and vivid. "Why do they hate us so much?" he whispered.

"I cannot say," Liall said kindly. "Perhaps it is more than simple hatred. I have seen massacres like this before, and the answer is always the same: Fear." He gazed steadfastly at Scarlet. "As weak in numbers as you are, what cause would the Aralyrin have to fear you? There is your answer."

Scarlet bit his lip and looked away. The Aralyrin had

once been Hilurin. Surely some of their elders must remember the Gift, and that Hilurin alone were able to speak to Deva and be heard. That was cause enough for fear.

Seeing Scarlet's distress, Liall put his arm around the pedlar in a friendly fashion, but Scarlet remembered the last time this man had tried to lay hands on him and pulled quickly away.

Liall looked gravely offended. "I would not offer you such an insult in your grief."

Scarlet was suddenly ashamed. This was the man who had saved his sister's life. "I crave your pardon," he mumbled without grace. "Please forgive me."

Liall sighed. "There's nothing to forgive, but let us get out of this wind before you freeze."

It was not very cold, and Scarlet had an idle thought that perhaps Liall was not very good at judging what a comfortable temperature for Byzans was. Liall motioned for him to follow. He obeyed, not really seeing where they were headed. Shortly, they arrived at a large blue yurt perched atop a wooden platform. On the platform was a tall pole adorned with a plain red banner without an emblem.

"This is Peysho's yurt," Liall said, holding aside the flap for him. Kio was there with a fresh bandage on his face, his golden eyes hooded and secret. Kio greeted them courteously before putting a fine silver cup into Liall's hand. Apparently, one could not go anywhere in a Kasiri camp without being offered food or drink of some kind.

"This is Scarlet," Liall said, pointing as he introduced him roughly. "Scarlet: Kio Sr'thanu."

Scarlet nodded at Kio. It was strange to be formally introduced to someone after you'd just had a knife fight with him. Liall motioned to a pile of soft furs near the small brazier and gave him a gentle push. Scarlet huddled gratefully into the furs without protest. Now that he had seen Annaya was safe, his own shock took over. He began to shiver violently.

Liall was talking in soft tones to Kio, but he did not understand what they were saying. The cup sagged in his hand and his eyelids drooped, and he jumped when he felt someone near him. Liall was bending close, taking the cup from him and pushing his shoulder.

"Go to sleep," Liall ordered. "You are safe. I will be here when you awaken."

Scarlet opened his mouth to object, to claim he was not tired, but in the space of one breath to the next the world went dark and he fell into dreams where he saw Scaja heaping ashes onto his head, mourning his children's fate, orphaned in the world and leaderless without him.

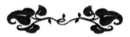

Scarlet had always been slow to awaken in the morning. *Sleepyhead,* Linhona had often named him. On the first morning after the attack, he woke in Peysho's yurt to discover that Liall had not left him. The atya was stretched out some feet away from the brazier, the whole giant length of him. Scarlet sat up and stared dully at the crack of light near the door flap while the events of yesterday settled in on him like rain clouds gathering over a valley. His head ached. He reached up to feel his temple and was surprised to find that his cut had been tended to while he slept. There was some kind of aromatic ointment spread over the wound, and someone had cleaned the blood off his face and neck.

Scarlet's eyes smarted fiercely. He rubbed them with the back of his hand and took a deep breath. You cannot cry, he scolded silently. *Annaya needs you.*

Liall stirred in his sleep and murmured, and then his pale blue eyes snapped open. He looked at Scarlet for a long, quiet moment before he sat up and began to lace his scuffed leather jacket closed and feel around for his boots. Not a sleepyhead at all. Liall seemed to flow from sleep to consciousness with the same effortless ease that he accomplished everything else. For once, the Kasiri's adroitness did not annoy Scarlet, and he began to see how he could learn from such a man, if Liall were willing to teach him. *Scarlet, you ninny, what are you thinking?*

His mouth twitched into a little smile. It was Linhona's voice in his head, not his own, and he was oddly comforted by it. He knew they would always be with him.

"Feeling better?"

He did not, really. Liall had risen and was scrounging in Peysho's supplies. There was no sign of Peysho or Kio.

"Yes, thank you," he replied automatically.

Liall stopped his rummaging long enough to throw him a curious glance. "Are you always so polite?"

He thought for a moment. "No."

Liall resumed his search. "Good. We stand on short ceremony here and we like to be quick about things. Manners take the long way around everything."

"That explains why Kasiri don't have any." He could have bit his tongue, but the look Liall gave him was one of amusement.

"Now *that* is the red-coat I know. Ah, here we go. Che." Liall held up a small linen bag and pulled its drawstrings open, then stuck his nose inside and sniffed. "Real southern blend, too. Peysho always has the best." He began to sprinkle some of the curled green leaves into the kettle.

"Won't he mind if–"

"Who, Peysho? Anything I have is his, and anything he

has is mine, save for Kio."

"Is that the Kasiri creed?"

Liall gave a huff of laughter. "No, but it is the creed between comrades, and we are that."

Something else Liall said nagged him. "You said Kio... does he own Kio?" He was apprehensive, remembering the boys in the slave market.

"Not at all, though there is a proprietary line there that only a very unwise man would cross." Liall poured the che and handed him a delicate enameled cup that had a chasing of green leaves around its white rim.

He sipped experimentally, and the taste of the che drove all further questions from his mind. It was green che, the same kind in Scaja's house, yet this had a subtle flavor and a mellowness he had never tasted before, without any of the bitterness that Byzantur che usually carried. There was also a hint of scent about it, like a delicate dusting of roses.

Liall took in Scarlet's widened eyes and startled expression. He smiled. "Good?"

"It's the best I've ever had," Scarlet said honestly, the incredible scent and fragile flavor lingering on his tongue and in his nose. "I didn't even know they could make something so wonderful." Then he felt awful. How could he be enjoying che when Scaja and Linhona were dead?

Liall sipped his che noisily, as Scarlet had seen other Kasiri do. "The world is bigger than any man can know in a dozen lifetimes, red-coat, and you have seen only a small part of it, no more than a thimble of sand on a broad beach."

The yurt flap opened and Peysho stood looking in. He nodded at Liall deferentially and then fixed his fearsome gaze on Scarlet. His gravelly voice was gentle. "Yer sister wants ye, lad. Better come."

To avoid going through the center of the camp and endure again the curious stares of the Kasiri, Scarlet took the longer route that skirted the outside of the wagons. The wagons were nearest the edges of the promontory where the land fell away steeply on all sides into the mountain. In his haste, Scarlet nearly tripped on a jutting rock and Liall caught him and steadied him on his feet.

"Byzan fool!" Liall's hands gripped his arms tightly, and Scarlet got the distinct impression the atya wanted to shake him for his carelessness. "Be more careful!"

"Annaya–"

"Is safe. Peysho would have said so if she were not. We have plenty of time. Slow down and keep your wits about you. There are cliffs all around here."

"I've been walking for a goodly time now," he retorted. Still, he slowed down.

They came to the yurt and Scarlet found he was strangely frozen, unable to mount the steps to go inside. Liall pushed on Scarlet's shoulder to urge him, and Scarlet went forward in a rush, only to freeze again when he pulled the flap open.

Annaya was huddled into a young man's arms, sobbing loudly. It took Scarlet a few moments to recognize him.

"Shansi?" he breathed. His feet carried him into the smoky interior, where he sank to his knees. "Oh, Deva, we thought you were done for."

"So did I," Shansi croaked, looking up at Scarlet from the dark tangle of Annaya's hair. His voice was coarse as winter winds, aged as an old man's, and his torn clothes were filthy with mud and ash. "I was down in Jerivet's new cellar near the village gate, fixing his side door

165

against robbers... you remember how he was feared of robbers, Scarlet? I never heard the Aralyrin come riding in, and only when they came for the stores did I spy 'em. I realized what was happening, because they could have never gotten by old Jerivet without him raising the alarm. I tried to get past them, wanting to get to my uncle, but one of the bastards hit me with his club."

Scarlet saw the wide gash on Shansi's forehead, healed a day or so, and his gut twisted in sympathy. Poor Jerivet, and poor Shansi, too: alone, underground, cornered.

"I don't remember much after that. Just darkness and the smell of smoke," Shansi said. His voice faltered but he forged ahead, and Scarlet realized that the words had been trapped inside Shansi since Lysia burned, and now they must come out, the poison must be drained. He settled back to listen, every bit as shaken as Shansi.

"The bastard must have rattled my brain for me, for when I woke up I didn't know where I was or what had happened. The cellar was empty. After they thought they killed me, they took everything and fired the building above me. The roof collapsed and that must have saved my life. It was pure luck I'd pulled away some of the side door built into the hill to repair it the day before, else I'd have had no air and be dead, too, like my uncle is."

"I'm sorry," Scarlet told him. He swallowed hard. Shansi had come to Lysia to become a blacksmith and instead had seen a massacre. At least he still had his parents, safely tucked away in Nantua. "We lost both Scaja and Linhona."

Shansi gave him a look of deep sympathy. "So Annaya has said. I'm so sorry. They would have been my family, too."

He took a deep breath, willing back tears. He had cried enough. "How did you get out?" He settled down closer to Annaya to hear the rest of Shansi's story, his heart thumping rapidly. Shansi's face had brought everything back to him: his first sight of the village, the smoke and ash rising from the pyre of bodies, his home, and somewhere underneath, Scaja and Linhona...

Scarlet shook his head to banish the images, trying to focus on Shansi's voice.

"I dug my way out," Shansi said, his hands combing through Annaya's hair. She had quieted and was holding on to him like he was a treasure returned to her, which Scarlet supposed he was. The smith's fingers were black with soot and earth and there were patches of raw flesh showing through.

Shansi saw the direction of his gaze. "Some of the timbers were still smoldering," he explained. "I lost a few fingernails, but I knew if I didn't get out right then, that cellar was going to be my tomb. The first place I looked was the smithy, but there was nowt left but ashes and bricks, so I went by your dad's place on Wainwright's Lane." He paused for a moment. "Ah, Scarlet..."

"I'm glad Deva saved you," Scarlet said bravely. "Annaya, at least, has someone returned to her."

"Deva saved all three of us, it seems."

"That wasn't Deva," Annaya said, stirring. She wiped her cheeks with the backs of her hands. "That was Liall, the Wolf."

Shansi blinked. "But... you mean he was telling the truth? I thought it was some bandit's boast, saying he had rescued you."

"That much is true," Annaya interjected when Scarlet would have spoken. She gave her brother an unblinking stare. "He did save me, him and the Morturii with the red eye."

"Peysho," he informed her. "And Kio and a few more, from what I hear."

"Scarlet, we're in their debt now," Annaya said,

amazing him. Just yesterday, he had doubted her will to survive, yet now her strength had returned along with her sense of Hilurin honor. Her voice shook and she needed a bath and a long sleep, but she was again in command of herself.

"I know that," Scarlet said reluctantly. He owed Liall a life twice over, but he no longer had any way to pay him, now that he had Annaya to take care of. "But how can we–"

"We honor our debts," Annaya went on. She turned and hugged Shansi fiercely, unaware of how he winced in pain and his shredded hands fluttered on her shoulders. "Oh Deva, to think I almost... but no, you're both alive, and we won't talk about that now. As long as there's life, there's hope."

Scarlet was highly unsettled. "I'll pay our debts, Annaya, even if he is a Kasiri," he promised. "If Scaja and Linhona were here, they'd be grateful even to a demon for saving us."

She smiled before she began to weep again, holding on to her young love.

Liall was waiting for him outside the yurt. Scarlet descended the short steps and faced west, filling his lungs with damp, chilly air. An early afternoon storm was gathering to the north, pushing a wave of steel-gray clouds before it. "You heard?"

"Not everything. I am pleased that your sister again wishes to live."

"More than that," he admitted. "She's reborn."

"It is good, Scarlet."

"I owe that to you," Scarlet said slowly, thinking it over. It was true enough. No matter how much he disliked this bandit, he owed him a great debt.

"I did not save the young man," Liall reminded him. "That was his doing."

"But you saved Annaya, and you saved me from Cadan."

"Only because I was there," Liall disagreed. "I could just as easily have been twenty leagues away."

"But you weren't," Scarlet persisted. "Deva put you there, and so Deva places the debt on me."

Liall tilted his head to look down on Scarlet. His tone turned subtly mocking. "Ah, so it was the will of your gods. Why thank me at all, then?"

"Because you had a choice," Scarlet returned plainly. He was unaccountably annoyed with Liall's logic. "You could've turned away, but you chose to help. *You* did. The gods had nothing to do with that part of it."

Liall grunted, eyeing him skeptically. "I do not believe in gods. If they exist at all, they do not answer *my* prayers, so what good are they?" He spat over the edge of the platform. "I piss on all of them."

This was such blasphemy that Scarlet gaped in shock. "You should not say such things," he whispered, scandalized.

Liall laughed and the skin around his eyes crinkled in merriment. For a moment, Scarlet was angry. Liall put his hand heavily on Scarlet's shoulder.

"Your goddess Deva commands you to remain chaste and to do good in the world, to be charitable to strangers, generous to travelers, kind to children, and respectful of all beasts, yet she fills her world with cutthroats and slavers and rapists and foulness of every sort. She looks on and does nothing while you Hilurin are beset on all sides by animals. Om-Ret converts more and more followers in Morturii and even Byzantur, and meanwhile you and your kind, faithful worshippers of Deva, are a pitiful minority slowly being swallowed alive by the world." He removed his hand. "No, boy, I fear no god's revenge. I am far more afraid of the cruelty of men."

Liall's words were like whips cutting into his wavering faith. "Still," he muttered, "I owe you a life debt and I will pay it somehow, on my honor."

Liall shrugged and looked at the sky, squinting as he assayed the clouds. "Honor does not concern an atya, only sky and wind and keeping his krait fed and an open road in front of them. You have nothing now, either way."

"One does not pay such a debt in coin alone," Scarlet said primly. "There is also service."

"Service?" Liall's pale eyebrows rose and his interest returned. "Do you wish to be my servant? To wait on me like Peysho's women, fetching and carrying my food and laundry. Is that it?"

"No!" he snapped. Gods, was the man totally ignorant?

"Then you will have to demonstrate this odd notion of service to me. I have no doubt it will be interesting." Liall turned suddenly sober. "But now, I have something to show you. Come with me."

Liall strode off, expecting to be obeyed, and Scarlet had no choice but to follow. They walked quickly through the camp with many eyes on them, but Liall spoke to no one. Scarlet saw that they were headed toward the atya's red platform, and his boots slowed. Liall ascended the short steps and looked back over his shoulder to see Scarlet still on the ground.

"Are you coming?"

Scarlet did not want to follow him inside. Sleeping in Peysho's yurt was one matter, being alone with Liall was quite another. Yet, as he was in the man's debt, he did not wish to offend. Liall looked at him steadily for a long moment, then opened the flap and ducked inside his yurt, leaving him to follow or not as he chose.

Feeling the eyes of several curious Kasiri on him, Scarlet went haltingly up the stairs and into the yurt. Liall was standing by the small, smoking brazier. A large, hinged box rested on a table beside him, and Liall had his hand on it. The box was painted in many colors and had a crimson vine crowned by a white flower inscribed on the lid, the Byzan symbol of the Flower Prince.

"I have this for you," Liall said as Scarlet let the canvas flap drop behind him. Liall's face was troubled and he patted the lid of the box before withdrawing his hand. "But I confess I do not know what to do with it."

Scarlet studied the box and stepped forward and would have touched it, but Liall seized his hand. "Do not open it," Liall said gently.

Scarlet stared at him, utterly at a loss. He shook his head, wondering if this was some new game, and if the old Wolf was back.

"I thought... it did not seem fitting to leave them there," Liall said.

The box seemed to loom darkly on the table. "What is it?"

"The bones of your parents."

It was a long moment before Scarlet was able to speak. "How?"

"Even in such a fire, something remains," Liall said. "I had my men sift the ashes of your father's house. This is the result."

Words failed Scarlet. He shook his head, aware that Liall still held his hand. Scarlet did not pull away. "Why?"

"I know how it feels when those you love suddenly die, and there is no opportunity to bury them or say farewell."

171

Liall cleared his throat, embarrassed of his confession. "There are many Byzan customs of burial, but I am ignorant of Hilurin tradition. I did not know what to do with them."

Scarlet gazed at the box and had absolutely no desire to open it. Liall looked at him with pity.

"Please tell me how to honor them."

Scarlet's voice shook. "We take the bodies of our dead to the priests of Deva."

"If there are no priests?" Liall prompted. They had all fled the raiders and were safe in Patra or Khurelen. "What then?"

"They're buried deep in the fields to nourish the soil. Scaja's father and mother are buried in the wheat field we sow every spring, the field where the family templon is."

"Shall we do that?" Liall asked, his voice uncommonly gentle. "Shall we bury them?"

The heavy rain clouds were perched over the valley by the time they made it on foot down the mountain path to Lysia. Peysho and Kio went with them, and Kio offered twice to carry the box, but Scarlet would let no one else bear it. He still could not bring himself to open it.

Liall was surprised that Annaya did not come with them. "She's a girl," Scarlet said, which explained nothing to a Kasiri. "Her business is bearing, not death. You can't expect her to do both. What kind of people are you?"

The matter was beyond Liall and he said so, but declined to argue the point. Out of respect, Scarlet supposed, and marveled.

Liall and Peysho had brought shovels, and together they

dug a hole in the earth as deep as a man, just a few feet from where the fence used to be, now trampled into the ground like everything else. A chilly, stinging rain started up just as they were finishing the hole, and Scarlet handed the box down to Liall.

"I will just open it and place it in the bottom of the grave. Is that well?" Liall asked. His bright hair was spattered with black mud and his face was filthy.

Scarlet nodded. It was a poor funeral, but he could think of nothing else. It seemed impossible that this man helping him put his parents to rest was the same man he had cursed as a brigand and murderer.

Scarlet helped Liall out of the grave, and thankfully Kio was shoveling rocky earth back into the hole before he got a clear look at the open box. Scarlet took up a shovel and joined Kio in his task, and Liall stood aside with Peysho, who watched the pedlar sympathetically with his strange, fractured eye.

When the grave was filled, Scarlet knelt on one knee in the mud, his head bowed as he carded through his memories: Scaja laughing as he taught him to seat a horse for the first time, Linhona waking him in the morning for breakfast, Scaja's soft eyes as he handed him his pipe in the evening, the feel of Linhona's warm hand on his cheek.

"Do you want to say something?" Liall asked, rousing him from the dark well of memory. The rain was cold on their heads and their clothes were soaked through.

"What is there to say?" He knew he sounded defeated and morose. "I'm not a priest. I only know the cantos that Scaja taught me to sing to Deva."

"Sing it," Liall urged.

He thought about it for a moment in the fading light, then looked up at the gray sky and began to sing in a pure, clear voice:

"On danaee Deva shani,
You brought us here,
You take us home
On danaee Deva shani
Noe drashen mor Anshali."

It was a simple song and he did not consider himself to be much of a singer, but Liall was staring at him.

"That was beautiful, Scarlet."

He shook his head and got to his feet.

Liall touched his arm as the rain drummed on their skulls, little needles of cold. "Come. Your sister will be waiting."

There was nothing to do but follow him. They marched back up the hill in silence. Finally, when they were about to turn the last bend that would take the field out of his sight, Scarlet stopped and looked back at the shallow depression in the earth. The raked soil was rapidly returning to mud. Soon, heavy rains and spring weeds would erase all evidence that they had disturbed the ground there. For a moment, it felt like Scaja and Linhona had never lived at all.

Liall was beside him. His hand was surprisingly warm on Scarlet's neck. "Would you like me to find a marker for their grave?"

Scarlet shook his head, shaking raindrops from the ends of his hair. Liall ducked his head a little to look Scarlet in the eye. His hand moved on Scarlet's neck in a soothing caress, his fingers kneading the tired, clenched muscles there.

Scarlet did not push him away as he would have a day ago, but he suddenly felt disturbingly vulnerable to that seductive alien countenance. In pure self-defense, he turned his face away and stared blindly at the summit of the Nerit. "All of Lysia is a grave."

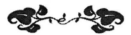

Two days passed before Annaya and Shansi were well enough to make the trip to Nantua. The previous night, Shansi had made known his plans to take her to his father's house across the river, far from where the Aralyrin raids were occurring. Scarlet had argued with him briefly, nurturing a forlorn hope that life could continue in Lysia.

"Scarlet, the place is a tomb," Shansi said gently. "Let it rest in peace."

"It's our home," Scarlet insisted. "Scaja wanted to see his grandchildren grow up there."

"That's not the point, now."

"Linhona wanted the same."

"Linhona had no love for Lysia, she only wanted us to stay close by," Annaya said. "She was no more happy about me going to live with Shansi than she was with you going off with the caravans."

"Still," he argued. "It's what they would have wanted."

"I'm not going to live in a slaughterhouse out of guilt," Annaya declared, putting an end to the debate. "I'll never go back to Lysia."

Scarlet saw from the set of her chin that it would be a battle to cross her. He gave in and went to sit with Liall and Kio on the steps of Peysho's yurt. There he sat quietly and twirled a stick in his hand as the two men conversed in an unknown dialect, some patois of Falx and Qaha that he could follow if he listened carefully, but he did not. The sun was setting and the Kasiri camp was in a shambles. All the oxen and horses had been brought out of their shelters and were tethered to half-filled wagons as the Longspur krait pulled up stakes and made ready to move on. Men cursed and trudged through the camp with heavy trunks and boxes on their backs as the last of the winter snow and ice slowly churned to gray slush under their boots. Not only had Lysia –the only nearby village to pressure tolls from– vanished into smoke, but the Aralyrin had genuinely hurt the Kasiri. Scarlet was ashamed to realize that he had not even asked Liall the names of the Kasiri who had died with Lysia.

"None who will not be mourned," Liall answered shortly. "How is your sister?"

He asked about her every day. Scarlet tried to wipe the glum look from his face as he snapped the stick in two. "Much better. Shansi will be taking her to Nantua."

"And do you approve of her choice?"

He shrugged. "She's got to marry someone, I suppose. Shansi will find another blacksmith to finish out his apprenticeship, and a smith makes good wages. A sensible lad and a sensible match."

"And will you go with them, make your new home in Nantua?"

He shrugged his shoulders. "I don't think so."

"What will you do, then?"

"I hadn't thought that far ahead."

"Yet, you must do something," Liall pressed, and for a dizzying moment, Scarlet believed Liall was going to ask him to remain with him and the Kasiri.

"Masdren is going to teach me leatherwork and tanning in Ankar," he said quickly. "He's got a shop in the souk."

"Masdren," Liall repeated oddly.

"Friend of my father's," he explained, then was angry at himself for explaining. What did he care what Liall thought? "He's old enough to be my dad."

Peysho strode past them as they sat in the orange light

of dusk and motioned for Kio to follow him. Kio went without a word and Scarlet stared after the two men, biting his lip.

"Curious about them, are you?"

Scarlet stared at the ground and said nothing. There were questions he wanted to ask, but they seemed scandalous when he thought about saying them. He settled for a shrug. "They make a... comfortable pair," he allowed. "Or they seem to."

"What an unromantic lot you are," Liall observed.

Scarlet sensed Liall was laughing at him again. He could do that without cracking a smile. "Why do you say that?"

"Comfortable, sensible, suitable," Liall quoted. "Have you never heard of passion?"

"Passion never put crops in the field." It was a saying of Scaja's.

"Never a Byzan field, at any rate. I'm sure of it."

Scarlet had no idea what Liall was on about, but then, he rarely did. The man had a mind like a weevil's path, all crossings and curls. "All I meant was they seem easy with one another."

"They are that. They're both former soldiers. Peysho will make a good atya when I'm gone, and Kio will help him."

Scarlet's head jerked up. "Gone? Where are you going?"

He may have said it too quickly, for Liall gave him an arch look. "Why do you want to know?"

"I just... I *don't* want to know," he said stubbornly. "If it's a secret, keep it to yourself. What do I care?"

"As you said, you are going to live in Ankar." Liall was staring at him blandly.

Scarlet scowled. "I thought these were your people."

"My people," Liall pursed his lips, seeming to mull the

notion over, "I am their leader, if that's a distinction you care to make. But, in many ways, I suppose I am a Kasiri by now."

"Then why are you leaving?"

"I've been called back to my homeland."

"Where's that?"

"Too far away for little Byzans ever to have heard of it," Liall assured, which annoyed him more. Liall grinned, but it seemed strained to Scarlet. "It is Norl Udur, as has been rumored, and I will get there by traveling to the port of Volkovoi across the Channel. I told you the word is a wide place. Where I come from, all men are giants like me and the land is wrapped in ice."

He could well believe that. "I have trouble seeing you as a journeyer."

"Kasiri are journeyers."

"That's different."

Liall chuckled a little. "Meaning thieving nomads are not the same as noble pedlars? You don't say much, Scarlet, and even when you do, what you *don't* say could fill a book."

Ha! Talk about pots and kettles. "When are you leaving?"

"In the morning."

Scarlet strove for a light tone, shaken for no reason he could name. "There's to be no celebration for the departing chieftain?"

Liall shook his head curtly. "It would not be proper after we have lost so many men. Also, it would mark a division between my rule of the krait and Peysho's, and I don't want to weaken his new stature by comparison."

Scarlet tossed the ends of the stick away, not knowing what to say. Just then, Kio whistled from across the camp, calling Liall to a spot where several men were gathered to right an overturned wagon. Liall stood up and slapped his palms together.

"Ready to get your hands dirty?"

Scarlet snorted and followed him. Hands dirty, indeed. Seven strong men had their hands knotted in ropes slung over the wagon's top on the other side of the camp, ready to pull. Liall took his place beside Kio and handed Scarlet a rope.

"This isn't a good idea," he said, taking his place beside the men and bracing his legs.

Torva, an elder tribesman with a scarred nose, laughed at him. "Kasiri have been traveling by wagon and yurt since Deva left the Otherworld to walk among mortals. What would you know about it?"

Liall was watching Scarlet with interest. Scarlet stole a quick peek under the wagon, saw the angle of the wheels, and then straightened. "At least one wheel will break on the felled side if we right the wagon this way," he judged. "Maybe both."

The Kasiri laughed and Peysho sang out a loud note. The men heaved and pushed. Minutes later, Scarlet was dusting off his hands and the Kasiri were casting him sheepish looks.

Kio walked over and gifted Scarlet with one of his rare smiles as he slapped dirt from his breeches. "One wheel snapped, the other cracked." He chuckled. "The pedlar knows his wagons." Kio watched Liall standing beside a knot of men, pointing and giving directions as Peysho listened with his customary solemnity that was never far from amusement.

"So," Kio said casually. "You'll be following the Wolf, then?"

Scarlet stared. "Why would I do that?"

Kio only smiled knowingly, as if he knew a secret, and left just as Liall walked up. The uppermost rim of the sun was sinking below the horizon and its dying light cast a final reddish glow on the mountain peaks all around them.

"This is your last night with the Kasiri," Liall said. "Mine, as well. Will you have dinner with me? I have more of that scented che you like."

Liall's gaze was unreadable and his neutral words gave Scarlet nothing to interpret. He swallowed in a dry throat. Not only was Liall his host, he was his sister's savior, and on the surface it was only a dinner invitation. Still, he thought nervously, *he wants more than company for a meal. He knows it and so do I and... gods, why must he be so plain that all he wants from me is to get between my legs? Why does he ask so damned little?*

It occurred to Scarlet then that Liall might not even like him at all, but might be only enamored of his face and the prospect of exploring his body, and all Liall's recent kindnesses but an extension of that lust. The unexpected hurt of that possibility rendered Scarlet speechless, and he stammered a clumsy refusal.

Liall's expression went hard. "Never mind," he said gruffly. "I recall I have some instructions to go over with Peysho before I leave. Good night, Scarlet."

"Good night," he replied. He did not know whether to be relieved or sad, and he retreated quickly back to Annaya's yurt, wondering if he should have said yes. Would it have been so terrible to have dinner with him? Even if he had wanted more, would that have been so bad? How could he judge, having no comparison?

When he returned to Annaya's yurt, there were sounds coming from the interior that he recognized. Traveling in the caravans, he had heard such sounds coming from tents where men and women slept together. Sometimes, when the night was still and the wind had died down in Lysia, these same sounds used to come from Scaja and Linhona's door.

Scarlet stood beside the short row of steps leading to the yurt and tried to summon his outrage. This was his only sister, an honored Hilurin virgin, not some Morturii ghilan whore or Aralyrin kitchen scut that a blacksmith's apprentice could use before marriage. It seemed he stood there for a long time, trying to gather enough anger to thrust his way inside and drag Shansi off her, throw him into the dirt and beat him with his fists for the insult.

In the end, he went to seek a spot by the large central campfire where he could huddle in his coat against the chilly spring night until he estimated enough time had passed. Rage had failed him. What did it matter? They might have both been killed in the attack. They had lost everything, including even a hut to live in. Annaya's body could have been nothing more than charred bones under the wrack of Lysia, and here he was worrying over her virtue like the hidebound Hilurin he had fought never to be.

At least she is following her heart, he thought sullenly. When have I ever done that?

So thinking, Scarlet found a wagon wheel to set his back to and tried not to notice that some of the Kasiri were peering at him in curiosity. Some stared at him outright. A lined woman bearing a wooden ladle, perhaps the official tender of a row of iron pots bubbling near the fire, glanced at him several times before she approached him boldly and squatted beside him. Her gray hair was like cobwebs about her face as she pointed the ladle toward Liall's platform on the other side of the camp.

"The Atya's yurt is there," she informed loudly.

"I see it."

"Much warmer in a man's furs than out here on the cold ground," she said slyly, her volume dropping.

"Thank you, woman," he retorted, staring her down.

She smirked. "My name is Eraph, little Byzan, Torva's

mate, and I was killin' Bledlanders when you were a squirt in yer da's britches, so don't be callin' me *woman* like I were your servant." Her old eyes gleamed. "Were I but younger, the Wolf might set his eye on me. You can be sure *I'll* not be freezing in my own skin if I can have the flesh of another warming my bones."

He drew the blanket up to his chin, saying nothing, and Eraph sighed as if he were a fool too ignorant to speak to. She left him alone to bear the inquisitive looks of the Kasiri until morning.

11.

Two Paths

Morning rumbled in with a sound like thunder. Liall, in his half-sleeping state, vaguely realized it really was thunder. A spring storm was over the Nerit. From the pattering sounds on the oiled walls of his yurt, it was a thin rain that would not last.

Masdren, Scarlet had said. A man old enough to be his father, he had taken care to add. Liall brooded on his decision not to answer back that he himself was old enough to be Scarlet's grandfather. Hells, was he that transparent? He told himself that he should be glad the pedlar had a plan for the future and some place to go to, but he could not summon that much grace. The port of Ankar was a filthy place and he could not convince himself that Scarlet belonged there. It was a sluttish city with a bhoros or ghilan on every third street, a harbor full of mercenary bravos, a large garrison of brutal Morturii soldiers, and a thriving slave trade in the great souk. Scarlet was not a total innocent, but he had a virtue about him that no amount of traveling had yet touched. Making a home in such a jaded place would ruin Scarlet, and Liall found he had come to care very much about that.

Would I remain in Byzantur if he agreed to stay with the krait? he wondered. Liall had toyed with the idea, but he could not forget the sting he felt when Scarlet immediately stated an intention to live in Ankar. What would I do if he stayed? he asked himself with amazement. Would I ignore the summons, turn my back on my true people?

Well, Scarlet was most assuredly not staying, so the matter was decided for him. It was also good fortune that Scarlet had refused his invitation last night.

His conscience would not allow him such blatant self-deception. It sneered at him: *Good fortune? Your phallus hasn't known the touch of any hand save yours in six months.*

Peysho came in while he was still under the furs and wandering in his thoughts. The enforcer grinned to see him awake. "Have I interrupted?"

"Oh, very funny." Liall showed him his hands were above the covers and not about whatever business Peysho thought. "Mocking a man with an empty bed is cruel, you know. I'm sure Om-Ret has a separate punishment in hell for that offense."

Peysho spared Liall further teasing and jerked his head toward the camp outside. "They're waiting. I told 'em ye didn't want a fuss. They wouldn't listen."

"Naturally." Liall pushed the furs off and swung his long legs over the side of the bed. He had not really believed he could take his leave of the boisterous Kasiri without at least a small amount of drama, but he had hoped. "Please tell me there will be no music."

"Nah." Peysho grinned. "It's rainin' and ditterns cost too much to bring out in the wet." He halted in the entrance a moment. "Take yer time, Wolf. We're in no hurry to see ye go."

Beneath the gray underbelly of sky, the whole of the Longspur krait was gathered in a loose crowd around the steps of Liall's yurt. Some, like old Dira and Umir, he had known for decades. They knew him well, and if they did not know his full heart, they knew what he was and that the krait had a strong leader in him. The faces Liall had known the longest were the most wary and anxious, and the ones he had known the least were melancholy and sweet-sad, for an atya leaving on a quest suited their romantic Kasiri souls.

As he went down the line of cheerless faces, he received a small clutch of white and yellow straw-flowers from the smiling midwife and a gold pin from Istri the ox-tender. One of Dira's whores kissed him passionately on the mouth and behaved like he was a beloved husband abandoning her before Dira pulled her off and pinched her for her nonsense.

Last of his goodbyes were Peysho and Kio, who stood together a little apart from the others, as it should be.

"Well," Liall sighed, not knowing what else to say. Kio was unsmiling, but Peysho clasped hands with Liall jovially. It was easy to see that Peysho did not believe in sad farewells.

"Nice mornin' fer it." Peysho laughed, rain soaking the shoulders of his gaudy coat.

Liall tilted his head to taste the rain, not feeling the chill. "Strange. I've longed for home for so many years. Now that it comes, I don't want to go."

"So stay," Peysho urged, quiet and earnest. His fingers pressed hard into Liall's forearm. "*Stay*, Liall."

There was no answer for it. Liall had been born knowing he would never be free in life, that he would be chained by duty and honor and family until his last breath, and then all that had changed. As a boy, he had fiercely desired freedom, and then suddenly he had too much of it. After many years with the Kasiri, he discovered that he was not even sure his desire was real, and that his longing for the thing itself had become a habit he could not break.

"Goodbye," Liall said. Liall saw that Kio's mouth was pinched and his golden eyes averted. "You have something to say?"

Kio shook his head tersely. Liall knew better than to

push him to reveal what he felt. It was not Kio's way. He reached into his jacket and brought out the white swan feather and handed it to Kio.

Kio took it curiously. "What's this, then?"

"An old custom. It's good luck, usually. But if you ever receive a message from the north with a feather like this one, look for my return."

Kio nodded thoughtfully and then closed his fingers around the feather, tucking it very carefully into his jacket. He patted the outline of it in his pocket before giving Liall a strained smile.

Peysho watched them. "Yer a romantic," he accused Liall, highly amused.

"Most likely," Liall conceded with a grin.

"Any final advice?"

He spoke to Peysho while looking boldly at Kio. "A man who cares for nothing does not necessarily make a poor leader. If anything, he is often a better one. But there's no joy in it, my friend. I should have taken a better lesson from you. You could have taught me much."

Peysho nodded in silence, and Liall saw that he understood him perfectly: eventually, Kio would have been a thorn between them. He embraced them both in the manner of Kasiri; brief and fierce and heartfelt. Liall left them standing together, Peysho's hand in Kio's, and turned his face resolutely toward the Sea Road.

He had dressed warm for the occasion: traveling boots of sewn leather, a long cloak of black wool over a thin jacket and a shirt of thick gray cotton, leather breeches, a sturdy journeying pack and a dark hat with a low brim that someone had decorated with scanty embroidery in red. It would keep his head warm and conceal his hair color. That was all he cared about.

He had barely turned the corner where the road bends temporarily out of sight of the camp when he saw Scarlet standing in the path, waiting for him. Scarlet wore his red coat and clutched a bright Kasiri blanket around his shoulders in the rain, standing in the lee of an old cypress to keep the worst of the downpour off his head.

Liall found his voice. "I didn't think to see you here, little redbird."

"There were a lot of people back there," Scarlet said, as if that explained it.

He realized that Scarlet had purposely waited for him here, away from the others. It silenced him for a moment, and in that space, Scarlet rushed on:

"I wanted to thank you once more," Scarlet said quickly. "For Annaya and for myself."

Liall recalled how they had met and he was again ashamed. "I wish I could have saved your parents, Scarlet. Your father greatly impressed me."

Scarlet ducked his head. "His name was Scaja."

"Scaja," Liall repeated gravely, though he had already known.

"And Linhona," he took care to say. "My parents." The rain came down harder and Scarlet shivered. "Well... Deva keep you on your travels. Have a safe journey, Atya."

"Liall."

Scarlet blinked. "What?"

"I know you want to repay your debt, but I must rob you of that. So give me this and say my name again."

It was not a normal request. Still, he had his honor.

"Liall," Scarlet said quietly.

The soft tones of Scarlet's Byzan accent made his name into a caress, and though it was not his true name, his birth name, Liall felt warmed.

"I'll never see you again, will I?" Scarlet asked, surprising him yet again.

"No. Almost certainly not."

Scarlet nodded. Then, unexpectedly, he reached forward and took Liall's hand and pressed it briefly to the side of his face. It was the Byzan sign of gratitude, a rare gesture that was never done lightly.

"You are most welcome," Liall said, deeply touched, and then he remembered: "Oh," he said. "Wait." He would have given anything to distract himself from the constricting feeling in his chest. "I have something for you." He opened his leather pack and dug in it until he came up with the dagger. "It's a good dagger," he said as he offered it hilt first. "You lost yours in the woods, you said, that morning with Cadan." It was a bright, handsome blade, not so large that men would mistake it for a fighting weapon, but not so small that Scarlet could not use it as one if the need arose. The haft was decorated with red enamel and a few lines of silver in a curling pattern.

Scarlet accepted the gift in silence. Their fingers brushed when Liall handed the dagger over, and the touch seemed to sing into his skin, crying out for more. Liall withdrew hastily and felt at the front of his coat, searching for the outlines of the two copper coins around his neck on their leather thong, the coins Scarlet had given him to pay his toll.

"Use it well," Liall said reluctantly, wishing he had the courage to take Scarlet's hand again. "And farewell, Scarlet of Lysia."

Scarlet bowed his head in a respectful farewell, hiding those expressive eyes. Liall turned and walked down the path to the Sea Road, more miserable than he had ever expected to feel at this parting.

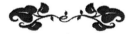

Scarlet found his old satchel with the broken strap on the floor of the valley outside of Lysia. It was empty, of course. Stragglers from the retreating Aralyrin army must have found it, or perhaps it was only looters come to pick the leavings from his murdered village. He had been keeping the last of the bone buttons Scaja had carved in a little pocket in the side. That, too, was empty. He sighed, telling himself it was for the best. Now he understood why Byzan women never wore their mother's jewelry, but gave it away to their own daughters as soon as they were old enough not to lose it or break it. He could never have worn the buttons, not without feeling Scaja's gentle hand on his wrist or brushing his throat, and that would not necessarily be a comfort.

The Kasiri abandoned Whetstone Pass when the wet weather broke, two days after Liall departed. The krait traveled with Scarlet, Shansi, and Annaya down the mountain and provided them with warm clothes and enough food to get to Nantua or even Ankar. Peysho hugged Scarlet impulsively and Kio pressed a few sellivars in his hand.

"For your sister," Kio said gruffly, and turned away.

Scarlet waved as their gaudy wagons and ribbon-bedecked oxen turned east toward Dorogi, and then the three of them turned north to Zarabek and thence on to Nantua, where Shansi's parents lived. But first, they had to cross what was left of Lysia.

They skirted the worst of the carnage by taking the wooded path around the northern side of the village, but the smell of smoke lingered. Occasionally, a puff of ash would drift by on the wind and Annaya's eyes would brim with tears that she impatiently wiped away. As for Scarlet, he was comforted by the weight of Liall's red dagger in his boot and the long-knives at his waist. He was done with weeping for his family, and vowed silently to protect the ones he had left with his life.

There was no avoiding the fields, and they had to walk through the raw, plowed earth that had been harrowed just weeks before and would now never be planted. They came to Jerivet's large field, then Imeno's, and then finally Scaja's.

Annaya halted without a word and Shansi stopped, looking at the pair of them with pity. Shansi probably did not know it was their father's land, but he sensed there was something of import here. Scarlet stood stiffly beside Annaya and grieved with her in silence. The little templon that Scaja had tended so carefully and lovingly throughout the years was tilted on its side. One of the tiny castle walls had been chopped off cleanly, as if struck by a sword. Inside, the god's paper clothing was all rain-soaked and coming apart.

There was no help for it, but Scarlet righted the templon and packed dirt around its base with his boot heel. Pure meanness, it was, to destroy even their shrines. Annaya looked around but could not find the missing piece of wall, and she stood helplessly with her hand in Shansi's. Scarlet realized she was waiting for him to pray.

The words of the cantos flowed through his mind: *On danaee Deva shani.* But they would not emerge from his throat.

"We are done here," Scarlet said, and strode off across the field.

They followed him. In short time, they were curving back down the hills to the east, toward the last bit of the Owl Road, which would take them to Tradepoint and thence to Skeld's Ferry. He had been dreading what they would find at Tradepoint, but as they drew near, he saw that the timbered building was still standing and that Deni was outside working. Zsu saw them walking and froze, then recognized Annaya.

Both girls shrieked each other's name and Scarlet shook Deni's hand as the girls hugged and danced around them.

"We'd given you up for dead," Deni grinned. He was Scarlet's age and a sturdy, typical Byzan lad, very loyal to his family. His father waved at them from the porch and smiled to see Zsu so happy.

"Thank Deva!" the elder called out. "Some of the villagers fled this way when the Aralyrin came, but not many." His face was grayer than Scarlet remembered, and much older. "Not many at all."

"Who?" he asked, eager to know.

Deni named several men and two women that were neither related to his family nor close to them.

Scarlet's heart sank. "Where did they say they were going?"

Deni shrugged. "They didn't." He waved his arm toward the river, encompassing the world outside Lysia. "Out there."

Scarlet nodded, vastly depressed. "We're on our way to Nantua. Annaya is going to marry Shansi and live there with his parents."

"Are you now?" the father exclaimed. "Congratulations, the both of you! Well, well. And what about you, Scarlet?" he asked. He shot a glance toward Zsu, who was chattering happily to Annaya and wiping away her tears. "We'd always hoped that Zsu and you one day would..." he trailed off.

"I'm bound for Ankar," Scarlet said, hoping the old man would let the matter drop. He was fond of Zsu but nothing more than that. "Going to learn leatherwork from Masdren."

"Ankar?" Deni's mouth turned down in disapproval. "Are you sure? If you worked for me and dad, carrying goods on the ferry-route, you could still travel the river as much as you pleased. We know you have the world-wild. We wouldn't try to pen you in."

He shook his head. "Zsu can do better than a pedlar who can't find his way home twice in a moon." It was excuse and he knew it. Zsu's prospects for a Hilurin husband had been sharply curtailed by the burning of Lysia. Now Deni and his father would have to accept that Zsu must go much further away than they were prepared for if she wanted to marry properly, or let her take up with some less-acceptable Aralyrin soldier or merchant who traveled the river. Neither prospect was appealing, if he knew Deni.

Deni's disappointment showed. "You'd be a partner in the business," he offered further. "Dad's thinking about buying out Skeld's Ferry too, since Kev is moving on with his sons. You'd never go hungry, Scarlet, and you'd be able to visit Annaya as much as you want, once the ferry and boats are ours."

The offer was more than fair: property and belonging and a decent Hilurin family who would welcome him as one of their own, no questions asked. Scarlet glanced at Zsu and saw that she and Annaya had fallen silent and were looking at him: Annaya with sadness and Zsu with some surprise.

"You will not find another Hilurin wife so easily," Deni urged.

He regarded Zsu, wavering in his decision, for he was fond of them all and she was probably the prettiest girl he had ever seen, next to Annaya. She had wild black hair that reached down to her knees and large dark eyes fringed with heavy lashes, so that when she raised her eyes quickly she had the aspect of a startled deer. She was not too fussy either, and liked to climb trees and go fishing and chase after the goats.

"And what do you want, Zsu?" he asked softly. "Would

you be happy with a wandering husband?"

She hesitated, shooting a look from her father to her brother and back to Scarlet before clasping her hands together in front of her and bowing her head. "No," she breathed.

"What?" Deni exclaimed, clearly not having considered she would have any objections or thoughts of her own. His father started to shout something or other, but suddenly Zsu raised her head, and there was fire in her black eyes.

"I said no," she stammered. She was scared but standing her ground. "I want to run the ferry myself, and when it's slow in the winter I want to travel to Zarabek and Patra and Morturii to sell goods to the army camps, just like you meant for Scarlet to do."

"Scarlet is a man!" her father roared, ponderous with his anger in the way that only old men can be.

Deni gaped in shock. "You'll do no such thing!"

"I will so!" Zsu shot back, her little hands balled into fists. "I've got the wilding and I'll do as I please, and if you try to stop me or marry me off or put me in chains I'll run far, far away and never come back!"

Scarlet could see that their visit had thrown a hornet's nest into the lap of Zsu's family. He apologized and promised a future visit and hurried toward Skeld's Ferry, hearing Deni's protests and the father's bellowing for nearly a mile.

Annaya smirked at him as they walked in the spring sun. The air was chilly but not too much, and moving kept them warm.

"What?"

"Zsu. You thought you could just take her or leave her." She smirked again, very satisfied.

"Did you know she had the wilding?"

"Oh yes," she said wisely. "I've always known."

"You might have told *me,*" he said crossly.

She only giggled again and whispered to Shansi behind her hand, and he was annoyed even more. Women! "I do like Zsu very much, you know."

"But you don't love her."

He had only Scaja's teachings to go by, a typical Hilurin who thought little of passion but much of loyalty and constancy. "Well, is that necessary?"

"It might be, to Zsu." She had some fire of her own, his sister, and it showed in her narrowed eyes. "Dad didn't know everything about women, you know. Mum just liked to let him think he did."

It irked him to suddenly realize that Linhona and Annaya had shared an altogether foreign, feminine world that excluded him and that he had never known about. Scarlet would hear no more disrespect to Scaja, so he set his teeth and walked faster, not speaking to Annaya until nightfall.

Annaya nearly drowned Scarlet with tears, but she could not convince him to stay in Nantua. It was a larger village than Lysia, the surrounding countryside flatter, and (he thought) uglier, with less color and also no high view from the foothills of the Nerit. The village itself was hardly prosperous, even less so than Lysia, and there had been a grain blight the previous year that left a deep scar on the place. Scarlet knew that he would never feel at home there, and six days after arriving in Nantua, he was ready to leave again.

"Ankar is no place for a Byzan," Annaya had argued in the warm, central room of Shansi's house. In the next room, Shansi's mother was putting the dishes on the table for supper. His parents had a large home, if a bit bare, and there was more than enough space for all of them. "What will you do for company? The only friend you have there is Masdren."

All true, but he was itching to get away and beyond reasoning. His old home was gone and he was not ready to try creating a new one. Life on the road had also lost its allure. He needed something different.

"Stay," Annaya begged. "We could build a house for the three of us, and you could still be a pedlar."

Scarlet thought privately that she was almost as sad as he that he was giving up the life of a pedlar. She had always loved hearing the stories of his adventures and near-misses on the road, and he told her things that he had never told Scaja. For the first time, he wondered what it might have been like for her, a Hilurin girl shut away in a house, knowing she would never have adventures of her own. She had lived her adventures through him, and now he was taking them away from her. He said as much to her, apologetically, and was surprised when she laughed at him and pushed his shoulder.

"Scarlet, you want-wit. If I'd wanted to run the roads, I would have. Do you think Scaja could have stopped me? He couldn't stop *you.*"

Again, he had misjudged her, and he stammered and his ears turned pink, angry at himself for making yet another wrong assumption about another. Would he never stop doing that?

"I don't have the wilding, love," she said. "I never did. We don't want the same things, and what's best for me isn't what's best for you. I want Shansi and my own home and children that I can teach to love everything Mum and Dad taught me to love. But you... you're scared, my brother. That's all. Just plain scared, and you're running to Ankar hoping Masdren will hide it for you."

"He's offered to teach me!"

"To do what?" she scorned. "Diaper his brats? You don't want to be a leathersmith, Scarlet, you're meant for the road!"

Had that ever been true? It was a question he could not ask her, because it was tied up in what he had suffered at Cadan's hands and the many dangers he had weathered in his travels before that. He sighed. "I'm just tired of it all, Annaya."

Her dark eyes narrowed. For a moment, she looked very much like Linhona in one of her moods. "This is about the Kasiri chieftain, isn't it?"

He looked away. "Don't be foolish, girl."

"Don't you *girl* me! I have eyes. You'd have stayed in the camp with him, but he left and now you've given up living to spite him." She smoothed her skirt and folded her white hands in her lap. "In case you hadn't noticed, he's not here to see you pout."

"Annaya!" he cried, shocked. Scaja had known about the difference in him, and perhaps Linhona, but he was certain Annaya had not.

"It's true. He's left and you're sulking. Why don't you just follow him, you ninny?"

Scarlet sat up straight as if he would bolt out of his chair, and his mouth opened and closed like a gaping fish. After a long moment of panic, he sank back in his seat. "He didn't ask me," he said at last. His chest ached a little, as if a soft lump of pain were lodged under his breastbone. "He didn't want me to come with him. What he wanted me for would have lasted only a single night. Beyond that, I was nothing to him."

Annaya reached for his hand. "I'm sorry."

"Don't be," he said, pulling away and standing. "At least he didn't lie to me. I couldn't have borne that." He could hear Shansi clearing his throat diplomatically in the next room. Supper was ready, but the smith must have been unwilling to intrude on the argument between siblings.

"Won't you stay? Even for a little while?"

He sighed heavily. Annaya meant well, but she was not thinking ahead to a time when a brother would be a bother, when there were children in the bed that was supposed to be his and not enough soup in the pot to go around. Her house would never be his parent's house, and Annaya was starting her own family with Shansi. Nantua could not be his new Lysia. All that was dead.

Annaya made one last reproach before he left. It was in the form of a gift: a leather pedlar's satchel with a deep pouch and sturdy pockets. On the oil-polished flap was a word in curling letters, deeply embossed in red dye.

He ran his hand over it admiringly, the bitterness of their last argument forgotten. "It's beautiful, Annaya. Did you have this done? What does it say?"

"I did it myself. It's your name, Scarlet."

His brow wrinkled in puzzlement. His sister could not read or write any more than he could. As far as he knew, neither could Shansi. "But how? Who helped you?"

"Linhona taught me. It was the one thing I ever asked her to teach me of reading."

She did not wait for him to speak, but embraced him tightly, her little hands digging into his shoulders. "Goodbye, brother."

So he left. It seemed that all he had done since meeting Liall was shed parts of his life that he had never intended to lose. He could not talk to Annaya about it, and it was more than not wanting to share how much pain he was in. He was not *able* to share it. Perhaps it was just the way the gods made him. He could not complain about that, but he regretted that he was parting with Annaya so badly.

She did not understand. With Annaya, it was always damn the winds and too bad if it rained harder. She had never been a quiet girl, and true to form, she was not about to start now. They spent the last night shouting at each other, and in the morning she had sent him off with a fierce hug and tears in her eyes. He crossed the river back into Byzantur at noon, and by the time he was too far down the road to Patra to turn back and apologize, he wanted to.

Sometimes the answer's right in front of us. We're just moving too fast to see it. They were Scaja's words, and he was shortly to discover how prophetic they were. If he had not been so lost in regret, he would have seen the faint smudges of color slipping through the edge of the woods alongside the path long before he drew near to them.

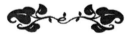

"Well, well! It's the wolf cub. We heard the gypsies had gone east. Did they leave you behind?"

Scarlet's mouth was suddenly dry and he knew he had been vastly stupid. It was scar-faced Cadan and three Aralyrin soldiers blocking his way on the Iron Path. They had come up so sudden from the trees that he had seen only shadows slipping from behind tree trunks, silent as wraiths in the quiet day. They were as fearsome as wraiths, too; armed men with a look of bored villainy.

No sense asking what they wanted. Scarlet tried to bluff

his way out. "Stand aside and let me pass."

"Bold orders from the bedmate of a thieving Kasiri," Cadan said, his palms resting on the hilts of his knives. His right leg was wrapped in some kind of leather splint below the knee and he stood with his heel up, not resting his full weight on it.

"I'm not–!" The denial was half out before he could stop it. He shook his head. "Get out of my way!" Scarlet's voice was brave, but inside he had begun to shiver. This former Kasiri soldier had meant to murder him once, for no more reason than revenge on another man. His fingers inched toward the long-knives at his hips, but Cadan only stared at him, smiling coldly in silence. There were four against one. To draw a weapon now would mean his death, and Cadan knew it.

He did not know what he expected Cadan to say, some threat or promise of harm perhaps. After how talkative Cadan had been in the past, this new silence was more frightening than any threat.

Scarlet risked a quick look behind him, hoping to see another traveler in the distance, but it was hopeless. After the last raid, there would be none coming north from the Salt Road. None but he, and he had lingered too long in Nantua.

Cadan saw the direction of Scarlet's glance and signaled to his men. Lame he might have been, but he still had his authority. "Bring him."

"Wait!" Scarlet said desperately to the soldiers. "Your captain, he was a Kasiri once."

One of the soldiers spat in the dust, unconcerned at the news. "Listen to him. Whey-faced Hilurin is what he is. First Tribe scum. Next, he'll lecture us about our duty as soldiers of the vine."

Another soldier gave a grunting laugh. "Soldiers of the vine! Do we look like country bumpkins to you, pedlar?

All that is past."

"You still swore to uphold the law," Scarlet said, shamed to hear his voice shaking. "You obey the Flower Prince."

"I obey whoever pays me, and lately, it ain't been a shit-arsed prince in silk pants."

Scarlet backed up a little. He had thought to reveal Cadan's past crimes to them and appeal to their sense of honor, but when he searched their faces, he found them as hard and carved as the stone statue at the Fate Dealer's. From then on, it was pride alone that held him silent.

Scarlet darted aside and tried to make a run for it, but as two of the soldiers stepped in opposite directions and expertly closed in on him, he froze in fear and hesitated for a moment. The soldiers fell on him, pinning his arms and stripping him of his pack and bundle, jerking the knife-belt from his waist and letting it drop in the road. He was dragged and shoved in silence into the thick stand of junipers lining the road. The scent of evergreen and springtime roses was thick in the air, and his only thought was relief that, whatever happened, Scaja and Linhona could not be hurt any more. He did not know who Cadan's comrades were, only that they were probably as foul as Cadan himself, and that they hated all Hilurin.

They arrived very quickly at a rough camp the soldiers had made in the woods: a canvas tent, a few bedrolls on the ground, and a heap of stones that circled a campfire dwindled down to ash and embers.

Cadan motioned to his men and they released Scarlet's arms. Scarlet had saved his strength and not struggled very much, and he stood glaring at them, his body trembling with stress and delayed fear. Still, Cadan did not speak, only kept staring with that even light in his eyes that did more to tear Scarlet down than any words could have.

"Where's your friend?"

Scarlet's mind went blank for a moment, still locked in

dread. "Who..."

"The Wolf. Where is he?"

Scarlet shook his head. "I don't know. He left."

Cadan stepped forward and struck him hard across the face. "I know he *left,* hill-brat! Where did he go? He wasn't with the Longspur krait when they made it to Dorogi. When did he leave them and where was he bound?"

Liall's words came back to him: *It is Norl Udur, as has been rumored, and I will get there by traveling to the port of Volkovoi across the Channel.*

A trickle of blood ran from Scarlet's nose. "He didn't tell me."

"Oh, did he not?" Cadan shifted a look from Scarlet to his men and back. "I figured you'd be in his yurt by now, playing cushion to the great chieftain's belly. He mustn't have been that interested in you, after all."

Scarlet kept his silence, refusing to take the bait.

"There's a price on his head, did you know? The word's spread to every port from here to Ankar and even in Khet. An envoy from Norl Udur came to the army garrison in Patra, carrying more silver than any soldier will see in a lifetime. It's all for the man who brings the White Wolf back in chains."

Scarlet fought to keep his mind clear, for Liall as much as for himself. "What do they want with him?"

Cadan hawked and spat into the dirt. "Doesn't matter. I can make you rich, pedlar. Rich enough to guarantee your safety anywhere. Then you'd be able to protect that pretty sister of yours." Cadan's grin was ugly with menace. "Nantua, is it? I wonder if that's far enough. I bet on a windy day, she can still smell the smoke from Lysia."

With a cry of rage, Scarlet bunched his fists and charged Cadan. The soldiers tackled him and knocked him to the ground. Cadan watched the struggling knot of them, smiling his pitiless smile. "There's plenty of time," he said. "If you won't tell me now, you'll tell me by tonight. Wait and see."

They dragged Scarlet up and two of the soldiers held his arms out straight as Cadan squared up to him. The last soldier sat down by the smoldering fire to watch.

"I told you, I don't know!"

Cadan drew back his arm and backhanded Scarlet. His head rocked back and his ears began ringing. He grunted in pain and focused on Cadan dizzily, just in time to see the soldier draw his fist back. Cadan punched him low in the gut.

The pain was worse than Scarlet could imagine. It felt like his stomach had been pushed back to his spine. His legs gave way and he retched, doubling over. Cadan's fist came down on the back of his neck.

He lost track of time. There was dirt against his face and the strong smell of earth and smoke. The soldiers hauled him back to his feet, and Cadan turned to nod to the man by the fire. The soldier slipped his knife from his belt and lodged the blade deep in the coals.

Cadan put his hands on Scarlet's shoulders. "Tell me where Liall is," he said almost pleasantly. "You owe him no loyalty. Come," he coaxed, patting Scarlet's cheek. "Tell me what I want to know."

Scarlet glanced to the man by the fire, watching him turn his knife to heat the blade evenly. He knew with a deadly certainty that if he did not give Cadan the information he wanted, the soldiers would kill him right here. It would not be a quick death.

He looked at the sky, the weight of the awful decision filling him with anguish. His life or Liall's? The world took on a peculiar brightness as he looked up at the dark, jagged scrawls of evergreen branches cutting through the warm blue calm of the sky. Despite everything, the murder of his parents, his home, the strong sense of loss when Liall said goodbye, now that he had come to it, he realized that he wanted very much to live.

But he desperately wanted Liall to live as well.

A small redbird drifted in the sky behind Cadan, journeying across the great disk of the sun in the span of an instant, and Scarlet thought: That is my life there, all the time that I have left. In a very little while, I'll be dead, and no one but Annaya or Liall will ever mourn me.

Scarlet thought of Liall's face –handsome, strong, and inscrutable– and wondered if the atya would make it to his homeland, and if not, would they meet again in the Otherworld? Would Deva keep them apart, or would she understand? I love him, Scarlet thought in wonder, amazed that he was the one person who had not seen that.

Then, in that stilled moment, Scarlet finally faced the truth of the fate of his people in Byzantur. They were all going to die, just as surely as he was going to die, and very soon. The Hilurin were few and they were feared and they were unwanted, and they had dared to rule. The coming war would be swift and decisive, its inevitable outcome already determined. Their fate was as plain to him as if it were written across the sky.

He was suddenly profoundly sorry that he had never truly lived his life as he wanted to, that he had never reached out to another's body for pleasure or comfort or warmth, and that he had been too afraid of his nature to learn what it might have been like to be loved by a man like Liall.

Why didn't Liall ask me to go with him? he thought mournfully. I would do it all differently now. I never had the wilding. I was only running away from myself, and now… I can't be the one to betray him, even if I die. Oh,

203

Deva, help me, I can't, I can't...

A shadow dipped across the sun, and the lazy-looking redbird darted aside, missing the razor claws of the hawk by so narrow a margin that it seemed, in that moment, a miracle that the prey had escaped. The hawk flew harmlessly past, and Scarlet stared transfixed at the disappearing outline of the predator, not even realizing that his body had gone limp in the soldier's grasp. The soldiers, perhaps not wanting to exert further effort into struggling that would soon be put to more enjoyable use, had loosened their holds on Scarlet's limbs. They held him lightly, just enough to keep him on his feet.

A thin thread of sound, silent as a falling cord of spider-silk, but so glorious that it seemed the sun had come alive to speak to him, reached his mind: *On danaee Deva shani.*

The soundless words seared through his limbs like liquid fire. Scarlet stared up at the sun, his eyes blind, his muscles like water, as Cadan's demanding voice faded into the sighing of the wind. Cadan's expression was languid with the pleasurable prospect of torment to come, his eyes heavy as if very weary, and his expression did not change in the slightest as Scarlet's unseeing gaze met his. Scarlet could hear the sound of Cadan's heart slowing down to a lazy, measured thump. A twig fell from the juniper and took an age to strike the ground.

The soldiers were barely holding him at all. He waited with the flames roaring in his blood as time crawled slowly around him, waited as Deva's holy voice whispered to his brain what he should do, what he *must* do if he wanted to live.

Cadan hit him again, a straight blow that landed on his chin and snapped his head back violently. Swift as a breath, Scarlet pretended to collapse. His eyes rolled up in his head and he let his knees buckle. The soldiers were taken by surprise and let him drop, but Scarlet only went to one knee. His fingertips grazed the haft of the dagger Liall had given him, safely hidden in the top of his boot.

The inferno in his veins threatened to burst out of his skin, to leave him ripped apart, bleeding and broken. It cried for him to let it free, to let it go before it tore him from within, and he did.

He let it *free*.

Scarlet rose as lightning-fast as the shadow of the hawk, and his left arm moved, the arm with the fragile, too-small hand that carried Deva's blessing. It moved seemingly independent of his brain, so quick that he could not have stopped it even if he wanted to. It was the hand of the goddess, not his own: her swiftness, not his, her power that slowed time itself around the core of their communion. Sudden warmth striped his face and neck. Cadan's expression did not change.

The soldiers cried out their shock in one voice and leapt away as if a dragon had dropped from the sky. The secret terror that all Aralyrin harbored against Hilurin, the fear of magic, had come to life among them, for the pedlar had moved faster than sight, so quick that it could only be sorcery, and now Cadan's neck was sprouting a dagger that seemed conjured from the very air. A small, bright dagger with a red-enameled hilt.

The Aralyrin soldiers fell back from the gout of Cadan's blood and from the enchanter come to life among them. Scarlet moved without thinking, without feeling, without emotion. His expression was almost sleepy as he whirled and vaulted past the two stunned men.

They could not catch him. No man could have.

He seized his packs and knives as he raced past, not even looking behind him as his feet found the road to Patra. Time resumed its natural pace. As he ran, the earth falling away beneath his boots, he gave thanks to Deva, blessing the creatures she had sent to show him the way, and in his mind the thought kept running over and over: I'm alive, I'm still alive, thank Deva I'm alive and I can save Liall...

12.

Volkovoi

The days that followed were a blur. Liall walked hard, aware that the weather was against him and he had lingered almost too long in Byzantur. In Rusa, he went to the harbormaster, seeking to find a vessel bound across the Channel for Khet and the port of Volkovoi. He was directed to a cargo vessel that he did not like the look of. The crew was a filthy lot. They looked to be either drugged with centaury or idiots or both, but their ship was the only vessel bound for Khet and there might not be another for days. Truly, the harbormaster advised him, the place was better avoided and was he sure he knew what he was doing?

The captain of the cargo ship was no better groomed than his crew, but Liall dickered for a small cabin below the main deck with a bunk that smelled of old wine and worse. He worried it might be infested with fleas. He had concealed his large coin pouch inside his shirt and kept only a few in his pockets to pay his passage, but the captain examined him with a narrow eye, as if trying to assess what else of value he might have.

They lifted anchor shortly after dawn the next day. Liall kept both his long-knives at hand once they were underway. When it grew dark, he locked himself in the stinking cabin, almost choking on the putrid smell of bilge. It would take two days to cross the wide Channel if the wind stayed fair, four if not. He had a good skin of water in his pack and the supplies Peysho had packed for him, so he would have few reasons to venture onto the deck. Many travelers from Byzantur who set out for Khet were never heard from again.

He was certain that one of the crew would try to come in at some point, and he was dozing on the second night when the hatch to his cabin was tried. Waking fully between one breath and another, Liall clasped a long-knife in one hand and rose soundlessly, waiting with his back to the wall. There was a scraping sound in the iron lock and the hatch creaked open. He waited until a head appeared, a shadow darker than the night, and then brought the iron hilt of his knife down.

The crewman sprawled dead-still in the hatchway. Mindful of tricks, Liall stayed where he was until a second figure appeared. Liall lunged forward and seized the man by the arm, jerking him forward so fast that the man's legs failed him and he was dragged into the cabin. Liall held the point of his blade just under the crewman's jaw.

The crewman was small but wiry. He froze when he felt steel against his skin.

"Get out," Liall said, ever so softly. "I want no trouble, but I'll kill you if you push me to it."

The man gulped and nodded nervously.

"Take this bastard with you."

Liall released him with a shove and stepped back and to the side in case the crewman changed his mind. He did not, but bent to drag his shipmate out of the hatchway.

"Close it."

When they were gone, Liall jammed a chair against the hatch. He sank down again onto the rough pallet he had made on the deck. Tomorrow, he would be off this stinking bucket and in Khet. Out of boiling water and into the flames, for the natives there were far more perilous than a half-starved merchant crew. With luck, he would not be there long. The night crawled on: anxious hours spent listening to the creak of timber and the lashing of waves against the hull. He tried to conjure images of his home and family, wondering what they looked like now and if they had changed very much, trying to rekindle his eagerness to see them again. Yet, the only image that filled his mind was Scarlet. All he could feel was a deep sense of regret and loss, as if he had held a precious jewel for only a short time before losing it through some gross lack of judgment on his part.

Volkovoi was what pirates called a cutthroat port. From a distance, it looked like a stack of sagging wooden boxes left out in the rain, though the landscape stayed roughly the same when one got nearer. The spring rains had come to Khet with a vengeance and everything was wet or had recently been wet or had stayed wet so long it was rotten. All the buildings were the color of mildewed straw and reeked of damp plaster, a fitting dwelling for its citizens: a mish-mash of whores, cutpurses, merchant sailors, deserters, professional thieves, and slavers. The town was dirty and cluttered, and a constant pelting of rain fell from the heavy gray layer of clouds perched over the Channel.

The Rshani brigantine was five days late so far. What little Volkovoi had to offer in the way of comfort had grated on Liall after one day, and he longed to be off. Yet, he must wait for the ship. There was no other way to get home, and it had to be an Rshani vessel. A foreign ship caught within sight of the capital port of Rshan would be fired on with cannon.

In Volkovoi, men with white hair and amber skin

were uncommon but not unknown, and even though the residents called them Norls or just Northmen, they knew little about where they came from, save that it was very far away and hostile. Liall saw none of his countrymen on the streets of the harbor the few times he ventured out, but his appearance caused little comment and no one gave him more than a second glance.

No one, that is, except the whore.

The boy looked scarcely old enough to be out by himself at night, much less being about the kind of business he so obviously was seeking. The only reason he caught Liall's eye was because he was slender and black-haired and he had a red cloak wrapped about him. The whore saw Liall's interest and cast a friendly smile at him, one without much hope. Liall was not walking with any purpose, just striding through the rain because he was tired of being penned up in his stinking chicken coop of a room. At least the wind blowing in from the Channel smelled fresh and had the clean tang of salt to it, and he enjoyed the sound of the loud swells booming against the wooden quay; a low, bass report that he could feel in the center of his chest.

Liall was standing under the flickering glow of a streetlamp filled with noxious, stinking whale oil. The boy strolled over to him and the lamp belched black smoke and threw greenish light down on them. The whore had an oiled woolen cloak wrapped around him to keep off the rain, and his hard eyes scanned Liall up and down as he drew nearer, uninvited.

"*Zadi,*" he said, giving Liall a Minh honorific as he stared at the strange coloring of the foreigner.

A whore received all kinds of trade in a port, but Rshani mariners rarely left the safety of their ships when visiting the Southern Continent. The old taboos and hatreds were still too great. Liall chanced a guess that this young one had never seen anyone quite like him before.

The whore had perused him, so it was only fair that he got to do the same. What he saw made him sad; slender beauty marred by dirt and weariness. Upon closer inspection, Liall saw that the brilliant red cloak was mildewed in places and that the boy's nails needed a good cleaning. His black hair was lank and dirty. Still, his smile was winsome if jaded, and he plucked at Liall's sleeve entreatingly.

"Looking for company?" the whore smiled, but his eyes –gray, not black– slid sideways to watch a pair of fair-haired Khet bravos in leather armor stroll by, tapping their clubs and giving Liall the eye in case he meant trouble for them later.

Liall knew the bravos' type; dumb muscle with no brain behind it to complicate matters. Good for keeping order in a place like Volkovoi, but bad news anywhere else. He ignored them and focused on the boy.

The rain began to come down harder and a peal of thunder spoke from the sky. The boy shivered a little in his shabby cloak and Liall felt a surge of pity for him. Desire, too, if he was being honest. In candlelight, after a meal and a good bath, he might have taken him for Scarlet.

He was on the verge of reaching for his coin pouch when the whore coughed. It was a wet, choking sound, and he saw that the boy was ill. Any blush in his cheeks would be from fever, not emotion, and the whore did not desire him, only his money. Liall saw it in the hard flash of greed in his eyes when his fingers moved toward his purse. It saddened him, and he drew out two silver bits –a week's pay for a groom in a noble house– and passed it into the boy's hand without a word.

The boy stared at the silver in his palm, and then pushed it with a finger as if testing it for solidity. Perhaps he thought it was the supernatural Fey gold that would vanish as soon as mortal hands touched it. He looked at Liall again, and this time there was fear in his eyes.

"What," he licked his lips, "what would you expect for this? I am not strong for the most part, and I do not enjoy pain."

Liall was further depressed. "Nothing," he said, shaking his head. "Just get off the street for one night. You will catch your death out here with that cough."

The whore's smile was tired and ages older than his flesh. "Would that be so bad?"

"What is your name, boy?"

"Laith," he answered. It meant laughter in Qaha, and was an odd dialect for a Byzan to speak.

"Go home, Laith," Liall ordered. "Buy yourself a meal. Get warm."

The slut bowed as elegantly as any courtier, but before he left, he took Liall's hand in his own and kissed it.

"Kind lord," he breathed over his skin, causing Liall to shiver with pity. How could he have fancied a resemblance to Scarlet? They were both pretty and dark-haired. That was all.

Liall watched the boy leave with his back to the mortared wall of an alley, his desire as shriveled as the wrinkled skin of his fingertips. He was chilled and soaked clean through and angry with himself. Little use he would be to anyone if he came down with lung-fever. Cursing, he pushed away from the wall to head back to the damned chicken coop, and ran straight into the bravos.

They blocked his way. Liall was tall, but they were only a little less so. They were both blue-eyed and had blond streaks in their coarse brown hair. Half-bloods, he thought. Some Rshani mariner stranded here a generation ago or more. They looked so alike they could have been brothers.

"Where are you going?" the first one inquired gruffly. He had a grizzled white scar streaking his brown beard and a swollen red pustule on his eyelid. He was a few years older than his companion, a barrel-chested brute with a jaw like a lantern. In the fashion of Khet mercenaries, they were both clad in leather armor capped with studs of metal, and they held hard clubs of oak meant for bludgeoning brawling soldiers and drunks.

Suddenly, the street seemed very empty. Liall did not fear them, but he knew he had been foolish.

"Only back to my inn," he replied, volunteering the simplest information he could. These men were born bullies and he knew firsthand that violence had a nasty habit of gaining momentum. "I'm waiting to take ship. I was only out for a stroll."

"In this?" The younger bravo indicated the sky. "You must be lying. Where are your papers?"

"Papers?" Liall laughed, abandoning good sense. "Who would need papers to come to this pigsty?"

The scarred bravo tapped Liall's chest with the butt of his club. "Here now, watch your ruttin' mouth."

Liall pushed the club away with the flat of his palm. "There is no need for this," he said. "I will return to the taberna and not trouble you further." He made to push past them, his chin high and proud, and thereby made his second mistake of the evening.

A club crashed into the back of his neck, dropping him to his knees. It was the last thing he expected from the bravos. To be fleeced of money, yes: questioned, intimidated, even roughed-up until he produced a few more sellivar for them. All of that was within what one could reasonably expect from harbor patrols, but this felt personal.

A hard kick to his ribs dropped Liall the rest of the way to the watery pavement before the heavy club landed again on his back. Beyond the pain, all he could feel was dismay and amazement and a vast sense of contempt for his own stupidity. Had he really thought he would be allowed to return to Rshan without incident? These men were not after money, but murder.

Blows rained down on him as his shaking hand fumbled at his waist, trying to draw one of his long-knives. He succeeded in getting his fingers around the handle and unsheathing the blade, but he was far too dazed and slow. A well-aimed kick numbed his wrist and sent his knife skittering across the cobblestones with a shining sound, far out of his reach, and he knew he was lost. He wanted to laugh. This was how he was to end? Beaten to a pulp in a stinking alley, his brains bashed in by a pair of hairy, mouth-breathing imbeciles. He had a lunatic moment where he wondered how much they had been paid to murder him, hoping they got a good price, but the next kick sent that out of his head altogether.

The bravos dragged him further into a dank, narrow alleyway flanked by two crumbling walls and began to beat him in earnest. He was on his belly in the gutter, filthy water rushing past his face. It bothered him that he should die like that, so he rolled over in time to see the younger bravo raise his club to bring down the final blow that would open his skull. He only hoped the rats would not find him until after he was dead.

The bravo raised his club for the killing blow and then was suddenly gone. A reddish blur crashed into the bravo and hurled him away. Liall blinked against the rain falling into his eyes, thinking there was some trick of light at work, but no, there was a scuffle happening that did not involve him.

He struggled to roll over and get his knees under him, grasping any chance for life, his body sluggish and unresponsive. He crouched on hands and knees and gaped stupidly around him, trying to focus on the knot of motion in the center of the alley, and was amazed.

The whore-boy in red had returned and was fighting off the bravos. He had a dark Morturii knife in each hand and the edge of one was against the younger bravo's throat while the scarred one yelled curses at him. The boy spoke in hushed, vicious tones, and the scarred bravo hurled abuse and threats, yet did not move, for the knife did not waver from its target. Liall, rattled as he was, could see the boy would kill the bravo if the elder did not back off. The bearded one heaped a final torrent of abuse on the boy, and then seemed to make a decision. He hefted his club, turned his back and walked away, heedless of the snarled curses of his comrade who had the long-knife at his throat.

Alone now, the boy and the bully conversed in tones too low to hear over the thudding rain, but Liall sensed the boy was promising murder if his terms were not met. Terms of release, he presumed.

"Don't do it," Liall croaked. He got to his feet, bleeding hands clawing the mortar of the wall for purchase. "He'll kill you the moment you let him go."

"Shut your face, fucker!" the bravo snarled.

The boy did not look at Liall, but shoved the bravo away from him so that the man impacted face-first with the wall and banged his nose. The bravo whirled, cursing, but the boy kicked the fallen club out of his reach and raised one of the Morturii knives in warning. The haft spun easily in his hands, whirling and glittering in the green lamplight, and he laughed when the bravo backed up to avoid the spinning edge. With a last, hate-filled look, the bravo spat a gobbet of phlegm at Liall's feet before he fled into the darkness.

Liall was alone with his savior. He began to chuckle, holding his sides against the ache. It was beyond ludicrous.

"Boy," he tittered, "if I had known I was speaking to a warrior, I would have shown you less silver and more respect."

The boy threw back the hood of his coat and stepped closer, his features clearly illuminated now. "What in Deva's shrieking hell are you talking about?"

"It's you!" Liall gaped, holding his bruised ribs.

"Of course it's me, you want-wit," he retorted mildly as he sheathed his knives. "Did they hit you on the head?" He spat in the direction of the bravo who had fled. "I broke my new walking stick over the first one's thick skull, damn him. Come on, we have to get off the streets!" He tugged on Liall's arm and half-dragged him along.

Aching as he was, Liall seized the boy's shoulders and swung him round as the cold rain poured over them. He was not surprised to feel his hands shaking.

"Scarlet," he whispered in wonder. "I thought I would never see you again."

Scarlet's hands tightened in Liall's cloak. He shivered and turned his face away. "Let's get out of this alley," Scarlet said, steering him toward the street.

Liall went without protest. Thunder rolled away from the port, vanishing somewhere over the Channel which leads to the sea.

Even the chicken coop was better than cold rain and the possibility of the bravos returning in force. Scarlet helped Liall navigate the rickety wooden stairs at the rear of the hostelry and into the stinking little den. The room was just a box, scantily furnished with a rump-sprung bed and a padded velvet chair that had seen better days, its worn surface shiny with oil and countless unmentionable uses.

Scarlet held Liall's arm until he was settled on the bed, then tried to strip him of his clothing to examine him. Liall pushed him away. "I'll be fine," he grumbled. Scarlet looked doubtful. "I've been hurt enough times to know. A few bruises, a lot of soreness. That's all."

"If they'd had the time, they would have done a lot worse," Scarlet reckoned. There were lines of anger around his mouth.

"Indeed." He felt dizzy and shaken and he was sure he had less than all his wits about him, but he managed to smile. "They were somewhat interrupted. You saved my life, Scarlet."

Scarlet dismissed that with a wave of his hand. "It's no more than you did for me." Always the pragmatist, Scarlet encompassed the room in one scornful glance and sighed. "The fire isn't even lit. A cave would serve you better than this." He knelt at the hearth and grabbed the poker.

"Don't bother. The chimney leaks and the wood is wet."

"We'll see." Scarlet ceased poking at the damp, charred wood and stood up. "Is there a kitchen in this sty?"

"Downstairs. The alewife will give you hot water if you ask, and you can buy food. Here." He handed Scarlet two silver bits, guessing his intent. "Leave your pedlar's coat. The bravo's friends may be looking for you by now."

Scarlet nodded and slung off the red leather and his pack. "I'll be right back."

When he had gone, Liall stripped off his wet cloak and shirt. He lay down on the sagging mattress and closed his eyes until the room stopped spinning. Well, perhaps he had not weathered as fair as he claimed. The club to his head could have concussed his skull, but that would not be evident at once. If he began to vomit or was not able to stay awake, Scarlet was going to have a devil of a time finding a curae in this place to heal him.

He dozed fitfully and awoke to Scarlet gently shaking his shoulder. A tin cup containing steaming liquid was being offered..

"It's che," Scarlet said. "Not very good, but it's hot. I added some powder of birch from my kit. Should take some of the pain away. I also bought waybread and a few apples, but I didn't trust buying meat in a place like this."

He nodded and accepted the che. "Wise of you. I noticed a distinct lack of alley cats in this port." To his surprise, he saw that Scarlet had succeeded in kindling the wet wood in the hearth and had a cheery orange fire going. "How did you manage that?"

Scarlet looked frightened for a moment, and Liall wondered why this would be so. "Oh, the fire? There were some coals underneath."

"There were? All I saw was a puddle."

Scarlet fidgeted, saying nothing, and Liall decided he was being inquisitive for no good reason. "I suppose you must simply be more skilled than I. You must have to kindle your own fire every night on the road."

Scarlet brightened. "True."

He drank and ate a little of the dry, chewy bread. The birch powder was acrid and did nothing for the taste of the tea, but it quickly took the sharp edge off his pain and he felt better. Presently, he stood up to test his legs. Solid enough, he decided. Despite the numerous bruises on his back and arms and one egg-sized lump on his skull, he concluded he would live. Scarlet was sipping his che by the door, his shoulder nudged against the grimy wall, watching Liall with worry.

"I suppose it would be rude of me to look a gift horse in the mouth," Liall said, sinking back down on the bed. He dragged a blanket over his shoulders.

"What?"

He shrugged and winced, rubbing his neck. "I forgot that Byzans do not have that expression. You would look a horse in the mouth in any case, whether it was a gift or not."

"Of course I would."

"Why did you follow me?"

Scarlet's face went carefully blank for a moment. "I didn't mean to. I'm... it was an accident."

Liall did not try to hide his skepticism. "No one comes to Volkovoi by accident."

Scarlet swirled his che in his cup. "I didn't mean it quite like that. I was bound for Ankar and I'd crossed the Iron River, heading north, when I ran into some Aralyrin soldiers. They asked me about you."

Liall's interest grew sharp. "What did they say?"

"Only that they were looking for you and that they'd had word you were trying to find passage north. They mentioned a price on your head in every port. I had to come and warn you."

Liall paled a little and he was silent for several moments. "It seems that machinations are already in place to prevent me from returning home. I suspected as much, but I'm not pleased to be proven correct." He sighed deeply and then dismissed worry from his mind. Men had been trying to assassinate him since he was ten years old. Tonight was no different.

Liall looked up and saw the worry on Scarlet's features. He smiled a little. "And what am I to do with you now, little pedlar?"

"I thought I'd come with you."

"Oh." Scarlet had succeeded in shocking him again.

"What about your plans in Ankar?"

"Plans change."

"And your sister? You would abandon Annaya when you know civil war is coming?" Scarlet winced, causing Liall to gentle his voice. "More than anyone in Lysia, you have known this for some time. It cannot end any other way."

"Annaya is in Nantua. It's not perfect, but it's safer than Byzantur. Besides, she wouldn't have come with me," Scarlet added quietly. "I know she wouldn't. She's too much like Scaja."

"I've been nothing but trouble to you since we met, brought you nothing but pain. Why do you care what happens to me?"

Scarlet bit his lip. "I don't really know how to answer that."

Liall sensed he was being put off. He set the che aside. "You're not telling me *all* of the truth here, Scarlet. Why did you really come?" Liall frowned. "This would not have anything to do with that life-debt nonsense you were spouting in my camp, would it?"

Scarlet shifted on his feet. "You can believe that if you like, but whatever you think, my debts are a matter of honor for me. I can't forget them just because you have a low opinion of Byzans, and I…" he trailed off. "I don't know why I care about you. I only know that I haven't been true to myself for a long time. Maybe when I'm with you, no matter how angry you make me, I feel like I'm getting nearer to who I want to be."

This was so close to how Liall himself privately felt about Scarlet that he was amazed. Yet, it was now too late to reveal that, and it would be unfair. He was leaving.

Liall's guilt returned as Scarlet watched him with an expression of mingled hurt and anticipation. Whatever Scarlet's reasons for coming to Volkovoi, it had been to his benefit, and now at least he had seen Scarlet once more. It was pointless to argue further. He smiled wanly. "You've worried over me?"

"With good reason, it seems."

"My savior," he agreed.

It was growing late, so he left off questioning and watched Scarlet busy himself about the room. The pedlar piled everything wet in one corner and hung Liall's clothing and his own wet coat from pegs on the walls, hoping aloud that the damp would leech out by morning. When Liall moved to help him, Scarlet gave him a warning glare.

"I can do it. Don't need you falling over and breaking your head again. Just drink your che. Put your boots by the fire if you want to be useful."

Scarlet was unusually quiet after that. When he was done shaking the rain from everything and tidying up, they were left staring at each other in the silence broken only by the constant patter of rain on the window and roof. Liall realized that this was the first time he had really been alone with Scarlet.

He stood up and held out his hand. The blanket dropped from his shoulders. "Come here."

Scarlet reached out to him tentatively and Liall quickly dragged him into his arms. He fits there perfectly, Liall thought, snug if a little small. Scarlet did not respond at first, tensing as if he would pull away, and for a moment Liall believed he had made a huge mistake. Then, surprisingly, Scarlet sighed and his arms went around Liall's back. Scarlet turned his head to rest his cheek against Liall's bare chest as they listened to the rain batten on the roof.

"Thank you for saving my life," Liall murmured. He considered carefully what to say next, knowing Scarlet had many boundaries. "You would really come with me?"

"I would." There was sincerity in his voice. "I *want* to come with you."

Liall's arms tightened around him. How many times must he say farewell to this impossible boy? "I regret, but no. It's too dangerous."

Scarlet tensed and pulled away from his embrace. He stepped away and turned his back, his posture stiff and wounded.

"What, more dangerous than being a pedlar and traveling on robber roads?" he asked resentfully. "Slavers sieve the north roads from Khurelen, and we've had brigands patrolling the river right next to Lysia since before I was born. And if that's not enough, my own countrymen are raiding every Hilurin village in Byzantur and burning it to the ground. The world is a dangerous place, Liall. Every breath I take is a risk."

Liall knew more about the evil of the world than most, because he had traveled more than most men alive. Thinking about how often Scarlet was in danger angered him. Damn this filthy place! he thought fiercely. And damn your bitch-goddess, too. Your Deva claims to prize purity, yet the world she hands you is full of evil and no fit place for innocents.

"I told you *no*. You're going to Ankar, like you planned."

Which was exactly the wrong thing to say.

"I'm not a child," Scarlet flared. "And you're not my lord. I'll go where I will."

"Scarlet!" Liall gripped his shoulders and tugged him around. "I know you've lost much, but are you deliberately trying to get yourself killed?"

That got his attention. "No."

"Then heed me. Go to Ankar, or even to your sister's house in Nantua, but go."

There was some fire in him yet. Then, Scarlet's eyes lit on the bright coin necklace around Liall's neck, and the heat of his anger seemed to gutter and die. He reached out and turned the copper coins thoughtfully in his fingers.

"I remember these," he said, his dark eyes very large. "Why have you done this?"

"To remind me."

Scarlet's voice was softer. "I can't go back to Byzantur, or even Ankar for that matter."

"What has happened?" Liall resisted an urge to shake him when he did not answer. "Tell me!"

"It's my business," he evaded, dropping the coins. "But I'm glad I found you. I wanted to see you one more time."

The admission dissolved Liall's anger in sudden warmth and robbed him of his resolution to get to the truth. He let Scarlet go and paced heavily to the window, wiping the beaded moisture away and peering into the night. Below the window, the squalid walkways ran with water and the green lamps made goblin shadows on all the walls.

"Here is the way of it," Liall said at last. "I've been summoned back to my homeland. This much you know. The journey by sea is long and perilous and I can take no one with me. I dare not take you, especially, for you would probably die on such a journey, and there will be... other dangers. I have many enemies." He turned to look at Scarlet. "Many powerful men who wish me dead, and who would not hesitate to kill you as well."

Scarlet was looking at him with new interest, and Liall was dismayed. He had already told Scarlet far more than he meant to, yet he was compelled by some unknown instinct to continue: "My family is also very powerful, and there has been, or will be, a change of kings in Norl Udur. I do not know if I will ever be permitted to return to Byzantur."

"Why you?" Scarlet asked. He was unsettled now. "Of all the men in the world this great family could have sent for, why'd they send for *you*?"

"That, I cannot tell you."

Scarlet laughed shortly. "For a moment, I thought we were starting to trust each other."

He would not be distracted. "This is not about trust. You cannot come with me. You must find your own way." It hurt to be so blunt, but he had to do it.

Scarlet tried to brazen it out. "Maybe I'm just going in your direction."

"I doubt that, and even if you were, you would find no ship willing to carry you. My people do not tolerate foreigners."

Scarlet looked stricken. Liall sighed and rubbed his face, wincing when his palm brushed a lump on his cheek. "Let us sleep on it. Matters will seem clearer in the light of day. Perhaps we will know what to do then. I will help as I can, but there is little time." He gestured. "Take the bed; I will be quite comfortable here."

"You're the one hurt."

"Don't argue."

Liall doused the lamp and reclined in the large velvet chair, a blanket over his shoulders and the two Morturii long-knives across his lap. After a long moment, Scarlet crossed the room. The bed creaked as he sat. There was a thump as his boots hit the floor and he sighed, reclining with his arm folded under his head for a pillow. The faint green glow of lamplight limned his form.

Liall watched from his chair. The multiple aches from his many bruises had settled into a dull roar. Minutes passed.

"Liall?" Scarlet whispered into the gloom.

Liall inhaled shakily. "No," he answered softly. He saw Scarlet rise up on his elbow to face him in the dim light.

"Why?"

Indeed, why? After all the effort he had put into seducing this young man, to refuse him now, when he was freely offering himself, seemed foolish. But why had Scarlet changed? What had happened to him since they parted on the Sea Road? He seemed more open than Liall had ever seen him, and he was finally at ease in his company. It was as if some mask or heavy burden had fallen away from him, allowing him to be at peace in his own skin. Scarlet had found himself, but now it was too late.

Liall's throat grew painfully tight. "I will not take something so precious from you only to abandon you afterwards. You have never had a lover before."

Scarlet's eyes glittered in the dark. "You don't know that."

Liall was silent, knowing he was right.

Scarlet sighed. "It doesn't matter. I want to."

"So do I, but then I would still have to leave you."

"I don't care."

"But I do."

Scarlet rolled over, facing the window. He looked very small on the bed, impossibly vulnerable, and Liall was again amazed at the resilience and strength of Byzans.

Rain slashed against the window with a hiss. Later, when Liall dreamed, he saw a horse-drawn sleigh racing over the snow, and the polished iron runners under the carriage hissed with a sound like steam.

13.

Into the North

The Rshani ship arrived sometime in the night. It was the calls from shipboard to shore that woke him: deep, boisterous voices shouting back and forth in Sinha, the language of Rshan. For a moment, Liall thought he was still dreaming of home, and then he recalled the last few days. He opened his eyes to search for Scarlet. The pedlar was asleep on the bed, one hand curled against his chest and breathing softly. Liall got up carefully, mindful of his many aches, and began to take down the dried clothing from the pegs. Scarlet slept like a cat, quiet and still, but lightly enough so that Liall's small movements woke him.

Scarlet blinked and looked around the musty room. "Liall? How do you feel?"

"I will live," he said, his back turned. "Don't concern yourself. Northmen heal very quickly."

"Well, I don't," he said as he stretched his arms over his head and yawned. "I think they must stuff the mattress with rocks hereabouts. That must be the single worst bed I've ever slept on."

"You must have not have slept in many beds during your travels."

Scarlet smiled ruefully and combed his black hair off his forehead with his fingers, clawing it into place. "I didn't. The ground was good enough for me, barring snow or wet. Beds cost money, even this one."

Liall knelt to push his rumpled cloak into one of the

packs and tied it closed, dusting his hands off as he stood. He bit back a groan as his muscles screamed protest, resigning himself to a slow but steady healing. At least the bruises would not stand out on his amber skin and he was not maimed or disfigured in any way.

"Hard to believe they can get away with charging for such as that," Liall said, "but it was worth it to be out of sight for the evening." He reached with both hands to rub a very sore spot on the small of his back. "Word has probably spread among the bravos that there's a fat bounty to be had."

Scarlet paused in the middle of slipping his boots on. "You'd better leave soon, then. When does your ship arrive?"

Liall noticed that Scarlet's socks were darned and worn paper thin at the toes, and he was glad he had stowed several gold *doges* –thick coins stamped with the vine of the Flower Prince– in Scarlet's pack as he slept. He pointed. "You mean that ship through yon window?"

Scarlet turned his head to see the brigantine. He made a little sound of awe at the size of it. It was a large ship. It had to be, to weather such a long and hazardous crossing.

"Just look at it," Scarlet whispered. "I've never seen a vessel so large, not ever. Look at all the sails! How many crewmen does she carry? What about–"

Liall held up his hand to stem the flow of words. "Those are the least of my concerns. The bravos will have staked out the dock by now."

Scarlet chewed his lip as he stared at the square-rigged ship and the great white sails. "What do we do?"

"We?"

"It's obvious you no longer have the time to help me find another path, as you put it, so I might as well help you."

"But what will you do? How will you live?" Liall fought off a surge of anxiety. By his own words, he was preparing to leave Scarlet to fate. What right did he have to begin questioning him now?

Scarlet waved that off. "Don't fret. I've been making my own way since I was fourteen."

"Scarlet."

"I'll be fine. Honest."

Liall saw the shine in his liquid eyes and the determined set of his mouth, and he realized that a final parting was upon him. "You're a curse on me, you fool of pedlar. You must be."

"Funny. I thought the same thing about you, once."

Against all sense and reason, Liall crossed the room to kneel at Scarlet's feet, startling him.

"I've dreamed about you many times since we met," he confessed. Scarlet's black eyebrows rose. Liall smiled. "And yes, some of those dreams do not bear repeating in polite company, which you most certainly are." Liall reached and cupped the pedlar's face, and Scarlet dipped his chin and brushed his cheek against Liall's palm, his eyes closing.

"I know thee," Liall whispered urgently. It felt like all of his heart was pouring out into these few short words, yearning hungrily toward Scarlet like a flower does toward the sun; a primal, natural hunger that would now never be consummated. "I've known you forever. You have not been absent from my thoughts for one hour since we met. Something in you calls out to me, demanding an answer, but I do not know how to respond."

Scarlet exhaled, his warm breath rushing against Liall's palm. He reached up to press Liall's hand closer to his skin. "And I've dreamed of you. I think I've been looking for you all of my life, and now you're leaving again."

Liall could not speak. From the quay, the sound of a

ship's bell rang out, and Scarlet opened his eyes. Liall forced himself to pull away.

"We must go."

Captain Qixa was an Rshani commoner who had a passing acquaintance with a few nobles in Rshan, enough to recognize that the man who sat before him was no merchant down on his luck or a traveling dandy with affected manners. Liall bought Qixa a drink in a dank, wood-paneled taberna that was lit by swinging yellow lamps made from ships' wheels. The crown of Qixa's head, bald as an eagle's egg, gleamed dully in the light. He was less tall than most Rshani, but had a broader chest and a longer reach. These traits bruited of his northern blood, the people of the Ged Fanorl.

Qixa downed the liquor –red *imbuo* and raw enough to peel skin from a man's throat– in one gulp and wiped his mouth on his sleeve. He nodded at Liall and ignored Scarlet, who sat close to Liall's elbow.

"You have heard a rumor," Liall judged, watching for Qixa's reaction. *Yes.* "A passenger waiting to take ship from this port. A very certain passenger." He leaned forward over the sticky, grimed table and watched how the captain's eyes drifted up to note the pure white color of his hair and his stone-hard features. If Qixa had any knowledge at all of certain families in Rshan, he would recognize the resemblance.

Liall raised his hand to show him the sapphire and platinum ring on his finger. "You see what I am," he said, deftly switching his *Sinha* dialect to match the hard northern burr in Qixa's, and the captain's chin lifted.

"I wish to take passage on your good ship. I will pay well," Liall concluded.

Qixa waved that aside as if it were nothing, though Liall knew he would accept the silver. "You are welcome to a good cabin on the *Ostre Sul,* noble *ser.* Food, too, we have, but, *ap kyning,* forgive me, if I defy the harbormaster or tangle with his bullies, I'll never be allowed to dock at Volkovoi again, and it's the last supply port in Khet before the sea."

Qixa was speaking of the bravos who had positioned themselves at the quay where the brigantine had made anchorage. He was risking much to help Liall.

"I will get past the bravos. You need only agree to carry me. I will remember your loyalty," he added.

Qixa slapped his hand on the table and stood. "Done. We leave in one hour. I will set a watch on the foredeck to keep an eye for you, but do not keep us waiting."

"One hour," Liall confirmed.

Qixa left them. He had not glanced at Scarlet once.

The hour passed too quickly. Liall had no time to come up with a workable plan and did not think it safe to hire thugs to take on the leather-armored men who lounged by the quay, waiting for a specific bruised, white-haired Rshani to show. Most of the thugs would be in tight with the bravos, or even related to them. He would find no help there.

There were eight bravos on the wharf: two by a wrecked loading platform that teetered precariously high over the water, and six more nearest the gangway to the ship. They sharply eyed each dockworker and pedestrian who came near their post, their heavy faces grim with determination.

"What are we going to do?" Scarlet hissed.

The rain had stopped and they were concealed between the wall of a crumbling factory and a stack of tar-soaked lumber twice as high as a man. From their vantage point, Liall could see the lookout on the forecastle, a blond mariner, tall and young and clearly of pure Rshani blood. The lookout's sharp eyes swept the docks, not too blatantly, and careful not to appear conspicuous.

"Peace, let me think," Liall growled.

Qixa appeared on the deck. He sent the docks a misgiving look and pointedly turned the hourglass near the wheel. As if signaled, the crew began to ready the sails to break harbor.

"Liall," Scarlet plucked his sleeve urgently, "they're going to leave without you."

"I'm thinking!" he snapped. Yes, Liall, think.

Scarlet waited another minute. The crew scurried faster, and then he blew his breath out in a huff and slung his pack at Liall.

"What—"

"Don't lose any of my things," Scarlet ordered. He took some heavier items out of his pockets: a flint and steel, a compass, and the two long-knives from his belt. When he would have ducked into the open street, Liall grabbed his arm and swung him around.

"What do you think you're doing?"

"You do intend to get on that ship don't you? Well, don't you?"

"Yes!"

"Then let me go."

He had no choice. In another minute the mariners would pull the gangway up and he would have to swim for it. He released Scarlet, who tossed him an easy grin.

"Don't worry. Just get aboard as soon as the way is clear."

"You're going to clear the dock of bravos on your own?"

"Looks like it."

He sighed, admiring in spite of his exasperation. "Scarlet, one back-alley brawl against men armed with clubs does not make you a warrior."

"No, but I'm not going to fight them, or not if I do this right."

"Gods grant me patience; you're going to give me a seizure!"

"You don't have time for that. Wait 'til after you're on the ship, eh?"

He gaped as Scarlet smoothly stepped into the foot traffic and made his way down the docks, to the quay where the *Ostre Sul* was anchored, stopping in open sight of the bravos, one of whom bore a plastered bandage on his flattened nose. They noticed him at once. How not, in that red coat? Scarlet stood with his hands on his hips and waved sunnily, then called out to them, his voice carrying over the hubbub of the wharf.

"Aye, it's me, ugly one. How's the nose?"

And that was it. The bravo with the plastered nose roared and tore after Scarlet, swinging his club. The remaining five bravos by the gangway dropped everything and followed and the two by the teetering platform tried to duck around and flank Scarlet, who stood almost lazily in the middle of the street. Scarlet waited until the six men moved fully away from the *Ostre Sul's* gangway and the other two bravos began closing in on him, and like a shot from a cannon, he was off.

Never had Liall seen anyone run so fast or so well, but then he had never seen a pedlar who walks for a living decide to stop walking and fly.

Scarlet was a deer fleeing the archer, a rabbit let loose in a market with the butcher on his heels. He turned and raced back up the docks, away from the brigantine, dodging pedestrians, leaping over anything that was in his way, seeming to flow through the press of people like water down a drainpipe. A ninth bravo, coming down the street purely by accident, almost ran headlong into Scarlet. He saw his fellows hard on Scarlet's trail and made a grab for him. Scarlet easily danced out of his range and took a turn down a long alley that led into another street running away from the docks, and as neat as that, Liall had a clear path.

Liall moved down the quay in a daze, hearing the crashing and shouts of the bravos on the parallel street as they pursued their quarry. His path to the ship was open and he took it, straight down the quay and up the wooden gangway, which the mariners pulled up after him at once. Qixa's face was urgent and angry. He barked orders at the crew and they cast off from the dock. The ship began to pull away from land, slow as sap in winter.

Liall went straight to the stern, dropped his packs to the deck. He leaned over the bulward to scan the docks, searching the crowd anxiously for a flash of red. Scarlet suddenly emerged from the small crowd, who had gathered in a knot on the wharf, running fast, the tails of his long coat flying behind him. One bravo blocked his way. He ducked the swinging club and shoved out with his arm, unbalancing the thug, who fell flat on his rump.

As Liall watched, Scarlet leapt over a pile of wooden crates and kept running. It looked like he was headed straight for the water. Was he going to swim? Liall turned his head to shout for ropes in case they were needed, and then Scarlet suddenly swerved and dodged to the right.

Oh, he would not...

He would. Scarlet took the rotted steps of the derelict loading platform two at a time, his feet barely touching the wood, and raced across the sagging planks that jutted high over the waterline, straight toward the slow-moving brigantine. Putting on a last burst of speed when he hit the top of the platform, he kept running until there was open space under one foot and wood under another, and pushed off. Scarlet leapt over the open water between the dock and the ship and crashed onto the deck, landing on his hands and knees and rolling to absorb some of the shock. The impact knocked the breath out of him and he lay there panting until Liall got over the shock and helped him to stand.

None of the crew had moved to their aid.

The bravos were gesturing angrily and screaming at the brigantine to come back, waving their clubs. Captain Qixa called back to them in Sinha, knowing they would not understand, but shrugging his shoulders and spreading his hands in a helpless gesture that said plainly; *what could I do?*

Scarlet was clutching his heaving sides and gasping, tired but proud of himself.

"I've never seen anything like that," Liall said truthfully, very awed at his skill.

Scarlet grinned. "Did you like it?"

"Yes, it was very brave." He sighed wearily, and some of the shining triumph sloughed off Scarlet. "But you *cannot* come with me."

"And you can't send me back to the port, they'll hang me."

"What?" Liall grabbed Scarlet's arm, his heart accelerating again. "Why would they do that? Certainly not for breaking a bravo's nose."

"I killed Cadan. I didn't want to but there it is, and the army knows it was me."

Liall's shoulders sagged. Fool! he raged inwardly. Oh lad, what have you done?

From the corner of his eye, Liall saw the Rshani crew begin to draw closer to them. Captain Qixa squared up to Liall, his quartermaster and the young man who had served as a lookout behind him. Slowly, Liall sensed the blanket of hostility folding around them, and he wondered at its cause, thinking for a moment that he had made a bad mistake in boarding the *Ostre Sul*. Then he saw their pale, hard eyes fixed on Scarlet and knew what was wrong.

"This was not part of our bargain," Qixa snarled in Sinha, jabbing a finger at Scarlet, who naturally did not understand a word of it.

Qixa was right. He had never asked permission to bring Scarlet on board, because he had never intended to. Yet, even if he had, it was doubtful he would have sought Qixa's consent. He could be that proud and used to getting his way. "Perhaps not," he allowed. "It is now."

"No! We do not carry *lenilyn* on this ship!"

Qixa used the old Sinha word for foreigner: *lenilyn*, which in some nuances could mean *non-person,* or even *animal*. Liall glanced pointedly around him at the shabby condition of the deck, the tarred ropes that were rat-gnawed, the smell of bilge and the gull droppings on the planks. "But you do evidently carry rats and lice."

"Better than *lenilyn*," the lookout reckoned. He wore his long hair vainly flowing around his shoulders, and he eyed Scarlet meanly before spitting into the scuppers. In another moment there would be violence. Liall forcibly kept his hand away from his knives and locked eyes with Qixa.

"This Byzan is not to be touched."

"Perhaps if he were not Hilurin, we could have made some arrangement," Qixa said in a conciliatory tone. "You understand, *ap kyning*? I regret, but it must be this way."

Qixa snapped his fingers and the crew hemmed them in closer, sixteen Rshani on the near deck and another fifty elsewhere on the ship, at least. Liall had no hope of fighting them all off.

He pushed Scarlet behind him with one arm and backed up to the bulward. Scarlet had gone quiet and watchful as a mouse, seeing only that they were in trouble and not knowing why, but wise enough to keep his mouth shut. In another moment, Qixa would order the crew to throw Scarlet overboard and –hell!– he was not even sure he could swim. Even if he could, there were the bravos on the docks, still within sight of the departing ship, who would be waiting for him.

The young mariner started forward and Liall gave him a cold stare. "You will not," he said, his voice low and lethal. "You dare not." His heartbeat had slowed and he was as calm as if sleeping soundly under a friendly sky. The weights of his Morturii knives were warm and reassuringly heavy where they touched his thighs. They would not lay hands on Scarlet.

It confused the mariner, one man against many who showed no fear and was confident he would be obeyed. Liall continued to look at Qixa as thunder rolled out of the sky and the ship tacked northeast into a gray horizon. A light, misty rain began drifting down.

"It belongs to me. My property," Liall said in Sinha, hoping that the rude claim of ownership would reach him where subtler arguments could not. "I give you the word of a Camira Druz that it will cause no trouble."

Qixa did not like it, but he backed down. Perhaps he simply did not want to be the man responsible for killing him. Gods knew there were enough waiting in line to do that once they made landfall in Rshan.

Qixa barked new orders and the crew dispersed with much grumbling. Liall relaxed and spat over the side to clear the sour taste from his mouth, his long hands trembling.

"What was that all about?" Scarlet inquired coolly.

He shrugged. "Nothing," he lied. "They're unaccustomed

to transporting foreigners on board, an old taboo. I gave my word to keep you in line."

"Me?" Scarlet eyed the fair-haired Rshani crew, their large size and the belligerent glares they cast at him. "Who's going to keep them in line?"

Who indeed? "Just stay clear of them and mind what you say. There are certain to be some who speak Bizye."

Scarlet brushed some grime from the shoulder of his coat where he had rolled on the deck. "If you say so, but I don't know how much good that will do." He brightened suddenly. "So, how long does it take to get to this land of yours?"

"Scarlet, Scarlet," he admonished, shaking his head. "Where I go, you cannot follow."

"But I am," Scarlet replied. He saw Liall's apprehensive expression and smiled slyly. "Unless you want me to drown or hang, and I see you don't." He poked Liall in the chest with a finger. "You care what happens to me."

"Yes, I do," Liall admitted freely. "I care so much that I will not allow you to go needlessly into death."

Scarlet looked up at Liall through black lashes, almost glowing with triumph from his near escape, and supremely confident. "I can see this is going to be a long journey. Now, how far is it?"

Liall's emotions were at war, tugging him between strong desire and good sense, yet he found the will to frown at Scarlet in rebuke. "You will be put ashore to the north above Morturii, where you should be safe from the Byzan army. You know enough of the language and customs to get by." He wondered who he was trying to convince.

Scarlet shrugged lightly and drew back with a smile, clearly not intending to be left behind anywhere. "You didn't answer me."

"Rshan na Ostre is a four month journey by sea."

Scarlet's teasing manner abruptly vanished. He thumped Liall hard on the arm. "That's not even a real place!"

He was so surprised that he laughed outright. "What do you mean, not real?"

Scarlet was indignant. "It's a fairy tale. Scaja used to tell me about it when I was no bigger than that barrel there. The Land of Demons, where the Shining Ones live," he scoffed. "Rshan! Do you take me for a fool?"

Liall was holding his aching arm and chuckling, and Scarlet looked a little guilty, knowing the bravos had kicked him there.

"I assure you, it is no fairy tale. And it is not called the Land of Demons, but the Land of Darkness, or Night. The words are the same in Sinha, you see. And the commoners in Byzantur just call it Norl Udur, the North Kingdom."

"The North Kingdom is not Rshan," Scarlet said patiently, enunciating clearly as if speaking to a very slow and dull-witted child. "It couldn't be."

"And just why not? Because you do not believe in Rshan, it cannot exist? That's very arrogant, little Byzan. Even for you."

Scarlet scowled blackly, his pretty eyes narrowed to slits of ebony. "Next you'll be telling me *you're* a Shining One." He waved his hand dismissively, highly annoyed. "Forget it, you great ox. If you don't want to tell me the truth, just shut up."

Liall laughed harder as the thin rain gathered strength and became a downpour. In a flash of rare joy, he threw his arms around Scarlet and planted a hard, passionate kiss on his mouth, grateful beyond measure to be alive, to sense the promise of a future waiting for him, to feel hope again. After a long, shocked moment, Scarlet moaned and responded. The last resistance in his muscles vanished, and his body —strong, young, and warm— melted against Liall.

The wind tugged at Liall's cloak with eager fingers as the sweet pull of Scarlet's mouth threatened to drive him past all caution. He forced himself to break the kiss.

"I will always tell you the truth," he whispered into Scarlet's hair, looking out over the choppy waves to the far horizon beyond. Liall blinked hard, his vision blurring, and told himself it was only the brisk wind blowing in from the north, but there was no hiding from the truth: after sixty years, the long-awaited journey to reclaim his true self was finally beginning.

The north, his heart sang. I'm going home. Finally, to home.

To be continued in *Scarlet and the White Wolf, Book 2: Mariner's Luck.*

Acknowledgments

A novel is never the sole product of one person alone. There are always people who, along the way, have contributed to its creation in some measure. With that in mind, I'd like to thank my buddies at the Livejournal SATWW community who patiently hung in there with me over the past year, offering encouragement and critique, keeping silent as deadline after deadline zipped by, and for being the kind of friends a writer can count on.

Heartfelt appreciation to:

keelywolfe, caras_galadhon, faramir_boromir, ashinae, cinzia, dameange, discord26, fatuorum, frogspace, glasshouseslive, gladio, gotham_syren, hrd02ca, imitari, ithiliana, jpolidori, lesadoreyl, macteague, moonwhip, neeteeus, ribby, sarcasticmissy, savageseraph, seleneheart, sffan, skripka, sneezer222, tipsy_scott, tmelange, rahalia_ cat, villeinage, zasjah, and also to Roy Batty and Simon Tam, for inspiration.

Special thanks to Analise Dubner, who bravely trudged through four edits of this story, until I got it right.

-Kirby Crow
September 19, 2005

Author's Bio

Kirby Crow worked as an entertainment editor and ghostwriter for several years before happily giving it up to bake more brownies, read more yaoi, play more video games, and write her own novels.

Changing weather patterns, watering bans, and pesticides have unhappily forced her to give up growing roses, alas.

Her published novels are **Prisoner of the Raven** (historical romance, Torquere Press, 2005), **Scarlet and the White Wolf: The Pedlar and the Bandit King** (fantasy romance, Torquere Press, 2006), **Mariner's Luck** (fantasy romance, Torquere Press, 2007), and **The Land of Night** (fantasy romance, Torquere Press, 2007). They are available from Torquere Books, most online book retailers, and Amazon.

Kirby is a Spectrum Book Awards nominee, and is hard at work on two more fantasy novels and one horror novel, to be announced on her website. http://kirbycrow.com

The Pedlar and the Bandit King

The Pedlar and the Bandit King

FEB 1 1 2010

LaVergne, TN USA
03 December 2009
165905LV00005B/36/P